W9-ABZ-224

DATE DUE

OC 0 ? ?		
OC 2 0 ??		

Demco

A DASH OF DRAGON

A Dash of Dragon

Heidi Lang & Kati Bartkowski

ALADDIN

New York London Toronto Sydney New Delhi

ALADDIN
An imprint of Simon & Schuster Children's Publishing Division
1230 Avenue of the Americas, New York, New York 10020
First Aladdin hardcover edition July 2017
Text copyright © 2017 by Heidi Lang and Kati Bartkowski
Jacket illustration copyright © 2017 by Angela Li
For information about special discounts for bulk purchases, please contact Simon & Schuster Special Sales at 1-866-506-1949 or business@simonandschuster.com.
The Simon & Schuster Speakers Bureau can bring authors to your live event. For more information or to book an event contact the Simon & Schuster Speakers Bureau at 1-866-248-3049 or visit our website at www.simonspeakers.com.
Jacket designed by Karin Paprocki
Book designed by Nina Simoneaux
The text of this book was set in Adobe Caslon Pro.
Manufactured in the United States of America 0617 FFG
2 4 6 8 10 9 7 5 3 1
This book has been cataloged with the Library of Congress.
ISBN 978-1-4814-7793-2 (hc)
ISBN 978-1-4814-7794-9 (eBook)

As children, we often played games of imagination. Writing a book together was just taking those games and putting them into words. This is for our parents, who encouraged our imaginations, our creativity, and our love of fantasy.

And for Ember, who is just starting to learn how to play make-believe. We can't wait to see what worlds you create.

1

Mystic Cooking

ailu flipped a large chef's knife end over end, scowling at the row of onions pinned to the far wall. She could have taken on another kraken or even a hydra right then—anything but this endless waiting. She almost didn't blame Master Slipshod for taking off and leaving her alone on opening day.

"Don't worry," she told her remaining batch of onions. "It will only hurt for a second." Definitely less than being chopped up, at any rate. As she selected a sweet yellow one, the bell above the front door chimed.

Lailu whipped around, the onion toppling onto the floor. Customers? She ducked past the curtain separating the kitchen from the dining room, straightening her fluffy white chef's hat as she went. "Welcome to Mystic Cooking. Our special today is . . ." Her eyes flicked to the man looming in her doorway, his maroon coat and black silk cravat practically blending in with the warm cherry-wood of the walls next to him. "Mr. Boss?" What was *he* doing here?

While she was barely over five feet tall, Mr. Boss ("Call me Victor") was not much taller, but his back was straight and his cane seemed more like a threatening prop than a tool. He looked like he might be in his sixties or seventies, his gray hair oiled back into a ponytail at the nape of his neck. She'd heard the rumors, of course, that he was actually 206 and that he bathed in the blood of young dragons every month to slow his aging. Lailu wasn't sure she bought that; she knew how hard it was to kill a dragon.

Mr. Boss turned slowly, taking in the spotless and very empty dining room. "Busy, I see."

Lailu flushed but refused to look away. It was only her first day, after all. Customers would come. They had to come. "Master Slipshod isn't here right now," she said, her voice shaking.

"So it would appear. Frankly, I'm surprised he left you here all alone, and you just a child."

"I'm old enough." Lailu stood up straighter, trying to look older than her thirteen years. "What do you want?"

Mr. Boss's smile widened as he studied the menu behind her. "Hmm. 'Kraken calamari in a creamy white wine sauce served over fettuccine, with a kraken seafood medley appetizer.'" He tapped his cane on the floor. "Well, now, that does sound fancy. I'll take it. On the house, of course."

"On . . . on the house?"

"Of course. Why should I pay? I mean, it would be almost like paying myself." He gave a dry chuckle.

"What does *that* mean?"

"Just that your mentor and I have a little . . . arrangement. I don't pay here."

Lailu gaped. "Do you have any idea what we went through to get that kraken?" Old Salty was a tough beast, and getting one of his delicious tentacles had cost Lailu two days and three bruised ribs, not to mention a brief glimpse of her own mortality. No way was she giving it away for free.

"I can't imagine why I'd care." Mr. Boss sat at one of her tables. "Well, girlie?" he demanded, tapping his cane again. "Get to it. I'm not getting any younger."

"That's not what I heard," Lailu muttered. Still, Mr. Boss was Master Slipshod's business associate, whatever that meant. She might not like him, but she had to be polite. And maybe her mentor *had* promised him free food, though she'd be sure to check as soon as he decided to show up. After a moment's hesitation she turned and stomped toward the kitchen, saying a silent prayer to Chushi, the God of Cookery, as she passed the small wooden shrine perched in the corner. Her father had carved it for her the day she'd been accepted into the academy.

Lailu had always looked up to her father. Much like the woods he carved, he could be firm and unyielding, but Lailu admired the way he worked hard in all aspects of his life. Before returning to their village, he'd told her how proud he was of her dedication to cooking and her determination to start this restaurant. He claimed the gods had granted her a gift that could change their world. If he believed that strongly in her abilities, then she could handle anything, including Mr. Boss.

In ten minutes she had a bowlful of her famous kraken seafood medley (well, one day it would be famous) with large slices of exotic fish fillet and kraken tentacles in a saffron broth. She carried it out, ducking carefully around the heavy blue curtain that hung from the kitchen doorway, then froze at the scene unfolding in her once-empty dining room.

"I hope you don't mind, Lailu my dear, but I invited a few friends to join me." Mr. Boss smiled wide enough to show off his gold molars.

"A few friends?" At least a dozen people were grouped around Mr. Boss, all watching her with unfriendly eyes. She only recognized one of them: the tall, gaunt man sitting to the left of Mr. Boss was Havoc McHackney, infamously known as "the Butcher," who slit the throats of those unfortunate enough to get in Mr. Boss's way.

As Lailu reluctantly moved forward, the Butcher eyed her up and down. "So you're training with Slipshod, are you?" His upper lip curled. "That wasted old fool."

Lailu stiffened, her ears burning. "Master Slipshod is a great chef. He literally wrote the book on dragon cuisine, and trained Head Chef Master Sanford, *and* he cooked for the king himself—"

Havoc made a rude sound, and the men around him laughed.

Lailu took a deep breath, then let it out slowly. This certainly wasn't the first time she'd heard insults against her mentor, but anyone could see Master Slipshod was one of the greats. True, he'd done all those things she'd mentioned years ago, but Lailu knew he still had it in him. She didn't need to waste her time explaining it to these fools.

"Here is your appetizer." Lailu placed the steaming bowl in front of Mr. Boss. "And the kraken calamari fettuccine will be out shortly."

As she turned to leave, one of the men in the back of the group caught her eye. Much younger than the rest, he was dark-haired and slender with laughing gray eyes. He winked mischievously.

Lailu flushed and took a step back, stopping when Mr. Boss hooked his cane through her arm. "I believe we still have business to discuss—"

The bell above the front door chimed.

Lailu's heart leaped. Master Slipshod, finally. He would set Mr. Boss straight. But when she glanced at the door, all hope of seeing her mentor disappeared as four figures strolled inside. Four tall, slender figures with high cheekbones and sharply pointed ears. Elves. Elves in *her* restaurant. "No . . . way . . . ," she whispered, her whole body frozen in place like the orc meat stashed in the cellar.

The elf in front bared his teeth in a feral smile. A green bandanna held hundreds of tiny blond braids back from his face, and his hand rested casually on the hilt of a wickedly curved dagger tucked into his belt. "Search it," he said, and the three elves behind him fanned out, heading straight for her kitchen.

"Hey!" Lailu stepped forward, the tip of Mr. Boss's cane slipping away from her and slapping against the floor. "Stay out of our kitchen!" She was stopped midstep by a dagger edge pointed at her chest. The elf had moved so fast she hadn't seen him draw his knife.

Lailu went very still, hardly daring to breathe as she stared at the blade aimed directly at her heart. Knowing the elves' reputation, she had no doubt this elf would use it on her if he thought it necessary, or even if he just felt like it. Almost twenty years ago, this ruthless gang of elves had systematically wiped out their goblin rivals in the city, destroying a whole block of buildings with them. The elves may have been driven to the outskirts of Twin Rivers now, but once they had owned all of this land, and they never forgot it. Anything in their way became just another obstacle to eliminate.

"It will just be a minute, little girl." He sheathed his dagger in one fluid motion, then glanced over at Mr. Boss. "Hello, Victor."

Mr. Boss tightened his lips into one thin line. The Butcher deliberately put his hand on the large meat cleaver at his hip, while the rest of the lackeys shifted uncomfortably in their seats.

"You have found nothing in any of my businesses, Eirad." Mr. Boss glared at the elf in front of Lailu. "This is harassment."

The elf inclined his head. "It's meant to be."

A loud crash came from the kitchen. Lailu jumped and stared at the blue curtain pulled across the kitchen entrance, her stomach filling with dread. What could they be doing in there? What was taking them so long? She took a deep breath, preparing to sprint over and defend her kitchen when the curtain flew open and the three elves moved back into the dining room. "Not here," one of the female elves muttered, chewing on something. Lailu eyed her suspiciously, certain she had been into the kraken.

"No?" Sadness tinged Eirad's voice.

"I told you, I have nothing of yours," Mr. Boss snapped.

"And I told you we don't believe you."

The Butcher stood abruptly, and Lailu cringed as his chair

scraped across their newly sanded, polished wood floor. "Are you calling him a liar?" He drew his meat cleaver.

Eirad smiled in anticipation. "Obviously. I can sense his lies, feel them clinging to him like maggots on meat."

"Havoc. Sit down." Mr. Boss's voice was like a whip. "As my backers, the elves have every right to inspect my establishments."

Havoc sat, his gaunt face impassive as he tucked the cleaver back into his belt.

Eirad looked disappointed. "You're not going to fight us on this?"

"No. Search all you like. You won't find anything."

Eirad's face grew still. "We could make a wager. If we find—"

"I am not so big a fool as to make a wager with the likes of you," Mr. Boss said quickly. "No, search my businesses and be done with it."

"Fine. Enjoy your meal, Victor. I'm sure we'll be seeing you again . . . soon." And just like that, the elves were gone.

"What was that all about?" Lailu demanded, rounding on Mr. Boss. She was still shaking all over.

Mr. Boss regarded her coolly. "It doesn't concern you."

"They searched my restaurant!"

"No, they searched *my* restaurant," he corrected, his knuckles whitening over the top of his cane.

"It is *not* your restaurant. Mystic Cooking belongs to me and Master Slipshod."

"Oh, does it now? And who do you and Master Slipshod belong to?" Mr. Boss's pale eyes narrowed.

"Ourselves," she said without hesitation.

"Really? So he hasn't told you yet?"

The first tiny pinpricks of fear raced up and down Lailu's spine. "T-told me what?"

"About our little deal?" Mr. Boss leaned forward. "You know, the deal that got you this fine establishment?"

Lailu swallowed. "Master Slipshod . . . He had connections. He said . . ."

Mr. Boss smiled. "*I'm* his connections, my dear girl. I loaned him the money. And in exchange . . ." He reached into his suit jacket and pulled out a roll of parchment, stretching it wide and reading, "I, Master Chef Sullivan Slipshod, do hereby promise to repay my loan in full within one year's time, or my apprentice, Lailu Logan-berry, and I will work for Mr. Victor Boss in perpetuity." Mr. Boss paused, his eyes meeting Lailu's. "That means 'forever.'"

2

Forever

*L*ailu felt the world closing in around her, sucking the air out of the room. The word *forever* buzzed through her ears. "N-no. He would never . . . That's a terrible deal. He wouldn't have agreed to that."

"No?" Mr. Boss turned the parchment around so Lailu could see Master Slipshod's scrawled signature, and next to that, a thumbprint marked in blood. Slipshod's thumbprint. Slipshod's blood. It was official and binding.

"But he can't promise me! Only I can do that."

"You, my poor, foolish girl, signed on as his apprentice. Meaning he is now legally responsible for you. He is quite within his rights to sign away your future."

Her heart lurched at the betrayal, and she kept shaking her head. She was the youngest master chef to graduate from the academy in more than three hundred years. Not every chef had what it took to master mystic cooking, those special skills needed to properly hunt and then cook mystical beasts. Of course, there weren't too many who actually tried, since making even one mistake in either the hunting or preparations usually resulted in a dead chef, or worse. Growing up in a small mountainous village far from the protections of the cities, Lailu had plenty of practice dealing with deadly beasts. And she was good at it. She'd known instinctively this was the kind of cooking she wanted to do, no matter the danger.

She had worked so hard and, according to her teachers, she had a great future ahead of her. Slipshod wouldn't have gambled it away like that, not after he had promised her father that he would take care of her. "It has to be a lie," she whispered. "It has to be."

"Ask him. Whenever he bothers to show up, that is." Mr. Boss grinned. "And now that we've settled that, my friends here are still hungry."

Lailu felt oddly disconnected from her body, like all of this was happening to someone else. "No."

"No?" He raised his eyebrows.

"I'm not giving away any more free food." She took a deep breath, then another. She'd ask Master Slipshod when he got back. They would straighten this all out. And she wasn't going to let some loan shark intimidate her and ruin their opening day in the meantime. "You might have lent Master Slipshod the money, but this is still our place."

"Is it, now? Well, in that case, I guess we'd better leave," Mr. Boss said.

Lailu blinked. "You're . . . leaving?" Could it really be that easy?

Mr. Boss stood, moving stiffly, and the rest of his lackeys followed suit. "Clearly we are not wanted in *your* establishment."

Lailu just watched him, too shocked to say anything else.

Mr. Boss nodded, but Lailu realized a moment too late that the nod had been meant for someone else. She turned as the Butcher whipped Mr. Boss's still-steaming bowl of kraken seafood medley across the room to shatter against the wall just above her.

She yelped, covering her head with her hands as hot broth and ceramic shards rained down on her, burning any exposed skin. For a second the pain was all she could think of, and when she looked up again the Butcher towered over her, a terrible smile twisting across his face. Lailu gasped as he grabbed her and pinned her against the wall, his fingers digging into her wrists, yanking them both above her head. She struggled, but it was like wrestling against a sea serpent. "Now," he breathed in her face, "should I start breaking fingers?"

Lailu whimpered, hating herself for making such a weak noise.

"Really, Victor, this is barbaric," someone whispered.

"Quiet, Ryon."

"You put so much money down for two master chefs, but what good is a chef if she doesn't have the use of her fingers to cook?"

Lailu looked past the Butcher and saw that the speaker was the young dark-haired man.

Silence, then the tap-tap of Mr. Boss's cane on the floor. "You bring up some good points. So . . . if not her fingers, what else should we break?"

Lailu sniffed and picked up a splinter of wood. She hadn't cried since the day Master Sanford pulled her aside and told her that she would have to leave the academy because the scholarship money was running out, and she wasn't going to start crying now. She'd shown them all, working tirelessly to graduate and earn her apprenticeship before the end of that year, and she'd show Mr. Boss, too.

The front door banged open and her mentor strolled in, a folded wad of papers tucked under one arm. He had been tall in his youth, but now he walked with his shoulders and back hunched forward protectively around his sagging middle, his long mane of thinning gray hair flopping loosely around his chubby face.

"Pigtails," he barked. "You up for a night hunt? I just got a great tip about a huge gaggle of batyrdactyls in the Velvet For—"

He stopped, his eyes widening as he took in Lailu's disheveled appearance. "What the blazes happened to you? Is that . . . is that your shrine?"

"It *was* my shrine." Lailu picked up another piece and put it in the bucket next to her. "Mr. Boss broke it. Just smashed it to pieces. Apparently I'm to consider *him* my new God of Cookery." Lailu repeated the words bitterly. She picked up another sliver, trying not to look too closely at it. Her dad had carved this shrine just for her, and it hurt to think of him now, of his aching hands working to make this beautiful monument, of the hope he had for her. She dropped the sliver in the bucket with the others and stood to face her mentor. It was time to get the truth.

"He also showed me the contract."

Master Slipshod's face went as gray as his hair. "H-he did?" he croaked, and Lailu could tell that it was true, it was all true.

She curled her hands into fists. "How could you? How could you gamble with my future like that and not even *tell* me?"

"I told you I was making a business arrangement with Mr. Boss. What did you think that meant?"

"I don't know, but not this! Not . . . not this." Truthfully Lailu hadn't thought much about it. She'd left all the business stuff to Slipshod, preferring to focus on the important things, like the cooking and hunting.

"I had no choice. You wanted to open a restaurant. Well, I opened a restaurant." He looked at her. "I did it for you."

Lailu's stomach clenched. "For me?"

"I didn't have any money, and I . . . I've made some mistakes in the past." Master Slipshod sank into a chair. "Lots of mistakes. I've burned bridges and lost connections; there weren't many people left who were willing to take a chance on an old chef like me. But we can pay Mr. Boss back. I believe in this place, Lailu. I believe in you. You've got more talent than I've ever seen in a chef of your age."

Lailu remembered the day Master Slipshod had taken her on as his apprentice. In order to achieve full Master Chef status, she needed to complete an apprenticeship with a qualified mentor after graduating, but everyone she'd sought out had said no. Some had turned her down because of her unusual restaurant idea—most graduates found jobs in wealthy households, but Lailu believed good cooking should be accessible to all. Others turned her down because she was too young, too inexperienced, too short. She'd heard it all. A week went by, then another, and even though she'd graduated at the top of her class, no mentors would take her.

Her father had come out for her graduation, and then stayed the extra weeks for support as she was rejected again and again. As she failed, again and again.

And then her favorite teacher at school told her about his old mentor. "What you need is an unconventional chef for your unconventional idea. Sullivan Slipshod's been out of the kitchen for a while now, but his mind is still as sharp as his knives," Master Sanford had said, passing her Slipshod's address. "See if you can't get him away from those card tables. His talents are wasted there." It had taken a lot to convince him, but finally, reluctantly, he'd agreed to at least meet her at school and sample her cooking.

"Okay, girl, you're up," Master Slipshod had told her as she stepped up to the academy stove. "Show me what cooking skills you've got."

"Let Chushi and Jiakin guide your hand," her father said, invoking the God of Cookery and the god he worshipped, the God of Hard Work. He kissed Lailu on the cheek, and in that rare moment of affection, Lailu knew she could do it. She would cook the best dish Master Slipshod had ever tasted. And she did.

After she cooked for him, Master Slipshod had signed her there on the spot. "You and me, Pigtails, we'll go places," he told her. And she had believed him.

She uncurled her fists. She believed him still.

"If you want to achieve great things, you have to be willing to take great risks," Master Slipshod added.

"But . . . forever? We'd be stuck working for him forever?"

"Only if we didn't pay him back."

"We haven't even had any customers. Isn't that a huge gamble?"

He gave her a ghost of a smile. "All of life's a gamble." He pushed himself up, moving slowly. "But with your talent, the odds are on our side." He glanced down at the paper in his hands. "I hate to bring even more bad news, but I decided to check out your friend's restaurant on my way back."

Lailu went hot, then cold. She knew exactly who Slipshod meant. "He's no friend of mine," she breathed, her nostrils flaring. She still couldn't believe she had entrusted him with her plans to open the first restaurant in Twin Rivers, just so he could turn around and copy her.

Master Slipshod shrugged. "He seems to think differently." He tossed her the folded paper.

Lailu unfolded it to reveal a black-and-white picture of a distinguished dark-haired man, his lined face filled with pride, his arm around a grinning boy's shoulders. Lailu would recognize that wide, obnoxious grin anywhere, not to mention that shaggy mop of hair. It looked terribly unprofessional, even crammed under the chef's hat. Apparently Greg hadn't changed at all in the six months since they'd graduated from the academy together.

Under the photo, a caption read *"Famous winemaker Dante LaSilvian with his nephew Gregorian Jocelyn LaSilvian."*

Below the picture, printed in tiny, perfect letters, were a few paragraphs. Squinting, Lailu read them quickly, then again, her hands shaking with the urge to tear the paper into thousands of pieces as she read the words a third time:

Youngest Master Chef
Cooks Up Huge Success

Dante LaSilvian opened the doors of his highly anticipated restaurant, LaSilvian's Kitchen, early this morning. Joining him is his talented nephew and protégé, Gregorian Jocelyn LaSilvian, the youngest chef to come out of the Chef Academy in three hundred years.

"Don't let his tender age fool you, Gregorian is a culinary genius," said Jonah Gumple, the first person inside. Gumple, who proposed to his longtime girlfriend in the restaurant, credits the food with her positive answer. "I've asked her four times already," he admitted. "This was the first time she said yes."

Gregorian prepared an excellent seafood feast for the first hundred people lucky enough to get in. When asked if he would be serving kraken, he scoffed. "No one's foolish enough to go after that kind of animal," he said, adding, "Skilly-wigs and stewed sea-orchids taste just as good, and are far easier to get ahold of, which means I don't have to overcharge my customers for them."

(story continued on page seven)

Lailu stopped reading and crumpled the paper into a tight ball, imagining it was Greg's head. "*The youngest chef?* How ... dare ... he!"

All through school she had been tied with Greg for top chef in their class. Lailu worked harder, and she knew her recipes were better prepared, but Greg was a favorite with most of the teachers and always seemed to pick up extra points. Greg, with his easy smile and aristocratic family. Greg, who unscrewed the caps of her seasonings, who added colored dye to her soups, who made up names for her and never, ever got in trouble because he was a LaSilvian. Greg . . .

She stood and threw the crumpled ball to the ground, all thoughts of Mr. Boss and Slipshod's betrayal vanishing in the wake of her anger. She had to beat Greg. She *had* to!

She looked up at her mentor. "What was this you were saying about a gaggle of batyrdactyls?"

Master Slipshod smiled. "That's the spirit." He stretched, then headed to the kitchen. Lailu followed him, pausing in front of the large steam-powered stove. A graduation gift from her father and two older brothers, it was made out of polished metal and glass and boasted eight burners as well as two stove openings wide enough for Lailu to crawl inside. A multitude of pipes burst from the top of it to puncture the wall and connect to the chimney in back, making their kitchen feel small, even though it was almost half the size of the rest of the restaurant.

Lailu traced the small letters, *SV*, engraved in the top left corner, sighing. Scientist Starling Volan was amazing and brilliant and creative. Almost two years ago she had visited the academy to unveil her new stoves, and Lailu had looked up to her ever since. Starling wasn't afraid to do things differently. No, she had revolutionized modern cooking with her marvelous steam-powered inventions, just as Lailu had wanted to revolutionize eating by opening the first restaurant ever in Twin Rivers.

Her mentor rummaged around in each of the shelves. "I got a tip that a gaggle of those bloodsuckers has been terrorizing the townsfolk on the edge of the Velvet Forest and could do with a bit of thinning out." He removed a small pouch that jingled mysteriously. "I have to do a few more things this afternoon, but I'll be back before dark, and we can go hunting then."

"I can hunt them myself." Greg probably hunted everything himself.

"No, batyrdactyls are dangerous."

Lailu snorted. "They're only a few feet tall."

"Yes, but they're bullies, always fighting in a group. Plus my contact said they're nesting close to the elves' tree fort, so we'd be treading a bit of dangerous territory. No, Pigtails, you need to wait for me. I won't be long."

But as Lailu cleaned up all the dirty dishes, and the sun sank below the horizon, Master Slipshod did not return. Finally, she headed up the creaky wooden stairs to her room above the restaurant. They'd still be able to hunt before opening tomorrow.

O God of Cookery, please bring people to our restaurant, Lailu prayed as she slipped under the blankets on her thin feather mattress. Then she remembered her broken shrine. Would Chushi even listen to her now? With that thought ringing through her head, she lay awake for a long time. Just as sleep came drifting over her, Lailu's eyes snapped open. There was . . . something. Something downstairs. She froze, listening intently. Was it Master Slipshod?

Thump! Crack! "Ow!"

Lailu went for the large butcher knife she kept in a quick-draw sheath next to her bed. The noise had come from the kitchen. Master Slipshod knew his way around that kitchen, even in the dark. It wasn't him down there.

She willed her heart to beat quieter, images of the Butcher flashing through her mind. A creak, then another. Someone climbing the stairs. Taking a deep breath, Lailu eased herself out of bed, her hand shaking from gripping the knife so hard.

The bedroom door opened.

Lailu lunged forward and grabbed a handful of cloth and hair in her free hand. She glimpsed a pair of familiar dark eyes widened in terror before the intruder shrieked and dropped her candle. It sputtered out, returning the room to darkness.

"H-Hannah?" Lailu asked, letting the intruder go.

She heard a deep, gasping breath, then, "Yes. Yes, it's just me," her best friend said shakily.

"What are you doing here?" Lailu crouched down and felt for the candle, then made her way over to the bedside dresser for some matches. As she relit the candle, she glanced back at her friend. Hannah remained standing awkwardly in the doorway, her borrowed secondhand school uniform disheveled where Lailu had grabbed it, a glittery emerald haircomb askew in her long black hair.

"C-can I stay here for the night?"

Lailu couldn't hide her surprise. Hannah had followed Lailu to the city from Clear Lakes, their snowy little mountain village.

But after being accepted into Twin Rivers's Finest, an elite boarding school for hairdressing and fashion, Hannah had been too busy to see Lailu much. Especially since she was living over on Gilded Island with the wealthy, whereas Lailu had moved from the academy all the way out to the opposite end of the city. "Why?" Lailu asked. "What's going on?"

"Just some nasty drama with the other girls at school." Hannah waved a hand casually, but her red-rimmed eyes and trembling lips were apparent in the flickering candlelight.

"Drama? What kind of drama?" Lailu had dealt with whispered insults and taunts from many of the girls in Clear Lakes, and was no stranger to the way words could cut a person into tiny pieces. But Hannah had never let things like that bother her before. What kind of drama would have such an effect on her?

"Oh, you know, just the usual." Hannah shrugged her overnight bag up higher on her shoulder. "But if it's too much trouble . . ."

"Of course you can stay." As if Lailu would tell Hannah no and send her back out into the night, especially since she was clearly shaken by whatever had happened. Lailu was dying to know more, but could tell Hannah wasn't in a talking mood.

Hannah gave her brightest smile and dropped her bag with a very final-sounding thump. "Whew. That was getting very heavy."

"But what happens if you're caught outside of school?" Lailu knew from experience that all the city's boarding schools had strict curfew policies.

Hannah shrugged. "I'll be back and in bed before Madame Pompadour even notices tomorrow morning." She pulled the sparkling emerald comb from her hair and carefully placed it on the night-stand, crawled into Lailu's bed, and blew out her candle. "Thank you," she mumbled, already drifting off to sleep. "You're the bestest. . . ."

Lailu sighed and squeezed in next to her friend. It wasn't exactly a large bed. The vanilla-and-cinnamon scent of Hannah's hairsprays and perfumes filled the room, tickling her nose. She tried to ignore it, waiting for sleep; then, when sleep didn't come, she waited for the sounds of her mentor returning so they could hunt. And waited. And waited. Then her thoughts started drifting to Greg, lines out the door of his own place . . .

"That's it," she muttered, easing herself out of bed. She was done lying around, waiting for her mentor as if she were some child. She was practically a master chef in her own right, and she could hunt by herself.

She smoothed down her black hair and gathered it back into pigtails, then dressed quietly in formfitting knit trousers and a matching long-sleeved top, both black. Grabbing her grappling hook and a belt of knives, she spared one last glance at her snoring friend before pulling a hat on over her ears and slipping out of the room.

Outside, the air had turned dark and crisp. A single lamp flickered across the street, illuminating a man staggering home from work to an old brick apartment building nearby. He looked defeated, his clothing worn and patched, his shoulders slumped, his bowl of a hat partially crumpled under one arm. It was a look shared by most of the citizens living this far on the outskirts of town, just yards away from the Velvet Forest.

Savoria was a wild country, full of the mystic beasts that Lailu used for her recipes. This made it a wonderful place for mystic chefs, but not as wonderful for farmers and village people just trying to live their lives. Many of them had slowly moved into the cities, where protection was provided either by local garrisons or, in the case of Savoria's capital city of Twin Rivers, the Heroes Academy. But the protection of the city came at a high price. Most poor citizens who wanted the safety of these city walls were eventually forced to deal with loan sharks like Mr. Boss or to bargain with the elves. It was hard to know which situation was worse or more dangerous: dealing with the beasts outside, or the ones inside.

When Lailu had first envisioned Mystic Cooking, she pictured it resting in a more populated area of the city, not shunted off to edge into the elves' territory. But it didn't matter; even here people would learn of their restaurant. They would have customers tomorrow. They *had* to have customers.

With a parting look at her small two-story restaurant, Lailu turned and slipped into the forest.

3

Solo Hunt

Shivering, Lailu steadied herself on a branch as she pulled her grappling hook out of the tangle above her. Up in the thinner branches of the oak trees, the wind whipped her pigtails into her face. She swung the hook gently in small loops, building up momentum, then stopped when she heard a sudden noise behind her.

It was a low screeching sound, increasing in pitch until it ended in a burbling shriek: the batyrdactyls' hunting call. The sound chilled her to her core, even though she had known she was getting close to their lair when she found a second bird corpse completely drained of blood.

Lailu turned, trying to make no noise as she balanced carefully on the branch. There was just enough light to make out the leathery snout, the bright red eyes, the teeth. The moonlight seemed to emphasize those teeth, all four of them, all unnaturally white and long and narrow, as the batyrdactyl settled on the tree behind her. Small gray feathers covered its plump body, while two large, leathery wings folded at its sides, both ending in hooked talons.

Lailu pulled a knife out of her leather belt. The batyrdactyl's wings opened slightly as it adjusted its claws on a branch not five feet away from her. It was a little on the short side, only about three feet tall, but it would make an excellent roast. She already had a special blend of seasonings mixed, not to mention plenty of sage and garlic. The leftover pieces would go well in a tasty soup, its bones flavoring the broth in a delightfully exotic way, a perfect appetizer. Her mouth watered thinking about it.

A scratching noise sounded behind her, and then another at her side, and Lailu pulled herself back into the present. There were now four batyrdactyls surrounding her, staring with those eerie red eyes. Most batyrdactyls hunted in smaller gaggles of only two or three; she hadn't been expecting to take on a group this size. Maybe she should have listened to her mentor and waited.

Lailu ignored her growing sense of unease and put the knife in her teeth, then pulled a second knife out. The forest seemed to hold its breath, a whole ocean of branches whispering quietly while the batyrdactyls watched her in the darkness.

Lailu turned back to the first creature, took aim, and threw her knife. As the blade left her hand, a screeching batyrdactyl slammed into her, raking her arms with its claws. Lailu threw herself to the side, flipping around upside down on her branch, and another one flew at her, its rubbery snout right against her face.

Her heart racing furiously, Lailu dropped down to the branch beneath her, ducking under the larger of the two creatures. She grabbed the knife from between her teeth and slashed at it, but as it fell, another one took its place, and suddenly it was like the forest was alive with batyrdactyls, all screeching that horrible burbling sound. Buffeted on all sides by wings and scraped by claws, Lailu turned and twisted, swinging her grappling hook in a circle around her, her knife clutched in her other hand. She could smell her own blood and knew it was drawing more of them. She was way too exposed up here.

Her hook jerked out of her hands and became embedded in the side of one of the circling creatures. The batyrdactyl howled and lunged at her. Lailu threw her knife, catching it neatly in one beady red eye. As it fell, she went for a third knife, but another batyrdactyl slammed into her from behind, knocking her forward. She caught the branch and wrapped her arms and legs around it. Sudden pain stabbed through the side of her neck as a batyrdactyl latched its teeth through her skin and slurped greedily, feeding on her blood.

Lailu screamed. Thrashing and flailing, she knew she'd never be able to get it off her that way. There was only one thing to do. She threw all her weight to the side and let go of the branch.

Lailu twisted as she fell, knocking the batyrdactyl away. She twisted again, reaching her hands out, desperately trying to hold on to branches that snapped and broke beneath her. She felt like she was falling forever, landing on a branch only to have it give under her.

A few seconds passed before Lailu realized she'd finally stopped falling. As she lay blinking up at the broken branches, she felt for the ground under her, but her bloody fingers dug into ropes instead.

Ropes. Gasping, Lailu sat up, trying to claw her way to a standing position as the net entangled her. Biting her lip to keep silent, she peered through the webbing of ropes beneath her, then groaned when she realized she was dangling only about six feet off the ground. She must have hit that trap perfectly.

"What are the odds," she said. She reached for a knife, her hand closing on thin air.

"No," she whispered, instinctively patting down her sides, before she remembered the feeling of the batyrdactyl clinging to her, its claws ripping into her arm. The knife belt must have torn off, which meant she was stuck here, weak and weaponless. Here, in the elves' territory, in what could only be one of their traps. It wasn't technically against any written rules to enter the forest; however, not all elves cared for humans, and not all trespassers made it out alive or fully intact.

Her heart sank. Master Slipshod would kill her—that is, if the elves didn't get her first. She remembered the cold blue eyes of the one from yesterday and shivered. "Oh God," she whispered, closing her eyes. "God of Cookery, if you'll just get me out of this, I'll . . ." She paused, not sure what she'd do in exchange.

As she sat there debating, she heard the soft crunch of boots on leaves. "Looks like you're in a bit of a pickle."

Lailu froze. *No. Way.*

This was a dream, this was all a horrible dream, a nightmare beyond epic proportions.

"Are you hoping if you keep your eyes closed, I'll just go away?" Lailu could clearly hear the smirk behind those words. "Not going to happen."

She realized he was probably right. He'd never gone away before. Why should now be any different? Lailu reluctantly opened her eyes and shifted, struggling to look down through the ropes below. It was dark, but with the dim moonlight filtering through the branches overhead, not dark enough as she stared at the last person she'd ever want to find her in this kind of predicament.

Lailu hid her face in her hands. "Hello, Greg," she mumbled.

4

RIVALS

ello, Lailu. Long time no see," Greg said.

Lailu kept her face hidden, embarrassment throbbing through her.

"So, whatcha doin'?" he asked.

"I'm knitting a sweater!" she snapped, finally looking at him. "What do you think I'm doing?"

"Look at you, all fire and brimstone." Greg smiled so wide she could see his teeth glinting in the moonlight. It reminded her unpleasantly of the bactyrdactyls. "That's the Lailu I know and love. I've missed you since graduation, you know. You never write. You never visit."

Lailu ground her teeth. She hated how Greg mocked her, always pretending they were old friends. "What are you doing here?"

"Hunting. Obviously."

"Well then, maybe you should get back to it."

"You know, you might want to be a little nicer to me."

"Yeah? And why would that be?"

Greg ran a hand through his unruly brown hair. "Oh, I don't know. Just seeing as you're stuck in there, and I have all your knives out here . . ." He fanned them out for her to see, her half-empty knife belt slung over his shoulder.

"My knives!"

"Here I am hunting, minding my own business, when I hear a whole gaggle of batyrdactyls screeching like their world's gone mad. Naturally, I had to investigate." Greg shifted so the moonlight gleamed off the edges of the knives in his hands. "Imagine my surprise when a dead batyrdactyl came sailing out of the trees toward me with this little beauty stuck inside it. Followed by a second, and then a whole knife belt." He reached up, wrapping his fingers around the bottom of the net. "Don't you know it's not a good idea to hunt batyrdactyls alone?"

"Says who?"

"Says everyone. I mean, even *I* remember them telling us that in Chef Academy. Makes me wonder just what that mentor of yours is teaching you." He shook his head.

"You're alone," Lailu pointed out.

"I'm not hunting batyrdactyls. Obviously."

Lailu launched herself forward, but all she managed to do was get more tangled than ever. After a few seconds of fruitless struggling, she collapsed, panting and furious, Greg's laughter ringing in her ears.

"Look at you, just look at you!" he crowed.

"Eat dirt, Greg," she muttered, but she felt drained, and even her anger slid away as sparks of light flashed in front of her eyes. All that struggling had reopened the scrapes along her hands, arms, and legs, and her neck was still bleeding. Dimly she remembered that batyrdactyl venom stopped the blood from clotting normally. She wondered what Greg was hunting, if not those bloodsuckers. Not that he'd tell her.

Greg stopped laughing. "Ask me nicely and I'll get you out of there."

She shook her head.

"Really? You can't ask me for help, even now?"

"I'd rather die," Lailu said, not looking at him.

Greg was silent for a moment, then said, "Suit yourself." She heard his footsteps crunching away and felt a pang of despair. For a second she debated calling out to him, but she couldn't, so instead she closed her eyes and willed herself not to cry. The forest seemed to close in around her, and she was alone. Alone with her scraped-up body, this horrible net, and . . . Lailu's eyes flew open as the net swayed. Then came the sound of snapping, and a few of the ropes gave way.

"You're so stubborn," Greg muttered, sawing the ropes with one of his trademark knives, a big straight blade with a serrated edge, like a glorified bread knife.

"I thought you'd left." She hated how weak her voice sounded.

Greg looked up, his eyes wide in the moonlight. "Did you really think I'd just leave you here?" All humor was gone from his face.

Lailu shrugged.

"You don't know me at all, do you?" he sighed, going back to his sawing. A few seconds later, the ropes entangling Lailu snapped, and she fell for the second time.

Greg caught her, setting her feet gently on the ground. She shoved away from him, then swayed, brushing off the hand he put out to steady her and taking a step back so she could see his face without craning her neck. She took a breath. Might as well get it over with. "Th-thanks," she managed.

"I guess you owe me one." Greg's eyes crinkled into slits.

"No," Lailu said quickly. "No, I never asked you for help." She had to keep blinking to stop the world from spinning, but she couldn't let this slide. She'd never owed Greg for anything before and she wasn't about to start now.

"Well, you didn't ask, but . . ." Greg frowned. "Are you all right?"

"Yes. Can I have my knives back?" It was taking all her strength not to lean against a tree trunk.

"Are you sure you're all right?"

"Knives?" Lailu repeated.

He passed them back to her, and she took the time to wipe each blade on her torn and bloody shirt before taking the knife belt back and sheathing them inside it. A chef's knives were her livelihood; no amount of blood loss was going to stop her from taking care of them. Head Chef Master Sanford had lost his eye in a deadly battle with a delicious manticore, and he still insisted on cleaning his knives before getting any medical help. Lailu could hardly do any different.

"So, how's the restaurant coming along?" Greg asked.

Lailu studied his face. It was a mask of innocence, but Greg had always been good at acting. What did he know about her business? Was he rubbing in the fact that his was booked solid on his first day, while hers was a dining graveyard? Or maybe he was just trying to have a friendly conversation? She narrowed her eyes. Unlikely.

"Master Slipshod dropped by my place yesterday. He told me your restaurant opened on the same day as mine," he continued. "What a coincidence."

"Coincidence my butt," Lailu muttered.

"What was that?"

"Nothing." She tried turning her grimace into a smile, but then gave it up as a lost cause. "Well?" she demanded. "What about it?"

Greg shrugged. "I was just surprised, since I didn't see anything on it in the papers."

"Well, maybe I was too busy cooking instead of posing for some ridiculous paper," she snarled, the sudden flash of anger giving her energy.

"What's that supposed—"

"And the youngest chef in three hundred years?" She cut him off. "What a joke."

"I never said that! I was misquoted."

"Whatever." She began limping away from him.

"Lailu, wait!"

She ignored him.

"Aren't you at least going to collect your batyrdactyls? You did almost die for them."

She turned reluctantly.

Greg gestured to a dark form lying on the ground several paces away from him and a second one sprawled nearby. Lailu hobbled over, grabbed each of the batyrdactyls by a foot, and started dragging them back toward her restaurant. She kept up a stony silence as she passed Greg again, concentrating on walking and trying to ignore all the aches and pains in her body.

She remembered the first time she'd hunted with Greg back at school, remembered how he'd tricked her.

"Let's be friends," he had said, and he'd looked earnest, his brown eyes wide and soft and warm like a puppy's. And Lailu, silly, young, and naive, took him at his word. "Want to hunt together?" he'd asked. And she'd been only too eager. Her first real hunt with another would-be chef. Her first real friend outside of her village.

Lailu shook her head, trying to rid herself of the memories, of the way he had left her there as bait, the sound of those chicken feet scraping, scraping as they surrounded her, and then, after it was all over, how he took all the credit for the hunt. The batyrdactlys might have taken a few chunks out of her today, but it was nothing compared to the pain of that long-ago hunt with Greg.

With her anger wrapped around her like a cloak, she managed to stomp through the forest until she was sure Greg couldn't see her anymore. Until it was safe to limp, slowly and painfully, the rest of the way home.

5

UNEXPECTED VISITORS

By the time Lailu got back to her restaurant and dragged the batyrdactyls into the kitchen, the sun was just peeking over the horizon. There was a quiet buzz to the air that let her know the city was waking up and would soon be hungry. The world swam in front of her eyes, but Lailu forced herself to stumble out back to the pump to wash up and get some water to clean the batyrdactyl carcasses.

Mystic Cooking's well and water pump sat about thirty feet behind the restaurant, just at the edge of the Velvet Forest. It was one of the reasons she and Master Slipshod chose this location; all the other buildings either had to share a water pump or were large brick apartment buildings well outside their budget.

As she pumped water into a wooden bucket, Lailu took a deep breath, enjoying the early-morning calm in spite of the way her whole body throbbed. When the bucket was mostly full, she hoisted it up and dumped it over her head, gasping as the freezing water streamed down her back.

Shaking the water out of her hair like a dog, Lailu tightened her pigtails before filling the bucket again and lifting it to bring inside. She had barely taken one step when she stopped. Someone was watching her.

A man leaned against a nearby tree, his arms crossed over his chest. "You," she whispered, taking in the shoulder-length black hair and laughing gray eyes.

"Me." He pushed away from the tree and gave her a little half bow.

He was really more of a boy than a man, Lailu decided as she studied his young face. Maybe fifteen or sixteen? His black slacks were tucked into well-worn black boots, and his matching shirt blended well with the early-morning shadows. He wore his outfit casually, his sleeves rolled up to just below his elbows and his gray vest unbuttoned to flap slightly in the breeze.

"You're one of Mr. Boss's lackeys." Lailu tightened her grip on her bucket.

The boy grimaced. "I suppose you could call me that," he admitted. "Although I prefer the term 'henchman.'"

Lailu narrowed her eyes. "You're the one who told Mr. Boss to break my shrine."

"Ah, but I also told him *not* to break your fingers. That has to count for something." He grinned. "Ryon, by the way. At your service."

Lailu scowled. True, she was glad to still have the full use of her hands, but that shrine had been hand-carved by her father out of lucky bamboo and blessed by her village's temple. The God of Cookery, not to mention her father, would be most displeased she'd let it get smashed to bits.

"What happened to you?"

Lailu looked down at her torn clothing dripping with blood and water, and covered in dirt and bits of twigs. "Nothing," she said irritably. "This is how I always look in the morning."

Ryon's lips quirked. "Fair enough."

Lailu shifted her grip on the bucket. "Why are you here?"

His smile widened. "Mr. Boss asked me to check up on you."

"Why?"

"He's concerned about your lack of business."

"We've only been open one day!"

"And did you have any customers?" He raised his eyebrows.

Lailu flushed and said nothing.

"Mr. Boss is just worried you and Slipshod won't be able to pay him back in a timely fashion."

"The first payment's not due till next year. Why should he be worried now?"

Ryon shrugged. "I am but a poor servant. I just do as I'm told."

"Yeah, right. Well then, you can tell Mr. Boss—"

"Tell him yourself. He'll be stopping by this evening."

"He'll be . . . what? Why?" She thought of the Butcher grabbing her again, and her stomach turned to overcooked pasta.

"He's having an important meeting, and he wants food for at least twelve people. Oh, and you'll have to close your restaurant for him." Ryon smiled as if this whole thing were a joke.

Lailu gaped. "Close our restaurant? Food for twelve?"

"You could always refuse. I wouldn't recommend it, though . . . no more shrines to break."

Lailu didn't have a good response, so she just walked back toward her restaurant, lugging her bucket. Maybe Master Slipshod would know what to do.

"Here, let me." Ryon reached for the bucket. She jerked away from him, water sloshing over the bucket's rim. "Or not."

"I don't need help." The memory of Greg having to save her still burned heavy on her mind, and she would be a cold, stiff corpse before accepting any help from a lackey of Mr. Boss.

As Lailu pushed the back door open, she spared one last glance back, then quickly stepped inside and let the door shut firmly behind her. Shivering, she put the bucket down. With Master Slipshod still out on his mysterious errands, Lailu knew she'd have to do all the prep work on her own.

She poured the water into a large steel basin and dumped one of the batyrdactyls in to soak. That would make it easier to de-feather. Grabbing the second batyrdactyl, she pushed the single chair in the kitchen off her throw rug, then kicked that aside and pried open the trapdoor hidden beneath it. After stumbling down the narrow staircase to the stone-lined cellar, she shoved the carcass inside the icebox towering in the corner, shutting the door quickly to keep everything as cold as possible.

Back in the kitchen, Lailu started all her prep work, then headed upstairs to get herself ready. After cleaning her scrapes, she dug her mother's special ointment out from one of her drawers and smeared it liberally over the wounds. The smell of mint filled her nose, and she could almost feel her mother's hands over her own. She closed her eyes, remembering those disastrous first hunts after she'd made up her mind to become a chef, and the gentle way her mother would tend to her injuries.

"It's good for you to be strong," her mother had told her after a particularly brutal failed hunt. "I want you to be strong. Women should be independent. But Lailu, my little one," her mother sighed, rubbing the ointment into a long scrape down Lailu's left arm, "women also need to be careful."

"I *was* careful," Lailu insisted. "But the blasted little pygem was faster than I thought."

"Well now. Either you need to be faster too, or you need to stop this hunting. The ideas that boy has put into your head."

"Vahn said I could be a chef. He thinks I could really be accepted into the academy." Lailu had never thought of leaving the village until the day an apprentice hero had saved her brother Lonnie from a vicious nest of vibbers. Not only was the stranger the most beautiful boy Lailu had ever seen, he also *loved* her cooking. She could still recall the way he'd asked for seconds, and then thirds, and as her brothers hassled him for stories of his heroic exploits, his attention had never wavered from his plate.

After dinner he'd told her all about the academy and its four fields of study: hero, artist, scholar, and chef. He was the one who said her cooking was excellent already, that if she could just improve her hunting, she could try applying to the academy's scholarship program.

"I know you feel Vahn can do no wrong after he saved our Lonnie, but just remember, one good deed does not make a good man." Her mother capped the ointment, then handed the small jar to Lailu.

"For me?" Lailu's heart beat faster. Her mother always kept her ointments locked up, secret, scarce.

"For you. I can see it in your eyes—you're never going to stop this." Her mother put her arms around her. Lailu could feel the strands of her mother's dark auburn hair sliding around her face, could smell the perfume she always wore, sweet and spicy. Comforting and exotic. "And I won't always be around to protect you."

She'd been gone the next day, gone for months, the weight of her absence pressing this last memory permanently into Lailu's heart. Even though her mother had vanished several times before, this was the first time Lailu began to wonder if she was ever coming back. Oh, she'd heard all about her mother's people, the Wanderers; had heard the longing in her mother's voice when she spoke of traveling the land with them before she fell in love with Lailu's father. But Lailu had never believed her mother might go back to that old life, might give up her family in exchange for extraordinary sights and distant shores.

When she finally came back, all smiles and hugs and acting like she hadn't just abandoned her family again, Lailu had never quite believed it. She had seen the truth now: her mother's heart was always longing to be elsewhere. Her family wasn't enough for her anymore.

Lailu shook her head, ridding herself of those ghosts. Her

mother had never been the most reliable person, but at least the ointments she made were dependable. Lailu ran her finger over the heart her mother had carved into the top of the ceramic container, then screwed it shut. She hadn't seen her mom in over a year. Her mother hadn't even bothered coming to Lailu's graduation.

Lailu shoved the ointment back into the drawer and closed it harder than necessary. Hannah rolled over in her sleep, muttering something about a comb. Ignoring her, Lailu pulled on a baggy, loosely knit shirt that fell to her knees, which she belted over a pair of tight-fitting trousers and her favorite soft-soled boots. As she finger-combed her hair into pigtails, she decided she looked presentable enough that Master Slipshod wouldn't know how disastrously her hunt had gone.

Bam! Bam! Bam!

Lailu jumped. She glanced at her bed, but Hannah snored softly on as whoever was at the door continued to pound away. Lailu turned and headed down the stairs, clutching at the rail as the world spun dizzily around her. The last thing she needed was another good fall.

Bam! Bam!

"I'm coming, I'm coming." Lailu pushed aside the curtain and stomped her way through the dining room, yanking the door open. "What now?" she demanded, then stopped. "Vahn?" For a moment she wondered if her memories had somehow pulled him here. Her hand was clenched around the doorknob to keep herself standing as her knees threatened to give way.

The boy standing in her doorway gave a small bow. "At your

service," he said gallantly, straightening and tossing his waves of honey-gold hair back behind his shoulders, looking every inch the hero he had set off to become.

His eyes were deep blue like a twilight sky, and Lailu remembered all those days she'd spent lost in them, waiting for him to notice her, and here he was, like something out of a dream, standing in the doorway of *her* restaurant. He was so tall the top of her head barely reached his chest, and his shoulders practically filled her doorway.

"Vahn, I–I mean, uh, that is . . ." Lailu stumbled, the words crashing into and over one another as her tongue seemed to fill her whole mouth.

Vahn flashed her a brilliant smile. "I often have that effect on people."

Lailu's face flushed, and she hoped he wouldn't notice. "Wh-what are you doing here?"

"I'm in the city on some business, and I promised Laurent I'd stop by and check on you." Vahn shifted his weight back and forth impatiently.

Lailu's heart sank. "That's all, huh?" Just checking up on her for her overbearing oldest brother. At sixteen, Laurent believed he knew everything, and he was always trying to oversee Lailu as if she couldn't handle things on her own. She just hoped Lonnie was giving him enough trouble for the two of them.

"Pretty much. But I must say, though, Lillie, you haven't changed a bit."

"Lailu," she corrected automatically. "It's Lailu."

"Of course it is," he said smoothly, adding, "You wouldn't happen to have any food on hand, would you?"

Lailu nodded. Someday he would remember, she promised herself as she led Vahn into the restaurant. Someday he would see her as more than just her brother's kid sister. He was only four years older than her, and that wasn't so much, not when they were meant to be together. Someday.

The door slammed shut, jolting Lailu out of her happy fantasy. "So, here's my place. Well, mine and Master Slipshod's. Welcome to Mystic Cooking." Nerves made her babble a little faster, and her voice came out in a high-pitched squeak.

"Master Slipshod, eh? So it's true. You *are* apprenticed to him."

"Yes."

"Interesting choice."

Lailu frowned. "What's that supposed to mean?"

"Nothing. It means nothing at all," Vahn said quickly. "So, how does this work? This whole *restaurant* thing?"

"It's for people who want a nice meal sometimes but can't afford to keep a household chef, or who want to try something different," Lailu explained. "We vary the specials every day, and people come in here and pay to eat them. Or at least I really hope they will." She took a deep breath, let it out. No need to tell Vahn all about their troubles.

"Sounds simple enough." Vahn ran his hands along one of the unlit candelabras that snaked along the wall, then paused to inspect the menu.

Lailu realized she was staring and gave herself a shake. "Feel free to sit anywhere, and I'll bring some food right out to you."

"Can't wait." Vahn flashed her another brilliant smile. "I remember what a great cook you always were."

She smiled up at him, way up at him. She wouldn't have minded her height so much if she were at least dainty, too, but she was built like her mother's people: solid and stocky, unlike the other native people of Clear Lakes, who were all tall and lean like Hannah. Maybe she'd grow a little more when she was older.

Back in the kitchen she got to work swiftly, de-feathering the soaked batyrdactyl with quick, practiced movements before transferring the meat to a cutting board. After preparing a dozen flaky meat pastries and putting them in the oven to bake, she took some of the batyrdactyl's chopped thigh meat and panfried it, letting it sizzle before dribbling olive oil and herbs all over it, the smell spilling out of her kitchen and into the main room. While waiting for the pastries to finish cooking, she figured she might as well get started on the lunch special. She wanted to prove to Master Slipshod that she had what it took to run a restaurant. She'd save the rest of the batyrdactyl, she decided, and reuse yesterday's ingredients in a delicious kraken hot pot.

Nodding to herself, Lailu began filling her special pot, a brass contraption practically big enough for her to sit in. Dials on its front adjusted the temperature and a small, narrow pipe wound along the side, letting steam escape without overheating the food. Once the hot pot was filled and set to a medium heat, she pulled the pastries out of the oven, setting them on a rack to cool, then transferring them to a plate for Vahn.

Out in the dining room, Lailu watched Vahn flip through pages of paper, the same kind of glossy white paper Greg's story had been written on. Hannah had told her it came from something called a "press." Lailu narrowed her eyes at it. No one had heard of the scientists until Starling Volan unveiled her line of stoves at the Chef Academy two years ago. Now it seemed like there was a new invention every week. Lailu thought Starling and her followers should just focus on cooking inventions and leave everything else alone.

She put the plate down in front of Vahn. "Breakfast."

"Thanks, Lola." His eyes didn't leave the paper.

"Lailu," she said, but he clearly wasn't listening. She frowned, then said again, "So, *breakfast*."

Vahn looked up, his blue eyes widening. "Sorry, distracted." He smiled, and Lailu felt her heart melt like butter. He could call her whatever he wanted as long as he smiled at her like that.

"That's all right," she said dreamily.

Vahn picked up a pastry and took a huge bite, chewed, swallowed, and took another bite. "Delicious," he said through a mouthful of food. Lailu almost swooned with happiness on the spot.

"Do you really think so?" She rested her elbows on his table.

"Would these lips lie?" He grinned, and Lailu found herself grinning back and leaning toward him.

A soft footstep, the creak of a floorboard, and she straightened, turning so fast her neck popped.

Greg stood there, one hand on the door like he'd been trying to slip out.

"Greg!" Lailu's cheeks burned. "What are you doing here?"

"I, uh, came to bring you your things," Greg mumbled, looking strangely subdued.

"My things?"

He held out his hand, showing her a dead batyrdactyl wrapped in her grappling hook. She must have killed a third one. "You left them this morning. I thought you might need them."

Lailu hesitated, then walked forward and took them. "Thanks."

His mouth twitched in a half smile. "That's two 'thanks' from you in one day. Be careful or it might become a habit."

"Don't count on it."

They stood there staring at each other, the dead batyrdactyl between them, and for a second Lailu wondered why she spent so much time hating this boy. He had helped her out twice today, and with Vahn sitting in her restaurant, enjoying her cooking, she was feeling a little more charitable than usual. "Greg," she began.

"Yes, Lailu?" Greg leaned in closer to her, close enough that she could see the dark circles under his eyes, proof he was actually working hard, was pouring his heart into his new business the same way she was. His curly hair looked crazier than usual, and his black shirt had a few small cuts in it, like he hadn't gone home at all since she last saw him.

"I was thinking—"

"Hey, you're that famous chef!" Vahn said loudly, coming up next to them.

"What?" Greg asked, surprised.

"Gregorian LaSilvian," Vahn continued. "I recognized you from the paper." He rattled the page between them, and Lailu, glancing down, saw another picture of Greg smiling on the front, his arms opened wide, customers pouring into his restaurant. YOUNGEST CHEF IN THREE HUNDRED YEARS PREPARING FOR SECOND DAY OF SUCCESS read the headline. Lailu scowled and turned away. *That* was why she hated him.

"Wait, Lailu!" Greg pushed past Vahn.

"I'm sorry, but I have customers to prepare for," she snapped as she hurried toward her kitchen.

"It doesn't look that way to me."

Lailu spun around and glared at him.

He stood there frozen, his hand halfway to his mouth. "I didn't mean that. I just meant—"

"Oh, stuff it. Just go away."

"Look, I just wanted to tell you the offer's still there, and I'd love to have your help. We could both benefit—"

"I told you once, and I'll tell you again: I am *not* working for you and your uncle. I might not have any money, but I still have some pride left. Now leave." She crossed her arms over her chest.

Greg shook his head. "I can tell you're in over your head. I heard you and your mentor borrowed money from Mr. Boss, and—"

"And it's none of your business." How did he know that when she'd just barely learned of it herself?

"Stop interrupting me and listen! He's bad news. You don't want to let that man own you, Lailu. I'm offering to help you here."

"You are, huh?" Her fingers clenched around the dead batyr-dactyl. Once she would have been happy to accept his help. But she wasn't the same naive village girl she'd been at the start of school.

"Well, I don't need any of your so-called help. You don't owe me anything, and I don't want to owe you anything in return. We're rivals. That's it."

Greg pressed his lips together. Next to him, Vahn looked back and forth between them, his expression curious, like this was a show they were putting on for his benefit.

"That's it, huh?" Greg said finally. "That's what you think?"

Lailu nodded. They stood there for a few more seconds, the time ticking by painfully, Greg's expression hard and unreadable. "Go back to your restaurant," Lailu whispered, breaking the awful silence. "I'm sure *you*, at least, really do have customers to see."

"Fine." He turned his back on her and stalked away.

"Hope you had fun slumming it over here!" Lailu yelled after him as he slammed the door. The dining room felt strangely quiet after that, and she stood there, breathing hard as if she'd been running.

"Well, that was dramatic." Vahn sounded as cheerful and unruffled as ever. When Lailu looked at him, he smiled and pointed to his empty plate. "Got any more pastries for me?"

Paying Customers

H e just waltzes in here, acting like he's better than me."
Lailu slammed more ingredients into her hot pot.
"Stupid aristocrat." She gave the bubbling pot a vigorous stir, then stomped back into the dining room, where even the sight of Vahn eating her cooking failed to cheer her up.

The bell above the door chimed.

Lailu's jaw dropped. Someone new stood in the doorway. A . . . customer?

"Is this restaurant open?" the man asked, glancing around the mostly empty room.

"Yes, it is." Lailu nervously pushed her fluffy white chef's hat straighter on her head, her anger evaporating like soup left too long on the stove. "Welcome to Mystic Cooking."

His face brightened. "So this *is* Mystic Cooking. It's so far from the center of town, I wasn't sure. I never would have found it if not for the referral."

"Referral?" Lailu asked.

"Yes, from that other chef, La—"

The door opened. "Sorry I'm late," a woman said breathlessly, clutching a tiny hat to her head, her skirts rustling. She paused in the doorway. "Oh, it's nicer inside than I thought."

Lailu wasn't sure how to take that. Should she be offended?

"Do your parents run this place?" the woman asked.

Definitely offended, Lailu decided. Still, a potential customer was a potential customer. She pasted a smile on her face. "No, I run it. Well, me and Master Slipshod."

"Oh! I've heard of this Slipshod." The woman closed her parasol and stepped forward, letting the door swing shut behind her. "Dragon cuisine, right? The finest in the land?"

"That's him," the man said, taking her parasol from her. "Is he around?"

Lailu bit her lip. "He'll be back shortly. Meanwhile, our special today is the kraken hot pot." She tried to sound calm, like people ordered the special all the time.

Their eyes widened. "So it's true, then. Now anyone can dine like royalty, at least for a meal. How times have changed," the man remarked.

Lailu supposed that was true; until very recently, only the wealthy could afford to have a private chef, and even now, most of the other students who graduated from the academy found jobs training in households with experienced master chefs. She was the one who helped open up the only restaurant in Twin Rivers. Well, it *had* been the only one, until that snaky Greg decided to go and copy her!

"Okay, I'll take an order of the special," the man decided.

"Me too," his companion chimed in, and Lailu had to exercise all her self-control to stop from dancing in place. They were staying! They wanted to eat her food! Oh, it was going to be a beautiful day.

Lailu smiled at her very first customers as they took seats in the corner, then had to refrain from skipping on her way back to the kitchen to check on the bubbling hot pot. She whistled as she cooked, stopping only when Hannah came downstairs.

Hannah flopped onto the kitchen chair, looking very colorful in a teal dress with little pink bows along the hem, her long black hair pinned back with that same gaudy emerald comb. Must be a new favorite, Lailu decided.

"You wouldn't believe it," Lailu whispered enthusiastically. "We have real, potentially paying customers!"

Hannah smiled. "I knew you could do it."

Lailu added some additional spices to the pot, then tasted the result. Almost perfect. It just needed to simmer for another few minutes. She glanced back at her friend, who was fiddling with one of the bows on her dress.

"So, you wanna tell me about it?" Lailu asked

"Tell you about what?"

"Why you needed to spend the night here? What drama with the other girls?"

Hannah sat straighter and opened and closed her mouth, like

she wanted to say something but wasn't sure. Finally, she looked away. "Just some baseless accusations. Really, there's not much to tell . . ."

The bell above the door chimed.

"Another customer?" Lailu poked her head out past the kitchen curtain. Three people, three whole, real live people, stood in the dining room, squinting at the sign that listed the special for the day. Much like the first couple, the middle-aged man and woman and their teenage daughter were all dressed far too nicely for this section of town. If anything, they looked like they would fit in well with the crowd on Gilded Island.

"—highly recommended, and it's cheaper than his place," the man was saying when he noticed Lailu standing there. "Oh! Hello."

"Hello, and welco—" Lailu began, when the door opened again and Master Slipshod ducked inside. "Master Slipshod!" She felt a rush of relief. She was very excited about having customers but also glad to know she wouldn't be facing them all alone.

He nodded briefly at Lailu, then turned to the customers, pulling a fluffy chef's hat out of his coat pocket and stuffing it on his head. "Welcome to Mystic Cooking."

"Does your hot pot really have kraken?" the woman asked. Her daughter shot her a look like she was too embarrassing for words, but Master Slipshod just grinned.

"Yes, it really has kraken."

"Wow," the man breathed, sharing a look with his wife. "Even LaSilvian's doesn't have kraken."

"He doesn't?" Master Slipshod said innocently. "I can't say I'm surprised. It takes a lot of nerve to catch kraken, and not every chef is as tough as my young apprentice." He nodded to Lailu, who stood a little taller.

As Master Slipshod seated the family, Lailu scurried back to the kitchen to scoop out bowls of kraken hot pot. Hannah, surprisingly, was still sitting there, staring at nothing.

"Shouldn't you be heading back to school?" Lailu asked. "I mean, don't you have to be back before Madame Poof—"

"Pompadour," Hannah corrected.

"—realizes you're gone?" Lailu finished.

Hannah waved her hands. "It's not important."

Lailu frowned. How could it not be important?

Hannah laughed. "Don't look so worried! I actually don't have class this morning."

"Really?"

"Really. In fact," Hannah said, climbing to her feet, "I can even help you with that." She picked up a tray, filling it with bowls and following Lailu back into the dining room.

Lailu took Vahn's food over to him personally while Hannah delivered the rest of the hot pots to their new customers. "Thanks, Lina." Vahn absently took a bite, then blinked, focusing on the food. "Wow! That's really good."

Lailu couldn't remember having a better day. "Thanks!" She watched him eat her cooking while across the restaurant Master Slipshod gave her a disapproving look before disappearing back into the kitchen. Lailu ignored him. She deserved this break. After all, she'd cooked up the hot pot all on her own. A quick glance around showed Vahn wasn't the only one who seemed to love it either.

And then Vahn put his empty bowl down and stood up.

"Y-you're not leaving, are you?"

Vahn chuckled. "Don't worry, kiddo, I'll be sticking around the city for a while. Got myself a quest."

Lailu's eyes widened. "You did? This is your first one, right?"

He nodded, his eyes sparkling. "My first chance to really prove myself." Like chefs, heroes typically took four years to complete their academy training, although Lailu managed to complete hers in only three. But where chefs apprenticed for up to two years, heroes stayed on as apprentices for at least four.

After Vahn completed his training at the Heroes Academy, he'd been apprenticed to the legendary Rhivanna, the most fearsome hero of Savoria. Lailu knew Vahn would end up being even more famous, though. After all, he had completed his training before his fourteenth birthday, just like Lailu, and he'd already finished his apprenticeship before his eighteenth. He was amazing.

"What kind of quest?" she asked eagerly. "I heard rumors that there's been a mountain dragon attack—"

He put a finger to his lips. "I can't talk about a current mission; it's part of the Hero Code of Ethics." He leaned in and whispered, "But it's not the dragon."

"Oh." Lailu felt strangely disappointed.

Vahn laughed. "It's bigger than a dragon," he reassured her. "I never thought I'd be doing a job for *this* particular group, but a hero goes where he's needed."

"Can you tell me about it when it's finished?"

Vahn grinned. "Tell you what: you cook me something nice, and I'll drop by to tell you all about it. All right?"

"It's a date," Lailu said, the words bursting out before she could stop them. She immediately flushed, but Vahn didn't seem to notice.

"That's my girl."

He called her his girl. Lailu couldn't help the goofy smile that crept across her face. And then Hannah walked by, and Vahn's eyes stuck to her like dried rice to a bowl.

"Hannah," he called, raising one hand in greeting.

Oh sure, Lailu thought darkly as Hannah walked over. Naturally he remembered *her* name.

"It's been a while." Vahn looked Hannah up and down approvingly while she preened under his gaze like some kind of exotic bird.

"Hello, Vahn." She tossed her head, that obnoxious emerald comb of hers catching the light.

"I swear, you grow prettier every time I see you." He took her hand and raised it to his lips.

Hannah blushed, then caught sight of Lailu's ugly look and quickly pulled her hand back. "Oh, er, uh," she began.

"I'm going to check on my other customers." Lailu stalked away, and when she glanced back, Vahn had already gone.

The next few hours passed with increasing busyness as more customers trickled inside, and Lailu forgot all about Vahn. To her surprise and gratitude, Hannah also continued to help, seating people, talking and laughing with the women, and flirting politely with the men. She was a natural. "No wonder that school took her in," Lailu whispered. She had always wondered how Hannah, with her eccentricities and silly, absentminded attitude, had gotten into an elite boarding school on Gilded Island. Now she understood, and she felt proud of her friend.

"Well," Hannah said when they were both back in the kitchen, Mystic Cooking closed for the day in preparation for Mr. Boss, "I've got to go now, but do you mind if I crash here again tonight? I've got the day off tomorrow, so we can hang out and I can help again."

Lailu frowned. "Is it really that bad?"

"Oh, you know." Hannah twirled a lock of her hair, and Lailu noticed she'd switched to an ugly silver comb in the shape of a butterfly. "I'm just letting things cool down a little."

Lailu had to wonder just what kind of trouble Hannah was having with her classmates, but knew she'd tell her on her own time. "Sure. We'd love to have your help again tomorrow."

Hannah yipped, throwing her arms around Lailu. "It will be like old times!" Lailu squirmed, and Hannah let her go. "Sorry, I know you don't like to be hugged."

"I . . . well. Personal space is very important." Lailu's mom had always given hugs way too freely, and Lailu had decided long ago that she didn't believe in such insincere displays of affection.

Giggling, Hannah sashayed across the restaurant, pausing at the door to wave before slipping out into the afternoon.

Lailu went back to work, scooping out the juices from the

marinated meat to use in a light gravy as Master Slipshod brought in the last of the dirty dishes from the dining room. "See, Pigtails? I told you. Customers."

"You said it." Lailu grinned.

"I notice the princess finally left." He piled the dishes in the corner.

Lailu frowned. She knew he was referring to Hannah, who had once made the mistake of questioning whether Slipshod was really the best choice for Lailu in front of Slipshod himself. He'd never quite forgiven her for that. "She doesn't act like a princess."

"She sure tries to dress like one." Slipshod snorted. "That hair-comb of hers is probably worth more than most people earn in a year."

"Really?"

"All those gaudy emeralds? Definitely."

"They're probably fake." Hannah didn't have much money, after all. "And you could be a little nicer. She did really help us today."

"Yeah, I suppose," he said grudgingly. "But cutting class to do it . . ."

"She had the morning off."

"Did she?" Master Slipshod looked unconvinced. "I don't remember Chef Academy ever giving a student a whole morning off."

"Well, her school is probably different."

"If you say so. I still say that girl's a whole lot of trouble, but if she wants to work here for free, I suppose even I can't complain."

Lailu shook her head, but that was probably the best she'd get.

"And speaking of not complaining," Master Slipshod cleared his throat. "I notice someone went hunting last night. Without me."

Lailu's ears burned and her body went icy. "Er," she tried.

"Er. That's what I thought." Slipshod's eyebrows drew close together. "Reckless, Pigtails. Very reckless."

"S-sorry."

"You won't do it again?"

"I won't do it again . . . as long as you come back when you say you're coming back."

He glared at her, then sniffed and went back to the dishes.

When it was obvious his lecture was over and he wasn't about to toss her in the street, Lailu relaxed and began stacking the leftovers off to the side. She couldn't feel too bad. It had been a successful hunt, after all. Well, more or less. She paused as the paper she'd cleared off Vahn's table earlier caught her eye. Leaning forward, she studied the picture of Greg.

It was obvious he came from money. LaSilvian's Kitchen was at least twice the size of Mystic Cooking, and even though the picture was in black and white, she could tell by all the different shades that his exterior was decorated with class. But what really caught her attention was how the picture did not look like some sort of painting. Oh no. The details of his annoyingly curly mop of hair and dimples were too perfect.

If Greg could get his picture in this paper thing to bring in the crowds, maybe she could do the same. She pushed the paper back farther on her counter, stashing the idea away for later, then stopped as another tiny article in the corner caught her eye.

Middle- and Lower-Class Businesses
Feeling the Elves' Pressure

The elves are cracking down on their businesses, and
an anonymous speculator has stated they believe that in
spite of this pressure, this notorious gang doesn't have
as much power as they once . . .

(see page five for continuation of article)

Lailu frowned, but before she could flip the page she heard the bell
chime, followed by the tapping of a cane. Mr. Boss had arrived.

MASTER SLIPSHOD DISAGREES

"est not to keep him waiting," Master Slipshod whispered. He squeezed Lailu's shoulder, then slipped past the curtain. As Lailu followed him, she could still feel the reassuring weight of his hand. She lifted her chin. They would be just fine.

Mr. Boss wore a sharp black suit with tails, a silvery cravat, and his favorite ruby pin, yet despite his polished attire, he looked exhausted, the wrinkles slowly gathering around his pinched-in face as he leaned heavily on his cane.

"Welcome to Mystic Cooking, Victor. Please sit wherever you would like." Master Slipshod gave an awkward half bow, then hovered nearby as Mr. Boss's people sat themselves at one of the larger tables.

Lailu kept a close eye on the Butcher as he sat to the right of Mr. Boss. She could still remember the feeling of helplessness, the way she'd been unable to stop him from destroying her shrine. Shuddering, she studied the rest of Mr. Boss's people. There weren't nearly as many as last time, only about a half dozen.

Ryon caught her eye as he pulled out his chair. He winked, and Lailu, scowling, looked away. Winking always made her uncomfortable. In her opinion, you couldn't trust a man who could close one eye at a time.

She glanced at the man to the left of Ryon. He resembled a drowned rat with his scrawny face, sharp nose, and rodentlike hands, the yellowed nails tapered to points. She didn't recognize him at all, but Slipshod did.

"Brennon, old boy! What are you doing here?" Master Slipshod clapped the rat man on the shoulder.

"Oh, Brennon's just been doing some work for me," Mr. Boss said with a sly smile.

Brennon shrugged, not quite meeting Slipshod's eyes as he sat.

"Is this everyone?" Lailu demanded.

Master Slipshod shot her a worried look, but she was too angry to care. They shut down their restaurant for him and just six of his people?

"Patience, my dear. There will be others joining us shortly." Mr. Boss leaned forward in his chair. "But we'll take some of your kraken calamari fettuccine while we're waiting."

Lailu shook her head. "We're all out."

"You're out?" His colorless eyes narrowed, taking in Lailu's disheveled appearance. "Ah. Customers today, I see."

"Oh yes. *Paying* customers."

"When are you going to make more fettuccine?" he asked Master Slipshod.

"Unfortunately, not for a while." At Mr. Boss's frown, he explained, "Kraken was this week's special, and the fettuccine was just for our opening day. The next special will feature something else."

"So what are you cooking next time?" the Butcher demanded. "It better not be something stupid, like fire-breathing chickens."

Lailu took a step back as if she'd been slapped. Did he *know*? She took a deep breath, her heart still pounding in her ears. "N-no. No chicken."

"Dragon?" Mr. Boss asked softly.

Lailu bit her lip. She wanted to hunt dragon more than anything, wanted to learn the secrets of creating a full-course feast from the dragon cuisine expert himself, but Master Slipshod kept putting her off.

Mr. Boss leaned forward, his hand tightening on the end of his cane. "I heard that dragon cuisine has longevity properties."

"It has what?" the Butcher asked.

"It helps you live longer," Ryon explained.

"Well," Master Slipshod began hesitantly, "it can help improve your health. For a bit. But the effects only last as long as it takes the food to digest."

Mr. Boss's eyes gleamed. "And isn't your specialty dragon cuisine?"

"It is," Slipshod admitted reluctantly.

"And," Mr. Boss added, "isn't there a dragon that's been harassing people on the outskirts of the city?"

"So I've heard." Slipshod shifted uncomfortably.

"Well then, doesn't that make it your duty as a master chef to take care of it?" Mr. Boss's smile was all sharp teeth and menace, and Slipshod looked away, his lips pressed together. "So . . . dragon next time."

Master Slipshod straightened, pulling his shoulders back until he towered at his full and considerable height. "No."

Mr. Boss's mouth opened in surprise. "No?" he managed to say, his face darkening. "*No?*"

"Not until we're better established. Dragon takes a long time to hunt and prepare correctly, and I want to wait until Lailu is ready for it."

"I—I'm ready," Lailu said quickly, unable to help herself. "I can learn—"

"No, Pigtails, you're not."

Lailu's heart sank. How could she not be ready? She'd faced krakens and manticores and all sorts of other mystical beasts. Why not dragons, too? She could do it. She *knew* she could do it.

"You're still a little too *reckless*," Slipshod added with a meaningful look.

Lailu winced. Had she ruined her chances at dragon? After one little solo hunt?

The bell chimed and a striking gentleman with thick salt-and-pepper hair stepped through the doorway. His cold green eyes took in everything, from the decorations of the restaurant to the people at the table, to Slipshod, and finally to Lailu herself. Lailu shivered, glad when the man's gaze moved back to Mr. Boss. The new arrival looked vaguely familiar and was clearly a man of money. Whereas Mr. Boss's clothing was flashy and loud, this man wore understated clothing of the finest cut and quality.

He strutted into the dining room flanked by two large men who were obviously his muscle, but he moved like he was dangerous, like he didn't need them. Lailu could feel Master Slipshod tense next to her, and her breath caught in her throat.

"Ah, Elister, my good friend." Mr. Boss rose to his feet. "Welcome."

"Victor," Elister said curtly. He towered a good foot and a half over Mr. Boss, and as he stared down at the smaller man, Lailu got the impression he was purposely emphasizing that fact. She frowned. As a short person, she hated when people made a big deal out of their height, like it somehow made them better.

"Please have a seat." Mr. Boss glanced at the two massive men with Elister, then indicated the empty chairs on the other side of the table. "For you gentlemen."

"We sit with Elister." One of them jerked a thumb over at Elister's side of the table.

"I hardly think he'll be attacked here," Mr. Boss said smoothly. "Relax, gentlemen. I own this place."

"Ahem." Lailu coughed. Mr. Boss flicked her a glance but didn't make a correction, and her blood boiled. She looked at Master Slipshod, but he was still staring at Elister, his lips pressed firmly together. Apparently it was up to her to correct Mr. Boss. "Actually—"

"We're going to need some wine," Ryon said, talking over her.

"Wine, yes. Wine." Master Slipshod seized on the idea. "Lailu, go fetch a few bottles."

"Maybe some LaSilvian," Elister remarked.

Lailu grimaced. Greg's uncle owned one of the largest vineyards in the country. She supposed his wine was okay, but with their most recent fight still so clear in her memory, it was all she could do to say politely, "Sorry, we don't keep LaSilvian wine here."

"No LaSilvian? Interesting." Elister finally seated himself next to Mr. Boss. His two men started forward, but Elister held out his hand, stopping them in their tracks like well-trained dogs. "Victor is quite right, boys. I do not require your presence next to me for this."

Boys? Lailu looked at the two men. Neither of them had been boys for a long time, that was for sure.

"But, Boss—"

"Please seat yourselves. I assure you I am quite safe." He smiled darkly, his eyes remaining cool and unamused. He turned those eyes back on Lailu. "Another brand of wine, then?"

Lailu just stared at him, her joints as rigid as the leftover kraken tentacle. She had finally remembered who he was: Lord Elister the Bloody.

The king's executioner.

8

ELISTER THE BLOODY

T'll make sure she brings us the good stuff." Ryon looped his arm through Lailu's and dragged her into the kitchen, pulling the curtain closed. "Lailu."

Lailu just stood there, unable to speak.

"Hey, snap out of it."

She was trembling so hard her teeth were knocking together. She couldn't stop; she just felt so cold, so cold, and Elister the Bloody was sitting there in the dining room. He was probably going to kill them all—

"Lailu!" Ryon smacked her lightly across the face.

Lailu blinked, stunned, and then the world snapped back into focus.

"That's better. Now where's your— Ouch! What did you do that for?" he demanded, rubbing his shin.

"You slapped me!"

"You were in a state of shock! You didn't have to kick me."

"Yeah well, you were in a state of deserving it." Lailu slid the chair over, kicked the rug out of the way, and grabbed the handle to the cellar trapdoor. "You're not allowed back here," she told Ryon.

He followed her down the narrow stairs anyway. She sighed but didn't argue. "We don't have LaSilvian. I wasn't lying about that."

"Really? I would think all chefs carried LaSilvian wine. Best in the land."

"That's a matter of opinion," Lailu sniffed. "Master Slipshod and I prefer Debonair wine." Actually, Master Slipshod preferred LaSilvian, but he'd chosen to purchase Debonair as a sign of support for Lailu.

Ryon shrugged. "Almost as good, I suppose." When Lailu scowled, he waved his hands at her as if to say get on with it.

Still scowling, Lailu grabbed a basket off a hook and scanned the wine shelf, ignoring the large gaps between bottles. Someday they'd have enough money to fill the whole rack with wine from all across the land. She chose one of their better bottles of wine, a Debonair red, gold label, which was every bit as good as that junk LaSilvian made. Hesitating, she grabbed a second and third bottle, just in case. She didn't want to take chances, not with *that man* sitting out there.

"What is Elister the Bloody doing here?" she asked, laying the bottles carefully in her basket.

Ryon's eyes widened. "Don't call him that."

"It's his title. It's what everyone calls him, ever since—"

"Shh."

Lailu lowered her voice. "Ever since *that night*." It had been four years ago; old King Salivar had died, and that same night Elister had taken it upon himself to execute two power-hungry uncles and a cousin so that Salivar's son's path to the throne would be clear and unchallenged. There had been some grumbling at the time. The nobles hadn't expected Elister to take his title of executioner quite so literally, but no one stepped forward to challenge him. No one dared. Especially after the queen herself gave him an official pardon.

Nowadays it was simply referred to as "that night," always in hushed tones.

"Yes, well, since people who call him that often disappear under mysterious and terrifying circumstances, let's just not, okay?" Ryon glanced nervously at the stairs, then back at her. "How do you know him?"

"I went to the Chef Academy, remember?"

"So?"

"*So*, we got to meet all the royal citizens. Including the king's executioner." And the king's spy, assassin, and dirty worker, she added silently. "I got to see his . . . work. Firsthand." She shivered. She could still remember the way he had moved that day, in front of all the students and teachers of every branch of the academy. Everyone from the heroes and chefs to the scholars and artists, but it was the chefs who had the front-row view. Lailu recalled the sharp glint of steel from Elister's twin curved blades, and the feeling of blood, warm and thick, spattering across her face from what had once been a teacher at the academy. Of course, he'd really been a spy for the Krigaen Empire, but still, the man certainly knew how to use rosemary to spice up a meal. Yet there had been no mercy for him when Elister the Bloody came to call.

"Let's go." Ryon put a hand on her back.

"Don't push me out of my own cellar." Lailu twisted away from his touch but climbed the stairs anyway. After all, she couldn't hide down there forever, much as she might want to. She shut the trapdoor and kicked the rug over it.

Ryon caught her shoulder as she turned to leave.

"What?" she asked, shrugging him off.

He glanced around, then leaned in. "Just keep your ears open, would you?"

Lailu frowned. "Is it even possible to close your ears?"

"Don't be cute. Something is going on with Mr. Boss."

"What do you mean?"

Ryon hesitated, then whispered, "He's having trouble paying his people."

"He is? Why?"

"I'm not sure."

Lailu recalled the sum he had loaned Master Slipshod. "I thought he had a lot of money," she said.

Ryon shrugged. "That's what I'm looking into."

Lailu narrowed her eyes. Why was Ryon telling her all this? "Aren't you supposed to be working for him?"

"Theoretically," he said with a wink. "After you." He swept a hand in front of him, and Lailu swallowed her questions as she pushed through the curtain, the basket handle clutched in her clammy fingers.

"Ah, there it is," Mr. Boss said with forced cheer.

"No LaSilvian," Ryon told Mr. Boss as he took his seat. "I checked. This is the best stuff they have."

Mr. Boss frowned, but Elister merely said, "Debonair is good enough."

Lailu put down the basket and opened two bottles, her hands shaking. Master Slipshod gently took them from her. "Why don't you fetch the appetizers?" he murmured as he poured the wine.

Lailu gratefully retreated to the nice, safe kitchen. She wished she could stay there, surrounded by the deliciously comforting smells of cooking spices and meat, but too soon the appetizers were ready to go.

Breathing deeply, Lailu put them on a tray and headed into the dining room, where Mr. Boss was talking very animatedly to a bored-looking Elister. ". . . like this restaurant," Lailu heard, pricking up her ears as she served everyone. "Seventeen businesses!" he continued. "And this is just the beginning. With your backing, and of course you'd get a cut of the profits from each one, I could take over this whole side of town within a year, two years tops."

"Why do you need my backing?" Elister asked. "If you're doing so well on your own, that is."

"I would be doing well, but it's those lousy elves."

"The elves?" Elister raised one brow. "Are they really causing so much trouble for you?"

"Oh, you know," Mr. Boss began, waving his cane causally.

"I assure you that I do not."

Mr. Boss frowned. "Well, they are demanding a cut of everything I own."

Lailu pulled a rag from her apron pocket and began wiping down a nearby table, listening carefully. Across from her, Master Slipshod picked up the empty tray and tucked it under one arm, clearly listening just as hard.

Elister shifted on his chair. "I'm afraid I don't quite understand you. You want me to back you, and in return for my backing, you will give me a cut of the businesses you have. But you already have this arrangement with the elves, do you not? And yet paying them is clearly chafing you. I don't see how paying me would be any different for you."

Mr. Boss's face reddened. "They are also repeatedly searching my establishments. Without cause, I might add. It's bad for business."

"Is that so?" Elister's long fingers tapped against the glossy wood of his table. "That is interesting. Perhaps I should ask them why."

"Th-that will not be necessary," Mr. Boss said quickly. "I know you're a busy man, and I hardly think you'd get the truth out of those creatures."

Elister's fingers stopped moving. "Those creatures?" His voice went so quiet Lailu found herself holding her breath. "As you know, *those creatures*"—his mouth twisted around the words—"are incapable of lying. Unlike certain humans I know."

"Yes, well, that is . . ." Mr. Boss slid a finger down his cravat, loosening it. "It would be a lot different with you as my backer. The elves may not be able to lie, but that hardly makes them honest. And I know *you* to be an honorable man."

"Ah, and that is, I'm afraid, where the real problem lies." Elister smiled, his green eyes cold. "You, Victor, are a rat. An overstuffed, overly pompous, social-climbing rat. I don't like rats. I don't want them clinging to my coattails, trying to scrape their way out of the sewers by attaching themselves to me. Do you understand?"

Mr. Boss's fingers tightened on his cane, and Havoc's hand went to his hip. The two men next to Havoc leaned forward eagerly. Brennon just looked frightened, his eyes rolling, those horrifying hands of his curling into little rodent fists, while at the other end of the table both bodyguards had come instantly alert. Only Ryon remained the same, reclining in his chair and sipping delicately at his wine.

"I said, do you understand me?" Elister repeated, his voice sharp.

"I . . . understand," Mr. Boss choked, quivering with fury.

Elister's smile widened, almost reaching his eyes. "Good. Now that that's settled, let's eat." And he slurped a large spoonful of batyrdactyl-and-roasted-herb soup.

Lailu was so distracted watching him that she dropped her towel, and when she went to pick it up, she accidentally slammed her head into a table. "This soup is amazing," Elister said, and Lailu slammed her head into the table a second time as she straightened up. "Where's the chef?"

"That would be my talented apprentice here," Master Slipshod said proudly, pushing Lailu forward.

Lailu adjusted her chef's hat and stared hard at her shoes. Her heart swelled with pride at Master Slipshod's compliment, but she was terrified of Elister's attention focused so intently on her.

"Come here, child," Elister ordered, and Lailu crept closer. He seemed to notice every detail about her, from the scratches down her neck to the hair escaping from her pigtails. Lailu reddened but lifted her chin. If she had known the king's royal executioner was coming into her restaurant, she would have cleaned herself up better. As it was, he got what he got.

"You're much younger than I would have expected. How old are you? Fourteen?"

"Thirteen. Sir," she added quickly. She wondered if she should curtsy, but her knees were locked in place.

"Thirteen and a master chef. Impressive. What's your name, girl?"

"Lailu, sir."

"Lailu Loganberry?"

Lailu started, surprised he knew her last name. "Yes."

Elister nodded. "I knew your mother. Enchanting woman. You take after her, except for the hair."

Lailu almost fell over in shock. The idea of this man knowing her eccentric mother was just too much. But why would he lie?

"H-how, sir?"

"Oh, she visited me once. In the city." And his eyes got a faraway look.

Lailu felt like he'd stabbed her in the heart. Her mom had visited Twin Rivers and never told her about it? She mustered a weak smile. She shouldn't be surprised, really. Her mom often disappeared for months on end, her nomadic blood calling to her, urging her to travel. That was one of the reasons Lailu had gotten into cooking in the first place. Her father and brothers were terrible at it, and Lailu was tired of eating only bland stews or crusty sandwiches every time her mother vanished. She supposed she should be thankful to her mother for helping her find her one true passion, but like those crusty sandwiches, it was hard to swallow.

"I look forward to trying your main course." Elister smiled at Lailu like she was a favorite niece. "Make mine to go, if you please."

Lailu watched in relief as Elister left their restaurant, trailed closely by his muscle men. At least that was over with. And then she caught sight of Mr. Boss's ugly expression and knew the worst part of her night was just beginning.

"I've been thinking," he started, his dinner lying untouched in front of him, "that perhaps I might have given you too good of an arrangement for this place."

Lailu froze. Next to her, Slipshod's breath caught in a wheezy gasp.

"Yes," Mr. Boss continued, his voice oozing from his lips like oil. "I was thinking that a year is way too long to pay off your loan. Wouldn't you agree?"

"We signed a contract," Master Slipshod croaked.

"Did we? I don't remember signing anything like that."

"But you showed me the contract," Lailu said quickly. "Right here, in this restaurant, you showed me."

Mr. Boss waved off their protests with one veiny hand. "Do either of *you* have a copy of this alleged contract?"

"A-a copy?" Lailu and Master Slipshod exchanged terrified glances.

"Yes, a copy," Mr. Boss repeated, carefully enunciating as if they were very foolish. At the moment, Lailu thought they must be. She shook her head.

Mr. Boss's lips stretched in a mockery of a smile. "That's what I thought. But I, on the other hand, have my own copy. A copy that says how much you owe me, as well as what you're prepared to give me if, that is to say when, you renege on your loan." He paused, letting those words sink in. "I think by the end of this moon cycle would be a good time for me to receive my payment . . . in full. What do you say?"

"I would say you are a lying weasel!" Lailu's hands curled into fists.

"Shh, Lailu," Master Slipshod cautioned.

"Don't *shh* me! He told us we would have an entire year before we had to pay, and we haven't even been here a week."

"No, I believe we agreed on payment by this moon cycle," Mr. Boss said. "Which gives you, what, almost three weeks?"

"Two," Lailu burst out. "Only two weeks."

"Well, there you go. That should be plenty of time. And if you can't pay up, well, I guess you'll just be working for me."

"No, I won't." Lailu had made up her mind. Legally binding contract or no, she wouldn't do it. She wouldn't work for a man like Mr. Boss.

"Lailu, we have no choice." Master Slipshod put a hand on her arm.

She yanked her arm free. "There's always a choice."

"Oh yes, my dear chef, there is always a choice." Mr. Boss leaned forward, a cold, hard rage filling his usually dead eyes. Lailu backed up half a step, suddenly afraid. "You can choose to work for me as you are, or you can choose to work for me in pieces. After all, a chef doesn't really need both ears, both eyes, both kidneys. . . ."

Lailu's mind filled with images of herself in chains, Mr. Boss holding the ends. She couldn't think of a way out of this, couldn't think of any way to save herself. All she could think was what a huge mistake Master Slipshod had made, going into business with this monster and dragging her down with him.

Mr. Boss must have taken her shocked silence for acceptance. "Good. I'm glad we could take care of that in such a dignified manner." He smiled wide, and Lailu saw with a start that he was missing his gold molars.

She took another step back as he stood, his chair scraping across the floor. At the door, he turned back one last time. "Remember, I always collect my debts. Always." The word hung in the air, a promise, a threat. Then the bell above the door chimed softly as they all filed out into the night. Brennon paused to shoot her and Slipshod a strange, hopeless look before the door slammed shut, leaving Lailu alone with her mentor.

9

The Scientists

The restaurant closed in around Lailu, its walls like a prison cell rather than the freedom they first represented.

"D-don't worry, Pigtails. I told your father I'd take care of you, and I will," Master Slipshod said.

Her father. For one fleeting second Lailu thought of writing to him, begging him to come get her and take her away from this. But no. Her contract with Master Slipshod was as legally binding as his contract with Mr. Boss, and if she wanted to be a true master chef, she couldn't run away at the first obstacle. No matter what, she would see this through.

"How, then?" she asked as she followed Master Slipshod into the kitchen. "How are you going to fix this?"

He glanced at her, his forehead beaded in sweat. "I . . . do have a plan," he admitted. "But you won't like it."

"What? Why?"

Instead of answering, Master Slipshod turned and raced up the stairs. She could hear rustling from one of the bedrooms above her, and then a minute later he was back with a small bag tucked under one arm. "I need to leave you again," he said gruffly, "but I'll be back early tomorrow morning."

"Wait, what kind of plan? Why won't I like it?" Lailu's heart lurched at the idea of being alone. She could still hear Mr. Boss threatening to take her unnecessary organs, and she had to force herself not to clutch at Slipshod as he headed to the door.

"I'll tell you later." He gave her a stern look. "No hunting this time while I'm gone, you hear me? The last thing I need right now is a dead apprentice." And then he was gone.

Lailu stood frozen in place as the minutes trickled by. She had no idea what to do, so when the front door opened again, she almost melted into a puddle of relief. "Hannah," she gasped.

"Hey." Hannah shut the door softly, her golden complexion pale, her eyes wide and wild. She had a small bag slung over one shoulder. "Mind if I leave some more things here?"

"Uh, sure, that's fine," Lailu said, momentarily forgetting her own troubles in the face of Hannah's obvious exhaustion. "Tough day at school?"

"Me? Pishposh." Hannah waved away the comment and started up the stairs. "How about you? You look way worse. No offense," she added quickly, "but what's going on?"

As they settled into her room upstairs, Lailu filled Hannah in on the night's events, from Elister the Bloody sitting at her table to Mr. Boss demanding full payment by the end of the current moon cycle. She left out the threat about him taking a kidney, eye, or ear, though. Hannah didn't really need to know all the grisly details.

Hannah frowned as she listened, her hands busy artfully arranging her pile of shiny haircombs and jewelry on the nightstand. She had a much larger collection than Lailu would have expected.

"Full payment," Hannah mused as she adjusted the angle of a butterfly comb. "Well, how much money is that?"

Lailu told her.

Hannah fell over.

"You don't need to be so dramatic about it." Lailu yanked her friend back up. "It's not *that* much money."

"Are you kidding me?" Hannah looked more serious than Lailu had ever seen her. "Lailu, honey, four hundred gold nuggets? That's a small fortune." Hannah shook her head, her haircombs clacking. "He really took you both for a ride, you know that?"

Lailu sighed and sank back into a chair. "According to Slipshod, no one else was willing to loan us the money."

"Maybe . . . maybe you should write to your dad."

"I can't do that!" Lailu's stomach clenched. True, she'd considered it in her first burst of panic, but it was a bad idea.

"He'd want to know."

Lailu shook her head firmly. "He doesn't have the money to help, and it would just make him worry."

Hannah hesitated. "What about . . . what about Greg?"

Lailu's temper flared. "Greg? Greg? No way! I'm not about to go crawling to him for help, not after he stormed out of here this morning."

"Oh, you guys got in another fight?"

"No." Lailu scowled. "We didn't get in *another* fight. It's the same one. The one that's been ongoing. The one where he's just a stuck-up jerk."

"But he has plenty of money. And connections."

Lailu crossed her arms over her chest. Hannah had met Greg a few times when she'd managed a visit to the academy, and the two of them had hit it off instantly, much to Lailu's extreme and continued annoyance.

Hannah exhaled. "Fine. I know there's no reasoning with you when you're like this. What are you going to do, then?"

"Slipshod will take care of it."

"And just where is your mentor?" Hannah studied her painted nails.

Lailu narrowed her eyes. It seemed like an innocent enough question, but she knew how Hannah felt about Master Slipshod. Hannah had wasted no time in telling her all the vicious rumors she'd heard about him from her time in the city. "Gambler, washed-up, lost his nerve" were some of her choice words. Unfortunately for Hannah, her final comment that Slipshod was "a few recipes short of a cookbook" was made just as Slipshod himself walked in the door. Their mutual disdain for each other after that was as obvious as mold on bread.

"He's working on a plan to help us take care of our little problem," Lailu said.

Hannah snorted. "You mean, he went out to take his mind off it all while increasing your debts."

"What do you mean?"

"Oh, you know . . ." She paused. "You do *know*, right?"

Lailu gave her a blank look, and Hannah threw her arms up, exasperated. "He's gone gambling again. Obviously."

"He wouldn't . . ." But after he had just gambled their future away—*her* future away—like that to Mr. Boss, Lailu no longer felt so sure about that anymore. The floor seemed to have dropped beneath her, taking her stomach with it. "He said . . . he promised, when I became apprenticed to him, that he wouldn't gamble anymore."

Hannah pursed her lips, like she was trying to keep her comments to herself, and Lailu realized how naive she'd been to believe that promise.

"Did he ever tell you why he took you on as his apprentice?" Hannah asked carefully.

"He said I had the most talent he'd ever seen. That together we would go places."

"And that's the problem," Hannah sighed. "He's using you to get to those places. Don't you see that?"

Lailu frowned. "No, that's not it at all. He's helping me."

"He's trying to regain some of his lost glory. He needs you, and your talent, because his own talent has dried up."

"That's not true!"

Hannah opened her mouth, then shut it again. "I'll never understand what you see in that man," she finally said.

Lailu didn't respond. How could she explain that Slipshod had believed in her when no one else would, had taken her on as his apprentice when everyone else turned her down? How could someone like Hannah understand what that was like? He wasn't perfect, but she couldn't believe he'd only taken her on for selfish reasons. She just couldn't. Still . . . "He probably *is* gambling again," she admitted.

"Don't worry." Hannah gripped Lailu's shoulders. "We don't need his help. We'll get the money ourselves." She looked suddenly determined. "I'll help. As much as I can."

"Really?"

Hannah nodded. "But you're going to have to close up shop tomorrow."

"What?" Lailu stood up so fast her chair fell over backward. "That's a terrible idea! I'll *lose* money doing that."

"But you'll gain a lot more than you'll lose. Trust me." Hannah smiled mysteriously. "Besides, if you're so worried about closing for a day, why don't you ask your mentor to cover for you?"

"Why? What are we going to be doing?" Lailu asked.

"You'll see."

Lailu recognized that look in Hannah's eye and knew her friend wouldn't tell her any more. "Fine," she decided. "But only if he agrees." Master Slipshod agree with Hannah? Lailu thought there was a better chance of a kraken learning to live in the desert.

Lailu could not believe it, but somehow Master Slipshod agreed with Hannah's plan. This was the first time he had agreed with Hannah on anything, as far as Lailu could remember.

"You can be the face of Mystic Cooking," he said, nodding enthusiastically. "Don't worry, Pigtails, I think I can handle the restaurant without you for a day."

"B-but—"

"Come on, Lailu, we've got to get you ready." Hannah clapped her hands together.

"Did she tell you where I'm going?" Lailu asked her mentor.

"Perhaps." He grinned.

"And?" Lailu prompted.

"And it's a surprise." Hannah pulled Lailu toward the stairs.

"Wait, Hannah," Slipshod called out.

Hannah blinked in surprise. "Yes?"

Master Slipshod hesitated, shifting his weight from foot to foot. "Never mind." He shuffled back to the kitchen.

Lailu and Hannah exchanged mystified looks, but then Hannah shrugged and they headed into Lailu's room, where Hannah proceeded to gleefully dress Lailu like a little doll.

Twenty minutes later they were out the door and on their way into the city proper. "I wish I was fighting those batyrdactyls again," Lailu muttered. Facing a gaggle of those beasts would have been more fun than this.

"Relax. You look adorable." Hannah beamed, looping her arm through Lailu's and pulling her along the city streets.

"Adorable my butt." Lailu glanced down at the flowing pink dress she'd been stuffed into. It belonged to Hannah, so the bodice was too tight and the skirt too long. Hannah had compensated for the last part by strapping a pair of very high-heeled silver shoes to

Lailu's feet. In order to hide Lailu's multiple wounds and scars, she'd also forced her to wear long, dainty gloves with a gauzy scarf, both of which were stifling in the summer heat. Lailu felt strange with her hair tumbling around her shoulders, and even stranger because she could feel the cold edges of the outrageous haircomb shoved into her dark locks.

"Stop messing with it." Hannah slapped at Lailu's hand, forcing her to leave the comb alone.

Sighing, Lailu studied the passing buildings, trying to ignore her discomfort. As they passed into the Industrial District, the apartments gave way to larger brick and metal buildings, and the people they brushed elbows with were dressed in worker threads and smocks, many of the men wearing bowl-shaped hats.

Lailu stopped to let a girl with a shock of strawberry-blond hair go by. The girl nodded gratefully, a triangular glass vial full of steaming purple liquid held carefully in both hands. A short man in a brown suit darted over, opening a door for the girl in one of the warehouse buildings.

Lailu narrowed her eyes. There was something familiar about that man . . .

The moment their eyes met Lailu gasped. She *did* know him! He was Slipshod's friend, Brennon. She recognized that rodentlike face.

Brennon inclined his head politely, one long-fingered hand touching the rim of his hat, and then he disappeared into the surging crowd around them. Was he following her? Was he spying for Mr. Boss? Shivering, Lailu wished Hannah hadn't made her leave her knife belt at home. It may have clashed with the dress, but without it Lailu felt vulnerable, and her mind kept replaying Mr. Boss's recent threats.

"Hurry up, Lailu!" Hannah waved impatiently, and Lailu sped after her, her skin crawling.

The shift from the middle-class district to the marketplace was subtle at first, the only difference in the buildings being the business signs hung next to every doorframe. BILLY'S BAKERY; PAULIE'S POTIONS AND CURSES; VIXEN: HAIRPINS AND COMBS ESSENTIALS. "Ooh, look at that!" Hannah pointed to one of the items on display in this last store window.

"I thought we were in a hurry," Lailu said, reluctantly stopping next to Hannah. She glanced behind her, still anxious.

"Stop doing that, you look twitchy," Hannah scolded. "Besides, even you have to admit that's a nice comb."

"I . . . suppose." Lailu studied the small jeweled piece. It was in the shape of a cat, the eyes made from chips of sapphire. Next to it, a pair of ornate silver chopsticks rested in a velvet holder.

"Hey, speaking of haircombs," Hannah said, not quite looking at Lailu, "I left a special haircomb on your nightstand yesterday, one with a lot of shiny emeralds and stuff on it. Have you seen it?"

Lailu shook her head. "I've only ever seen it on you."

Hannah frowned.

"Was it with the ones you brought last night?"

"No, I thought I left it there earlier. But maybe not . . ."

"I'm sorry. Is it important?"

Hannah waved that away. "It's fine, it's fine," she began, her words drowned by a rushing sound, like water boiling in a teakettle, only fifty times louder.

Lailu whipped around as a strange contraption roared closer. It looked almost like a normal carriage, with four wheels and a driver sitting in the front, but no horses pulled the gaudy red-and-yellow-striped body, which was clearly painted metal with an open top. A huge plume of steam shot out behind it.

As the monstrosity moved alongside them, Hannah waved to the driver and he tipped his black bowl of a hat at her before rumbling past.

"Did you see that?" she exclaimed excitedly.

"Hard to miss, wasn't it?"

Hannah ignored Lailu's sarcasm. "That was one of the scientists, trying out his newest invention. They're starting to become real popular on Gilded Island." Hannah raised her husky voice to be heard over the buzz of other gossipers on the street. "I heard Beolann is full of amazing creations; practically everyone there is a scientist, and they have to come up with at least one new invention a year."

"Why are there scientists living here, then? I mean, if their home country is such a great place, why would they leave?"

Hannah shrugged. "Too much pressure? Not enough fame? I don't know. I've never had a chance to ask. But I do know Beolann doesn't actually *let* anyone in or out of their country. They don't want us stealing their inventions." She leaned in closer. "I heard this group of scientists had to sneak out disguised as fishermen."

"Do you mean Starling Volan's group?" Lailu thought of her idol.

"Of course. They're the only group that matters."

"How do you know all this?"

"Everyone gossips when they're getting their hair done. I hear things." Hannah grinned. "Anyhow, I'm glad they escaped. They're also the ones who came up with the printing press, you know."

"Really?" Before Lailu could ask more questions, though, Hannah tugged on her arm.

"Oh, look. I can see the bridge."

"Why're you so excited?" Lailu grumbled. "You go to school here every day." Lailu recognized that bridge only too well; they were nearing Gilded Island, the home of the richest citizens of Twin Rivers. Greg's home.

As Hannah happily dragged her through the crowds and onto the bridge, Lailu was forced to focus on walking, her ankles wobbling in her outrageous shoes. The only real benefit that Lailu could see in wearing heeled shoes was that she could now stare at people's chins rather than their chests.

"Hey, there's Vahn!" Hannah pointed.

Vahn stood against the main wall about ten feet away, talking to . . . Ryon? Lailu would recognize that roguish face anywhere. She kept an eye on them as she let the crowd push her along.

". . . can't just go barging into people's houses," Vahn was saying. "If they do that, I'm out. You understand that, right? No more violence. Nothing illegal; I could lose my license."

"Vahn!" Hannah hollered.

Vahn started and glanced around, then smiled at Hannah as they walked toward him. "Well, I was hoping I'd run into you again." As he pushed away from the wall, Ryon slipped into the crowds behind him.

Lailu frowned. "Where's Ryon going?"

Vahn glanced down at her. "Oh, ah, Lita, you're here too, huh?"

Lailu's frown deepened. "Lailu. And yes, I'm here too."

"I almost didn't recognize you. You look so . . . different."

"I dressed her up," Hannah said proudly, patting Lailu on the head like she was some kind of fancy pet. "Doesn't she look beautiful?"

Vahn studied her, and Lailu found herself blushing the same color as her awful dress. "Absolutely breathtaking." He smiled at Lailu, then transferred that smile over to Hannah. "You can make anyone look good."

Ouch, Lailu thought, stung.

"Oh, Lailu didn't need my help," Hannah said quickly. "She's always so cute on her own. I just thought she could wear something special since I'm taking her to get her picture taken for the papers."

"Picture taken? Me?" Lailu asked. Suddenly, Master Slipshod's comment about her being the face of Mystic Cooking made a lot more sense. Her stomach tightened, and she couldn't decide if she was excited or anxious. "D-does it hurt?"

Hannah giggled. "It's painless. I think."

"You think?"

"Well, I've never done it personally." Hannah shrugged. "But, you know, if *Greg* could do it . . ."

"Let's go," Lailu said immediately.

"How about I walk you ladies over there?" Vahn asked.

"That would be very nice of you," Hannah said. Vahn offered her his arm, but she shook her head. "I think Lailu could use help more than me. She's like a baby elephant on stilts in those shoes."

"Thanks, Hannah," Lailu grumbled, but when Vahn offered her his arm she was happy to take it. Around her, the crowd seemed to part, letting them walk through. Then an uneven cobblestone caught her by surprise and her ridiculous shoe twisted under her. Lailu stumbled, flailing about with her other arm while clutching at Vahn.

"Careful there." He caught her and set her upright, holding her steady.

Lailu flushed. "Sorry," she mumbled, trying not to be too embarrassed as a group of women on the other side laughed.

"Oh, no problem, kiddo. At least I was here to catch you."

"Are you coming?" Hannah turned around, then blinked, clearly surprised to see Lailu looking flushed, one arm looped through Vahn's, his other hand on her shoulder. "Am I interrupting?" A small crease formed between her lovely brown eyes.

Vahn grinned. "Not at all. Lala here was just showing me her baby elephant impersonation."

Lailu flushed even brighter and didn't bother to correct her name. Consequently, Vahn called her Lala for the rest of the walk.

Finally, Hannah stopped in front of a line of small, expensive shops. This was clearly where the wealthy went when they didn't want to make the trip all the way out to the main market. All the buildings were notably larger than Mystic Cooking, but smaller than the surrounding houses and estates. The one they stood in front of had the same brightly colored shingles and turrets as its neighbors, but thick black curtains blocked out all the windows, almost like the house itself was in mourning.

"Here it is," Hannah said.

Lailu exhaled in relief. She felt so embarrassed, she was sure her face would be tomato-red for the rest of her life. Letting go of Vahn's arm, she turned and walked as carefully as she could to her friend.

"Thanks for walking us," Hannah said.

"Oh, it was my pleasure." Vahn gave her a slow smile.

Lailu stared back and forth, her embarrassment boiling over into anger. "Ahem," she said.

Hannah jumped guiltily, but Vahn just transferred his smile to Lailu, who froze under all that charm. "Well, Lala, I'll see you around. I'm still planning on collecting that breakfast you promised me."

"Y-yeah?" Lailu felt strangely elated at his words, and then immediately annoyed with herself for her reaction. *Get a grip, Lailu,* she told herself firmly. Still, he wanted to come and see *her*, eat *her* cooking. She couldn't stop the silly smile that crossed her face.

"Oh, definitely. And in the meantime, maybe you can get your graceful friend here to give you lessons on walking in heels. Trust me, it's something every woman needs to learn." Lailu's smile wilted like lettuce left out overnight. "I mean, right now it's fine if you don't, but when you're grown-up, you'll be expected to," he continued, giving her his best "big brother" tone.

"Oh, *Lailu's* plenty grown-up," Hannah cut in.

Lailu walked away from them both, feeling completely dejected. Behind her she heard Hannah asking Vahn about delivering a message to someone. Lailu didn't stick around to listen to his response, but kept walking until she reached a pair of bronze doors stamped with a strange engraving: a large box with a circle in front.

Hannah caught up to her. She glanced sideways at Lailu and bit her lip, then pushed the door open. "Let's go in."

Lailu spared one final look at Vahn before following Hannah inside.

10

THE APOLOGY

As the door shut behind them, Lailu blinked, adjusting to the dim lighting. It felt good to hide in the dark.

"Really, Lailu, don't worry about it," Hannah said softly. "I mean, he doesn't know any better. He's just a stupid boy, after all."

"Who says I'm worried?" Lailu snapped. "I don't care."

"Honey, you're the color of an overripe cherry."

"You can tell that in here?"

"It's dark, but colors are my specialty. And trust me, your skin tone is totally clashing with that lovely dress right now."

Lailu turned away from her. "What is this place?"

"The dim room." Thick, dark curtains were draped all around the walls, making it feel as if they were inside a stuffy velvet box. The floor was solid marble, and the only light came from a single wide candle placed on a small table in the center of the room.

"Excuse me, excuse me," a nasal voice chirped, as someone stuck a balding head around the curtains. "You can't just go barging in here like a bunch of hoodlums. You need an appointment."

"Oh, but we do have an appointment," Hannah said smoothly. "You must be Albert?"

"I was Albert," the man said proudly, stepping around the curtain and holding himself up as tall as he could. Lailu was surprised to see that he was even shorter than her, but he made up for his lack of size upward by having a ball of a stomach in front. "But as of yesterday, I shall now be known"—he paused dramatically before finishing—"as Neon!" He struck a pose, and Lailu snorted, trying to keep from laughing. "Or you can just call me N. E. for short."

"Neon?" Hannah asked. "Wow, sounds impressive." She shot Lailu a warning look before explaining, "This brilliant man here is the inventor of the camera."

"The camera?" The word came out a little distorted, having sounded foreign to Lailu. "What's that?"

"Only the most ingenious invention known to man," Neon, formerly Albert, stated haughtily.

"It's this sort of machine thing that can capture black-and-white images more accurately than any master painter," Hannah explained, and Lailu remembered the picture of Greg she'd seen in the paper. "Al—I mean, Neon here—is the most brilliant of the scientists." Hannah beamed at the man, adding, "Aren't you, Neon?"

"Well, I . . . ," he mumbled, seeming to stand a bit taller as he fidgeted with a gold pocket watch. "I try not to make the others feel bad."

What a piece of work. Lailu shook her head. "What about that man we saw earlier riding that horseless carriage thing?"

"Carbon?" the little man hollered. "He has nothing on me! Nothing, you hear me? Any idiot could design a carriage like that, but it takes a *real* master to invent something that captures images."

"Okay, okay." Lailu held up her hands placatingly. "He has nothing. I get it."

"And if you must know," Neon added darkly, "that lying cheat stole *my* design."

"So *you're* the idiot who *really* invented it, then," Lailu said brightly. Neon scowled, and Hannah elbowed her in the ribs. "Ouch. I mean, er . . . you're the genius who . . . well, you know what I meant."

"She's not used to being around such amazing people," Hannah confided, stepping in front of Lailu. "Your genius dazzles her."

Neon gave a pompous little nod of his head and Lailu snorted, but quietly; her ribs hurt and she didn't want Hannah to elbow her again. Staring up at Hannah, Neon continued, "So, you had an appointment with me. You must be Hannah, then."

Hannah smiled. "That's me. I was told you were the one to see about getting a picture in the paper."

He nodded again.

"Well, my friend here has a restaurant that we would like to advertise. It's a phenomenal place that's just not getting the attention it deserves."

"A restaurant, eh?"

"Yes. It's kind of a new thing—" Hannah began.

"I know what a restaurant is," Neon snapped irritably. "What kind of restaurant?"

"It specializes in mystical cuisine."

"Is that so? Like that LaSilvian restaurant, eh?"

Lailu scowled, but at a sharp look from Hannah she managed to keep her mouth shut.

"You know, I got to eat there the other day, and it was pretty good." Neon shifted his small bulk from foot to foot. "But I was a bit disappointed he didn't cook any kraken. I'm told their meat is the best in the sea . . . well, right after sea dragon."

"The very best indeed," Lailu said, unable to keep silent any longer. "And for *our* opening, we actually served kraken."

"Hmm . . ." Neon flipped open the gold pocket watch, then, with a click, snapped it shut again. "Let's step outside to get some light, and we'll talk. I think we should be able to come up with some sort of arrangement."

"Look, don't think of it as a free meal," Hannah said as they started back through town. She twirled something on her finger that looked suspiciously like the gold watch Neon had been playing with. "Think of it as paying in trade." In order to get flyers printed and an article in the paper, Lailu had promised to serve a fancy meal for Neon and a few of his friends during the next moon cycle, on the house.

"Master Slipshod's going to flip. At this rate, *no one* is going to be paying for their meals," Lailu fumed.

"Oh, he'll get over it. After all, he's the one who got you into this mess. And it's not like you had any money to actually pay any of them."

Lailu growled.

Hannah pocketed the watch, laughing. "Well, you didn't! Besides, just look at these flyers. They're gorgeous! And when the article comes out in the paper, the lines'll be out the door. Trust me."

"I don't even look like me." Lailu glanced at the front of the glossy sheet of paper. A small, fair-skinned girl with shoulder-length black hair, pale eyes, and a delicately cleft chin smiled reluctantly out at the world. Even in black and white, Lailu thought it was obvious her dress was a horrid shade of pink, and there was no getting around that awful comb. Underneath her photo was a description of the restaurant, as well as some of the upcoming specials. The only thing she really liked about the flyer was the bold star in the corner, where it said in dark letters, "*I* actually serve kraken."

"And now comes the fun part," Hannah declared.

"Oh, good. I was just waiting for the fun part to begin," Lailu grumbled.

Hannah chuckled. "Well, my grouchy friend, now we get to put these flyers up."

Several hours later, Lailu was forced to reevaluate Hannah's idea of "fun." Lailu was exhausted, hungry, sweaty, and definitely ready to be back in the kitchen before Hannah finally agreed they could leave Gilded Island. "We'll want to put a few more up around the city proper, too," Hannah said.

Lailu groaned and trudged after her. "I am never wearing heeled shoes again."

Hannah hesitated at the bridge, looking back over her shoulder.

"What?" Lailu whirled around, thoughts of Brennon flashing through her mind. Was he behind them? Or the Butcher? Or some other lackey of Mr. Boss's?

"Oh, nothing. I thought he'd meet us here . . ."

"Who?"

Hannah shrugged. "I guess it doesn't matter."

"Leaving?" the guard at the bridge asked.

Hannah nodded, starting forward; then she paused and turned back. "Hey, let your friends know about this, would you?" She handed him a flyer. "It's a really, really good restaurant, and if you bring at least three friends with you, we'll give you appetizers on the house."

Lailu made a choking noise before Hannah quickly pulled her away. "What are you doing? Trying to bankrupt me?"

"Relax, honey. You're already bankrupt, remember?"

"But we have to pay Mr. Boss soon. We can't be giving away even more free food."

"It'll be worth it in the end," Hannah said soothingly. "You're building a client base. Jeez, did they teach you nothing in that school of yours?"

"They taught me how to hunt and cook!"

"Well, that's not going to be much help for you if you don't have anyone to hunt and cook *for*."

As they stepped off the bridge and into the city proper, Lailu thought of all the food she'd have to bust her butt to get and then give away. Those flyers had better be worth it, she thought irritably.

"Hey! Hey, Lailu!"

Lailu looked around. "Did you hear that?"

Hannah grinned. "About time, too."

"About time for wha— *Greg?*" Lailu took a step back, almost falling as her shoe wobbled. She caught herself just in time. Thankfully. She could just picture how that would look, her on her face in front of Greg. What the spatula was he doing here anyhow, chasing after her?

He stopped a few feet away, his eyes wide. "What happened to you? It looks like you fought a garden and lost."

Lailu flushed, crossing her arms over her chest. This was why she didn't try to wear nice things. They never looked right on her.

"I dressed her up," Hannah said coldly.

"Oh. Well. She looks very. Well." He cleared his throat. "Anyway, I came. Just like you asked me to."

Lailu glanced around but realized Greg was looking at her. "Like *I* asked you to? Me?" Then she remembered hearing Hannah and Vahn talking about a message. She turned on her friend, her eyes narrowed to slits. "Did you send Greg a message from me?"

"Well, ha-ha, I guess that's my cue!" Hannah snatched all the flyers away from Lailu. "I'm just gonna go and put the rest of these up. See you at home!" She flashed Lailu a quick smile and then took off, moving so fast she was practically running.

Lailu shook her head.

"I take it you didn't call me out here to apologize, then," Greg muttered.

"Me? Apologize to *you*? You're the one who should apologize."

"Me?" Greg's nostrils flared. "For what? Saving you in your last hunt? Delivering your kills to your door? Offering to help you out? Which of those things should I apologize for?"

"All of them!"

"All of them." Greg made a point of thinking, exaggeratedly running a finger along his chin. "Hmm, yes, I can see how me trying to once again save your butt from the frying pan is worthy of apology. I'm sorry, Lailu. I know how you like to make things hard on yourself."

"Excuse me?" Lailu took a step forward, fury washing over her. He was using that tone of his, that I'm-better-than-everyone tone. It made her want to punch him in his smug, arrogant, aristocratic face. "You think I'm doing this to myself?"

"No, I know you're doing it to yourself. How else can you get everyone's sympathy? The poor little girl from the poor little village—"

"You better stop it, Greg."

"All alone, friendless, abandoned," he continued, still in that mocking voice.

"I said knock it off," Lailu warned.

"Trying to make her fortune in the big city, all on her own."

This time Lailu was silent, and Greg's voice drifted to a halt, some of his condescension evaporating into uncertainty when there was no retaliating remark.

Lailu took deep, shuddering breaths. Back at school, occasionally Greg would be nice to her. Occasionally she would forget what a jerk he was. Like that time she agreed to hunt with him . . . and he set her up as bait and took the credit for the kill. And that time she went ingredient gathering with him . . . and he tricked her into getting the wrong kind of mandrake root, costing her three fingernails and her place at the top of that class. Or that time she told him about her restaurant idea . . . and he stole it and was more successful in his first day than she'd probably be in her first month. Or first year.

Her fists were clenched so hard her arms ached, and she forced herself to relax. She would never forget again. She wouldn't let Greg trick her anymore into thinking he was her friend. "Have you considered," she finally said, her voice cold and steady, "that maybe I have to do things on my own? If I take your help, it means I'm just another charity case, that I can't make it myself. It means I'm not really a master chef."

"Lailu," Greg began, reaching for her. She jerked away.

"No, I'm done listening to you. You and your perfect life and your perfect restaurant. You don't have to prove yourself to anyone. Everyone already thinks you're so great." She sniffed. "Except me."

Greg's hand dropped, his eyes filled with hurt. Lailu turned and walked away from him. She waited until she was around the corner before wiping her face on her sleeve. After that she just walked blindly in the direction of home, the city blurring in front of her as she replayed their conversation again and again. Other insults came to mind, things she wished she'd said. Then she wished she hadn't said anything to him at all.

She scrubbed at her face, took a deep breath, let it out. And only then Lailu realized she was wandering in the Industrial District. It was more than a little creepy, with all the buildings looking like large, windowless blocks pressed against one another. She could smell sulfur mixed with something sharper in the air.

As the sun sank over the horizon, it filled the streets and alleys with pools of shadows that made Lailu itch to pull out a knife. Biting her lip, she stopped at an intersection to peer up at the street signs. "Steam Avenue," she read aloud, squinting, "and . . . Iron Way." Was she supposed to take Iron? Or was it Steel Lane she was looking for? She hesitated, looking up and down the street, when a sudden flash of light blinded her.

Shielding her watering eyes, Lailu blinked rapidly. The whole street was lit up brighter than a summer's day by a series of glowing glass orbs mounted on the sides of each building. And as her vision cleared, she realized she was not alone in the little alleyway.

11

Starling Volan

*G*knew you'd come back this way."

Lailu yelped and jumped back. Her shoe twisted, sending her sprawling to the floor. She reached instinctively for a knife she wasn't wearing as her eyes strained to make out the shape in front of her. Brennon's ratlike features slowly swam into focus against the backdrop of light, and she scrambled away.

"I've been watching you, you know," he said, his eyes rolling, the whites showing all around. "I saw you with that man, that hero, back on Gilded Island. Your friend?"

Lailu stopped her mad scramble and instead yanked the shoes off her feet, holding one in each hand like mini clubs as she stood up. "S-stay away from me."

"I'm not going to hurt you."

"No, you're not." Lailu shifted her weight, the shoes nice and solid in her hands. She'd tackled a kraken; she could take this one small man.

"I came to warn you."

Lailu froze. "Warn me? About what?"

Brennon twitched, jerking his head around to check if they were alone, then took a step closer.

"You can stop right there," Lailu said.

He stopped, but lowered his voice to a hoarse whisper. "Mr. Boss won't let you go; you or Sullivan. Even if you pay him back, he'll find other ways to make you owe him money. And then he'll make you work for him, do things for him . . . terrible things. The things I've done . . ." He shuddered, then breathed, "He has my family."

"He what?" Lailu swallowed hard, fighting the urge to run.

"And he'll find something you care about, or someone, and use it against you too. I thought you should know. I mean, I knew what I was getting myself into, borrowing money from that man, but you, you're just a child. Sullivan should never have mixed you up in that business."

"I'm not just a child. I'm a master chef."

He gave her a pitying look. Reaching into his suit pocket, he pulled out a small glass jar filled with hissing purple liquid. He regarded Lailu for a moment, then tossed the jar at her.

Instinctively, Lailu dropped the shoes and caught the jar in both hands, surprised at the heat radiating from it. "What is this?"

"I stole it today. I'm supposed to get it to Mr. Boss."

"You stole it?"

"From a girl, probably younger than you, even." Brennon shook his head. "It's the reason Mr. Boss won't . . . *can't* let you go. He's bankrupting himself to buy this junk from the scientists. And now he can't afford to pay for it, so he's forcing us to steal it for him."

Lailu stared at the jar, mesmerized by the way the purple inside caught the light. So beautiful.

When she looked up she realized Brennon had moved closer, much too close. Before she had time to think, he grabbed her by both shoulders, holding her in place. "Get that to your friend. The hero. It should help him."

"Vahn? Why? I—I don't understand."

"I saw what it was made out of. I shouldn't have . . . I was never meant to know." His hands clenched her shoulders harder, the yellow pointed nails digging painfully into her skin, but Lailu didn't flinch.

"What's it made out of?"

"The less you know, the better."

"What's it for?"

But he just let her go, then backed up, his eyes on her. "Hurry," he whispered. "Hurry, they're coming." Then he turned and ran.

Lailu stood there for several long moments, uncertainty pinning her in place.

"But, *Mama*," a girl's voice whined from up ahead.

Lailu jumped. She couldn't see anyone. Yet. But she realized she didn't want to be caught here, at night, holding a jar of . . . of . . . well. That was the problem. She didn't know what she was holding. The glass vial in her hand felt uncomfortably hot now, and distinctly alive. She hiked up one part of her dress and wrapped it around the jar, hiding it from view, but she could still hear it. *Bubble, bubble, hiss, hiss.* It made her shiver unpleasantly, like the sound of a fork scraping against a plate.

"Stop. Just stop. You know I can't stand whining," a woman said, her voice smooth and cool with just the hint of an accent. Lailu craned her neck. That accent . . .

"Mama, I said I was sorry."

"You seem to say that a lot. Don't be sorry, just use your head."

The voices were getting closer now. In this district with the weird metal buildings, sound echoed in strange ways. Lailu wasn't sure exactly which way to go. She scrambled back, stopping to pick up her shoes in her free hand, then padded along barefoot.

"As it turns out, the thief may have done us a favor," the woman continued. "I knew the specimen had been growing unstable, but this is a level of desperation I had *not* anticipated."

"But how is that a favor?"

Lailu ducked down a side street, practically holding her breath.

"It tells me that our experiments won't be properly funded for much longer," the woman said. Was her voice getting louder? Lailu hesitated, worried she was actually moving closer to the pair. "And since we are running low on mal-cantation powder, it might be time to abort this experiment."

"But our progress—"

"Better to abort than risk exposure. We can always find new specimens later. We have better connections now, after all."

Lailu turned another corner, caught a glimpse of two silhouettes, and ducked back, her heart hammering. Had they seen her? She waited, but there was no outcry. They must have been too busy with their conversation.

"I hope I don't regret this," the woman sighed, "but I want you to be the one to see the process through."

"Me? Mama, you really mean it? You trust *me* to do this?" The girl sounded almost painfully happy.

"I trust no one. But you have the proper skills for this job, and you need to learn." A brief pause. "Besides, here's your chance to prove that your acting classes were not a waste."

Lailu pressed her back against the building behind her as the two figures strolled into view.

"And what about the thief?" the smaller figure asked.

"He will be dealt with. One way or another." The woman's voice was still cool, but there was iron under it now, as hard and unyielding as one of Lailu's favorite cooking pans.

Lailu held her breath, but they walked past her side street without giving her a glance. From this angle she could only see one of the figures clearly: a tall woman with very red hair, her cheekbones sharp as steak knives. She strode purposefully, her slender body wrapped in a tailored suit, the jacket billowing out in the hint of a skirt.

Lailu choked down a gasp. She *knew* that person. She could still recall the exact moment she'd met her, a little over two years ago. The academy had held a special unveiling ceremony, a line of brand-new steam-powered stoves. And at the front of the crowded room, a tall woman with reddish hair spoke confidently: "This will change your lives, and it will revolutionize cooking." She'd been elegant, her voice cool with just a bit of an accent, her face full of enthusiasm.

And she'd smiled right at Lailu. "You," she had said, "have the eyes of a true chef."

Lailu's chest filled with warmth even now as she thought of that moment.

She blinked and the woman was gone, the warmth of the memory fading. Lailu bit her lip. Why was Starling Volan—the most brilliant inventor in Savoria—skulking around the Industrial District at night?

Mr. Boss is bankrupting himself to buy this junk from the scientists.

Lailu stared at her jar of bubbling liquid as the sun finished its slow descent, plunging the world into darkness. Only the Industrial District stayed illuminated, its false light buzzing and humming. Mr. Boss . . . and the scientists. What in the name of cutlery had she stumbled into?

12

Hannah's Secret

Lailu did not sleep well that night. Her head was full of questions about Starling Volan and Brennon. Even after she'd temporarily stashed the mystery jar out of sight in an old pixy paprika spice container, she kept thinking of Brennon's words, of the desperation in his eyes, the way he'd whispered about his family. She still missed her family greatly, but for the first time she was glad they lived so far away. The only one who could be used against her easily was Hannah. Hannah, who did not return that night.

The next morning, trying not to feel sick even as her stomach wriggled and writhed like a nest of slythers, Lailu forced herself to go downstairs and begin cooking. But no matter how much she told herself Hannah was just back at school, her mind was not on the job. Twice she almost put the wrong seasonings on her batyrdactyl slices, and her sun-dried cherry sauce was definitely not shaping up to be her best work.

The door chimed, and Lailu's eyes widened at the sight of a family of four in her doorway, the father clutching a black-and-white flyer.

"A-are you open?" The father anxiously shifted his weight from foot to foot.

"I told you it said lunch and dinner only," his wife hissed next to him.

Lailu debated for a second, knowing that Slipshod wouldn't be down to help for at least an hour, but in the end customers were customers. "Welcome to Mystic Cooking," she told the family, adding, "Today we're open for breakfast, too. Table for four?"

"Yes, please." The father looked relieved as Lailu seated them at a comfortable table near the window.

"It will be a bit of a wait." Lailu headed into her kitchen, her mind racing. If she was going to get breakfast served by herself and also have time to start lunch and dinner preparations, she would have to move, and move fast. Mentally she went over all her ingredients and was just deciding on a course of action when the bell above the door chimed again. More customers! What the spatula was going on? Were Hannah's flyers really *that* effective?

After the breakfast and lunch rush ended, Lailu flipped over the sign on their window to CLOSED. She sank into a nearby chair, glad of the break until dinner. Their busiest day yet, and she had managed to handle it all by herself. She felt a twinge of pride battling with annoyance at her mentor for choosing to sleep in so late. On the other hand, he'd covered for her yesterday. Maybe this was just fair.

A soft knock sounded at the door. Lailu's heart lurched and, for the first time ever, she hoped it wasn't a customer. She had no food left to feed anyone.

The knock came again, more hesitantly this time. Lailu pushed herself to her feet, pulling the door open just a crack to reveal a young boy, his huge blue eyes partially obscured by a mop of blond hair. "Are you the owner of Mystic Cooking?"

"More or less," Lailu said slowly, opening the door wider. The boy was dressed very nicely for this section of the city, in a purple tunic belted over baggy breeches, fine silk stockings, and shiny black shoes. A page? Here?

"Then I'm supposed to give you this." He held out a scroll. When she hesitated, he added, "From my lord Elister."

Lailu gingerly took the scroll, her muscles turning to jelly. Why would Elister be sending her something? The boy bowed, then shut the door quietly behind him. Lailu barely noticed he had gone, too intent on the rolled-up parchment in her hand.

She wandered over to a nearby table, about to sit down to read, when she noticed a tall figure reclining in the far corner, his feet propped up insolently on the table in front of him. He wore brown camouflage tucked into knee-high brown boots, and gold rings glinted all the way up one of his long, pointed ears. "Finally noticed me, I see." He bared his sharp white teeth in a dreadfully familiar smile.

Lailu felt the blood drain right out of her face. He put aside the bandanna, but there was no mistaking that cascade of long golden braids or the icy blue eyes. It was the elf who had barged into her restaurant on opening day. The one who'd threatened her. She swallowed. At least this time he was alone. Hopefully. "S-sorry, Mystic Cooking is closed."

He cocked his head. "And yet the door is unlocked."

"Well, yes. But I mean, we're not serving food right now."

"I'm not here for food."

Lailu's fear increased, buzzing until her whole body seemed to thrum with it. "W-what," she began. She took a breath, let it out, tried again. "What are you here for?"

"Something far more valuable than food." He stood so suddenly that Lailu staggered back a step. "You appear to be in quite a predicament in regard to our mutual acquaintance, Victor Boss. *I* could help you out of that predicament."

"How?" The word came out as barely more than a whisper.

The elf ran a finger down the row of golden rings in his ear, considering. "Years ago I would have offered you wealth in exchange for your imagination."

"My *what*?"

"Or maybe just the warmth of all your summer days. Or the memory of your parents' love. Or . . . let's see." He tapped his chin. "Your ability to dream. Yes. That would have been worth a nice pile of gold."

"Y-you can't have any of that!" Lailu took another step back and crossed her arms protectively.

"No, I can't," the elf grumbled. "Fahr, in his misguided wisdom, has decreed that we are not to take Intangibles from you mortals anymore. It only works on children, and he has decided it is . . . in poor taste. Instead, I am authorized only to deal in a trade of years. So. I could offer you the money you owe Victor in exchange for, say . . . five years?"

"Five years of what?"

"Of life," he answered. "The last five years you wouldn't even know you missed."

Lailu's jaw dropped.

"Don't look so shocked. It's a fairly common arrangement in this part of town." His smile was back, colder than ever. "We give money to the poor unfortunates who come crawling to us, and in exchange we take the years at the end of their lives."

"For what?"

"Magic isn't free." He spread his long-fingered hands. "Nothing is free."

"So . . . you steal years to create your magic?" Lailu had known elven magic was evil, but this was more horrifying than she'd ever have guessed.

"Oh no, little chef, you have it all wrong. These years must be freely given, not taken by force." He tilted his head, his braids whispering down his back. "So. Do we have a deal?"

Lailu shook her head.

"Pity. It would have saved more than just yourself."

"And what does that mean?"

"Does Hannah live here now?"

Lailu wiped her sweaty palms down the sides of her apron, surprised by the sudden change of subject. "No."

His face went still, a beautiful, glittering mask. "Are you sure about that?"

It wasn't a good idea to lie to them. Elves were incapable of lying themselves, but Lailu heard they could also sense the lies of others, too. Staring into those pitiless blue eyes, eyes that seemed to go straight through her, Lailu believed it. "She doesn't live here, but she's over here often," she amended.

"Good. Then tell her I expect to see her three days from now with the item she took from us."

"What item?"

"She'll know what I'm talking about." And then he was gone, the bell above the door chiming softly behind him.

Lailu let herself sag into a chair. She would have stayed there all afternoon, but someone had to do the dishes.

ANGRY WORDS

*L*ailu was busy reducing the hodgepodge of fresh vegetables and spices from her latest market delivery into something edible for the dinner crowd when Master Slipshod finally appeared in the kitchen, blurry-eyed and tousle-haired.

"Late night." Master Slipshod yawned hugely, pouring mandrake oil into a pan and tossing in the last of the kraken. The mixture hissed and spit, filling the kitchen with the delicious smell of cooking fish. "I managed to add to our money collection, though."

"How? Are you gambling again?" Lailu failed to keep the anger from her voice.

Master Slipshod shrugged. "It's only gambling if you're losing, Pigtails. Remember that."

Lailu started to argue with that ridiculous statement when the door chimed and Hannah waltzed in, all smiles. "Hey there."

Lailu put down her knife. "Hey there," she repeated flatly.

Hannah plopped down in the chair like nothing was wrong. "So, what's going on?" She adjusted the ornate chopsticks holding back half her dark locks.

"What's going on?" Lailu slammed the bowl of cut vegetables down next to the stove, then grabbed handfuls and tossed them into the pan, on top of the crackling kraken. She sprinkled in rather more spices than usual, her irritation making her careless, which in turn made her more irritated.

"Easy on the spices." Slipshod glanced at Hannah, then back at Lailu, and sighed. "I'll be in the dining room."

"You seem a little . . . tense," Hannah said when he was gone. "Is this about Greg? Because I thought if you just saw him again, the two of you would be able to work things out."

Lailu's jaw dropped. "When has *that* ever worked?"

Hannah waved a hand halfheartedly. "It was a spontaneous plan. Anyhow, I'm sorry for meddling."

"Well, Greg's not the problem . . . at the moment." Truthfully, she'd forgotten all about Greg, along with Hannah's little message trick.

"Hmm. It's just, you seem like you're wound tighter than Madame Pompadour's horribly permed hair."

"I can't imagine why." Lailu dropped her lebinola spice jar on the counter with a sharp clank. "Maybe because we're just about out of food and don't have time to hunt more before the dinner rush. Or maybe it's because, even though we're getting busier, there's no way we're going to have enough money to pay Mr. Boss back before the next moon. Or maybe," she said, slamming the spatula down on the counter, "it's because we've just been invited to cater a meal for Elister the Bloody at his mansion on Gilded Island in two days."

"Cater a meal for Lord Elister? Wow, you're in the big time, aren't you?"

"Maybe. I don't know! I mean, why would he choose us? After all, the king has over a dozen master chefs in his household, and I'm sure Lord Elister has his own too. Why look outside of it?" Lailu shook her head, then dove into her cupboards for the rice.

"Will the king be there?"

Lailu bumped her head on a shelf in the cupboard. She hadn't even considered that the king might be there. What a terrifying thought. Of course, he was just a young king, hardly older than she was . . .

She got ahold of the bag of rice and closed the cupboard with a snap. "I don't think he'll be there," she said slowly. "I don't think he really leaves the academy. The Scholar Academy requires six years of training before students move on to their apprenticeships, and he's pretty deep into his studies now; I doubt he'd leave for some dinner party."

"That is a pity." Hannah sighed deeply. "He's supposed to be so handsome. I was hoping you could check him out and report back." She grinned, but at Lailu's tense look her smile faltered and then slipped off altogether. "Er, well, I can see how all that might be stressful," she added.

"Oh, I haven't even gotten to the stressful part yet." Lailu dumped the rice in a pot of boiling water. "No," she continued, her voice tight, "the stressful part is when a visitor came here for you earlier today."

Hannah stiffened. "Who?" she breathed.

"It was one of the elves. He said they wanted the item returned three days from today."

Hannah seemed to melt into the chair like a cake left out on a hot day. "Oh no. Oh no."

"What item, Hannah? What is he talking about?"

Hannah straightened, her face ashen, her hands fluttering around her head. "I . . . borrowed . . . a haircomb. Missing."

"Borrowed?" Lailu recalled that emerald haircomb Hannah had been asking about. And then her eyes narrowed as she studied those chopsticks in Hannah's hair. Chopsticks she knew Hannah did not have money for, and suddenly she remembered other items: Neon's pocket watch . . . all those expensive haircombs she'd brought over . . . all the shiny jewelry Hannah couldn't possibly afford. Lailu staggered. "No, not borrowed, was it?" One look at Hannah and she knew all her suspicions were correct. "Oh, Hannah, I can't believe you. You've been stealing. And from the *elves*? Why? I mean, how stupid can you get?"

"Like you're one to talk." Hannah rose in a flurry of dark hair and crimson skirts.

"Oh no. Unlike you, I'm actually trying to make something of my life!" Even as the words left Lailu's mouth, she knew they were harsh, but she couldn't help it. She shook with anger, her hands curled into fists.

"You're in over your head with this restaurant, so don't go

around pretending you're better than I am. Because you're not." Hannah stomped out of the kitchen.

"And where do you think you're going now?" Lailu demanded, following her.

"To school!" Hannah slammed the door shut behind her.

Slipshod glanced up from the paper he was reading in the corner, his eyebrows raised, but wisely he did not comment. He just stood and headed back into the kitchen, the paper tucked under his arm. Lailu caught a headline proclaiming: TWO MORE MISSING IN POSSIBLE MOUNTAIN DRAGON ATTACK, but for once she didn't care.

Even under her anger, her stomach twisted itself into knots. She'd never fought with Hannah before, not like this. "I never said I was better," she whispered, but she knew that wasn't true. She hadn't said those words out loud, but she'd thought them, hadn't she? She'd always considered Hannah a flake, a pretty little thing flitting through life without a care, expecting the people around her to help her out. "Well, it's true." Lailu scowled furiously, turning back to the kitchen. But she still felt terrible, and all through the dinner rush she kept glancing up, hoping to see Hannah appear through the door, but she never did.

The cool night air wrapped around Lailu as she lost herself among the trees.

"See what I mean, Pigtails? There's nothing quite like a little nighttime hunting to take your mind off things," Master Slipshod said, trotting next to her like a large white shadow.

Lailu didn't answer. She kept thinking of her fight with Hannah that afternoon, the words she'd hurled at her friend echoing over and over and over in her head until her stomach felt sick with guilt. Hannah had always been there for her. Always.

The first time Lailu had woken up and found her mother gone, she'd been six. Days passed, then weeks. Everyone talked about it. Their village was small, only about fifty different families, and news traveled fast—especially such juicy news. "Did you hear? Lianna Loganberry up and left. Just left! Can you imagine?"

Lailu's father ignored all of it, retreating to his workroom and carving for hours upon hours until Lailu felt like she'd lost both her parents. Her mother's absence felt like a hole where a tooth should be, and the village was a tongue, constantly probing.

"It's no one else's business," her father would say, always in that quiet voice of his. "Whispers will go away like wasps in winter."

But that was hard for Lailu to believe when there was nothing but whispers around her all the time. "Her mother's a foreigner, what can you expect?" they'd say. And, "It's too bad her mother's gone. She's already so boyish, and it'll just get worse." Or the worst, the absolute worst, "She's so weird. It's no wonder her mother left her."

This one was whispered by the other girls Lailu's age, the ones who'd never really understood her. To be fair, Lailu had never understood them, either. She was too interested in hunting and building forts with her brothers, too busy learning how to use knives with her father. Too messy, too dirty, too strange to be friends with the other girls. And now they had another reason to shun her. They'd whisper just loudly enough that Lailu could hear and then giggle when she ran off, crying.

Then, one day, Hannah—tall, beautiful Hannah—had sauntered over, pushing through the girls clustered near Lailu. "Don't you have somewhere better to be?" she asked them, her lovely face filled with scorn. At seven, she still managed to carry herself like an adult, her head tilted just so, lips pursed. "Oh, I forgot. You don't."

The girls scattered, none of them daring to talk back to Hannah. Everyone was a little in awe of her. The perfect daughter of the village headman, always more mature than the rest of them, more confident. But perfection and responsibility brought their own form of isolation.

"I know what it's like," she'd whispered, taking Lailu's hands in hers. "All those eyes, those whispers. But don't worry. None of them matter." And then she'd smiled and asked if Lailu wanted to play with her wooden chess set. "My mother says chess is for boys, but I like it," she admitted.

"I'll play," Lailu said. She knew how; her father had carved the pieces.

And just like that, they were friends.

Lailu stumbled over a root, the memory dissolving like salt in water as the forest crashed back into focus around her.

Slipshod frowned. "You okay?"

"Just . . . just thinking," Lailu said.

"Well, stop it. You're giving *me* a headache. And we have some serious work ahead of us."

Lailu shrugged.

Slipshod frowned and stopped walking, throwing out an arm to stop Lailu too. "Look, Hannah's a good girl in her own way, I'm sure. But let's be honest, her impulsiveness *was* distracting you from your full chef potential. Maybe you're better off without her. I mean, stealing—" He stopped abruptly. But Lailu didn't want to talk about Hannah with her mentor, so she pushed past him and headed farther into the forest.

"So, what are we hunting?" she asked.

"Basilisk fish," he panted, jogging after her.

"Basilisk fish?"

"Yes. The meanest, toughest fish of lakes anywhere."

Lailu remembered reading about them at the academy. The only other fish that was worse was the medusa fish, a close relative that lived in the oceans. Both species had to be fished using a blindfold. If they caught your eye, they could turn parts of you to stone while they feasted on the remaining fleshy parts. Mean little suckers, they grew to be six feet long with two rows of long, serrated teeth, making them dangerous enough even if you didn't have to hunt them blind.

At least basilisk fish only had the one mouth to worry about, whereas medusa fish usually had as many as seven or eight, and in one rare instance over a dozen. Someday Lailu wanted to take one of them on. But not yet.

"If this doesn't take your mind off your woes, Pigtails, then nothing will." Slipshod clapped Lailu on the shoulder as the trees opened up ahead of them, revealing a large lake.

Moonlight glittered across the lake's dark, sparkling water, making it look more like a miniature ocean. With the trees rustling and whispering around it, Lailu felt strangely at peace. She breathed deeply, tasting the night air with its mingling sweetness of lebinola and pine, then joined Slipshod at the edge of a rocky outcropping. He handed her a fishing line and some rubbery, slimy batyrdactyl innards. Lailu wasn't a huge fan of the way they felt, but she knew a true chef wouldn't be reluctant to get her hands dirty. Ignoring the pungent smell, she carefully secured the innards to the fishing line and waited for the next step.

Master Slipshod pulled out two blindfolds. "Are you ready for this?"

Lailu swallowed hard, then nodded. She'd never hunted anything blind before.

"You don't really need your eyes, girl. Use your other senses." He slipped the blindfold over her eyes, tying it securely so only the faintest trickle of light from the full moon shone through.

"O God of Cookery, help us out this one time," Lailu said quietly as Master Slipshod wrapped her hands around the fishing pole and nudged her toward the lake's edge. "I really don't want to be fish food."

Slipshod chuckled.

Lailu cast the line out before settling down on the rocks to wait, her fishing pole secure in her hands, her knives loose in their sheathes around her waist. The breeze picked up, and her shoulder blades prickled like someone was watching her.

A few minutes passed with nothing but the hooting of an owl in the distance and the rustling of some small creature in the grasses a few feet away. She could hear Master Slipshod breathing softly next to her. That, and the gentle lapping of the lake in the breeze, the clicking of the insects, the croaking of a frog nearby, and—

Splash!

Lailu barely had time to steady herself before her line went zooming, and she knew it was on.

"I've got something," she cried out, all thoughts of anyone watching them forgotten.

"Good, haul her in!"

Lailu didn't need Slipshod's words to spur her into action. She spun the fishing reel as fast as she could, her shoulders burning like a stove top from the effort. She could picture the thing fighting her; from the strength of its resistance she was sure it had to be one of the six-footers, longer than she was tall.

Lailu's line suddenly went slack.

She froze, confused, until a tremendous splash made her realize the fish had stopped fighting the pull and was using the momentum to launch itself from the water. For one terrifying moment she imagined all those rows and rows of needle-sharp teeth coming straight at her face. Then her training kicked in and she ducked, feeling the fish swoosh over her head. Before it landed, Lailu had her cleaver drawn. She could hear the gnashing of its teeth as it thrashed toward her, and she let her knife fly. A soft thunk echoed in the quiet night, followed by the wet thud of the basilisk fish hitting the ground.

"Way to go, Lailu!" Slipshod roared, applauding.

Lailu undo her blindfold to see that Slipshod had already taken his off. "You saw?" she asked.

"Of course I saw! I wanted to see my amazing protégé in action." He beamed at her.

"Isn't that dangerous? What if it looked at you?"

"Oh, it did." He held up his left hand to show fingers that had gone gray, the skin hard and bumpy like granite all the way down to his palm. "Blasted fish caught my eye in its dying moment." He seemed completely unfazed, but Lailu knew if that fish had held his gaze for longer than a second, he would have more than just a few stone fingers to worry about. That kind of confidence in her ability made her feel pleased as pie, if not a little worried.

"Anyway, it's nothing one of Paulie's potions can't cure. And look at the size of the beast, just look! It's worth a few fingers, I'd say. Temporarily, at least."

Lailu looked down at her kill. The fish's head was neatly severed, its golden eyes open but harmless in death, the teeth bared in a last snarl of defiance. Lailu let her gaze sweep down the body. It was a fat one, two handspans wide, the scales shimmering with reflected moonlight. It looked delicious.

Slipshod threw an arm around Lailu's shoulders. "And you took it down in a single stroke without any help from me. One of these days, Pigtails, you're going to make history."

14

DEALS WITH THE ENEMY

"elcome to Mystic Cooking. Please have a seat wherever you like." Despite her wide smile, Lailu felt like she was asleep on the inside. Still, business today was going pretty well. In addition to the basilisk fish, which they were saving for Elister, Lailu and Master Slipshod had caught some very delicious freshwater carper fish last night. Granted, the only mystical thing about them was that they lit up like lightning bugs at night, but they were still tender and juicy, and had been baked to perfection for the carpe diem special.

"Hey there, Lulu," called a familiar voice

Lailu's heart stuttered. Vahn leaned against the open doorway, his hair flowing down his back in dark gold waves that stood out against his teal shirt.

"H-hey, Vahn." She mentally went over her own appearance.

Her hair was plastered down in its usual pigtails under a fluffy white cloud of a hat, but she knew there were circles under her eyes and her outfit was slightly less than clean. Still, no hope for it now. "Are you here to eat?" she asked, then immediately regretted the question. Of *course* he was here to eat. Why else would he stop by? Not to see her, surely.

"I'm here to see you, actually."

Lailu gasped.

"But I'll take some food, too," Vahn added. "As I recall, you owe me a meal."

"I—I do?"

"We had a deal, remember, kiddo? I was going to regale you with stories of my current heroic deeds, and you were going to feed me a delicious meal."

"Oh! Right, I remember," she said quickly.

"Of course you do."

"Uh, does that mean you're done? I mean, did you finish your quest?" Lailu's heart sank. If Vahn was done here, who knew when she'd see him again?

Vahn glanced around at the nearest diners, then leaned in closer, so close Lailu could smell him, all soap, sunshine, sweat, and . . .

". . . almost finished, but I can't quite figure it out," Vahn was saying. Lailu mentally cursed herself for being distracted.

"Figure what out?"

He ran a hand through his long hair. "Where they are being held," he muttered, "or how. But I think . . . I think I know who." He was quiet for a second, and Lailu could hear the sounds of people happily eating her cooking in the background. "Which is why, Lailu, I'm here to see you." He flashed her another brilliant smile.

Lailu almost fell over. "My name."

He raised an eyebrow.

"You got my name right." Suddenly she was nervous. *Why* did he get her name right? Whatever it was he had to talk to her about, it must be very important. "Well, uh, let me just get your food going, and, uh, sit wherever you like." She felt her face flush, and she fled back to the kitchen.

"You all right there, Pigtails?" Master Slipshod asked.

Lailu nodded, then loaded up a tray of food.

Slipshod's eyes narrowed. "That blond boy out there again?"

"W-what blond boy?" Lailu's heart clenched. Had Master Slipshod noticed?

"Don't play dumb, Pigtails. I know I didn't pick a dumb apprentice. That hero, the one you keep giving free meals to."

"Uh . . ." Lailu glanced down at her heavily loaded tray. "He's a family friend. And anyway, you've been giving free food to Mr. Boss."

Master Slipshod stiffened. "That is hardly a fair . . . totally below the belt . . . not at all the same thing," he spluttered. "Fine. Feed the idiot boy, for all the good it'll do you. See if I care." He turned his back on her and tenderized the carper fish more vigorously than necessary.

Lailu escaped back into the dining room, but before she'd gone two steps she saw that Vahn was no longer alone.

An elf sat with him. *The* elf. The one with the blond braids and the cruel smile.

The tray rattled in Lailu's hands and she thought she might be sick. Was he here about Hannah? Had something . . . Did he do something to her? But he said three days! It hadn't been three days.

She took a shaky step forward, then another, and the elf glanced up at her. His eyes narrowed and he said something to Vahn before standing in one smooth, angry motion and leaving the restaurant.

"W-what was that about?" Lailu set the tray down on Vahn's table. Her hands felt numb and she didn't want to drop it.

"Oh, nothing too important." Vahn smiled, but his eyes were lined with worry. Lailu suddenly realized how tired he looked, how strained. "Sorry, kiddo, duty calls. I'll have to collect that scrumptious meal of yours at a later date."

As he disappeared out the door, Lailu was left with nothing but questions and an uneasy feeling pooling in her stomach. Vahn and the elves. Nothing good could come of that.

The rest of the day passed in a mindless, tired fog. When the last customers trailed out, Lailu gratefully flipped the sign over to CLOSED.

"I'm meeting someone tonight," Master Slipshod said, tossing the paper at her. "Don't wait up."

"Who are you—" But he was already gone.

Frowning, Lailu flipped open the paper. Greg's smug face practically filled the first page under the headline: ALL DAY, LASILVIAN'S FLAMING FYRIAN CHICKEN FEAST. Lailu knew he was just trying to insult her and rub in her slight weakness for those horrid creatures, and after finding her own advertisement squeezed in the back, she ripped the paper to shreds.

She threw away the pieces, then started sweeping the floors as the sun crept well below the horizon, but still no Hannah. Lailu tried not to feel lonely. She told herself it was better this way. "You don't need them," she said, her broom whispering across the floor in time with her words. "You don't need any of them."

Still, when the bell above the door chimed, Lailu was actually relieved, even if it was only Ryon. "What are you doing here?" she asked.

"Besides enjoying your pleasant company?" He winked.

"Would you stop winking so much?"

"Now, why would I do that when it obviously makes you so uncomfortable?" He winked again. Lailu flushed, and Ryon's smile broadened. "What can I say, I just love making a pretty girl blush."

Pretty girl. He'd called her a pretty girl. Lailu hurriedly fished a rag out of her apron and started scrubbing tables, her face now so hot it was a wonder her hat wasn't smoking.

"So, how's your friend doing today?" he asked. "Did she find the item she . . . misplaced?"

Lailu froze. "How do you know about Hannah?"

"I know many things."

"What kind of answer is that?"

"A purposely vague answer. I could throw in another wink, too, but I'm showing restraint."

Lailu sighed and resumed her scrubbing. "I don't know if she found it yet. We got into a fight yesterday and I haven't seen her since."

"I hope she has, for her sake." His eyes were no longer laughing.

"What's so important about a silly haircomb?"

Ryon studied his fingernails. "Well, to start, it's an expensive heirloom that has been passed down in the oldest elven family for generations."

Lailu shuddered.

"How she got ahold of it . . ." He shook his head. "Right off Livea's head while she was paying a social call to Madame Pompadour. The girl's got guts, I'll give her that." He actually sounded impressed.

"How do you know how she got it?"

"It's my job to know these things," he said. "Look, I'm telling you this as a friend—"

"Yeah, right."

"—but the elves are serious about getting it back. If she doesn't return it, they will make her pay, and pay dearly. You need to find her and warn her."

"I'll . . . I'll let her know," Lailu croaked. "Next time I see her." *If I see her,* she silently amended. Maybe Hannah would never come back here again. Maybe she had cut Lailu out of her life for good. That thought hurt too much. Lailu had to keep moving, had to keep working, just to stop her chest from aching so much.

Turning her back on Ryon, she headed to the kitchen, where a mountain of dishes waited for her. Might as well get started there. She grabbed two empty buckets, then opened the back door and trudged toward the well.

It was a dark night, the moon mostly hidden behind a veil of clouds. A chill wind picked up, smelling crisp and woodsy like the start of autumn. Back home they'd probably had their first snowfall already, Lailu reflected with a sudden pang of homesickness. She loved the first snowfall, how it coated everything, wrapping the world in silence and peace like icing wraps a cake.

Lailu could picture her brothers out chopping firewood, having to work extra hard to make up for her absence. That made her smile. Between the extra chores and the bland, burned food she was sure they were eating, they'd definitely be missing her. Especially Lonnie. Lonnie was only one year older than her, and he'd been her best friend before Hannah. He'd have no one to help set snow traps for their oldest brother, no one to complain to when Laurent got all bossy, no one to build ice forts with . . .

Lailu's smile fell away. She told herself she was doing what she always wanted to do; there was no reason to be sad. But without Hannah around, her village seemed so much farther away. Lailu shivered as she filled up the first bucket and tried not to feel so alone. She put that bucket down and filled up the second, suddenly uncomfortably aware of the silence.

Lailu glanced around. The night sounds had definitely stopped. Someone was there. Someone *had* to be there. "Probably Ryon," she whispered, but her heart had jumped up its pace. She grabbed both buckets and hurried toward the door, water sloshing over the sides and spilling on her legs in icy rivers. *Almost there*, she urged. *Almost—*

Movement out of the corner of her eye had her turning, but not fast enough. Like something out of a bad dream, a large calloused hand grabbed the front of her shirt, slamming her against the side of the restaurant.

15

BLACKMAILED

"Now you listen, and you listen well, you filthy little upstart cook," Lailu's attacker snarled, his breath hot against her face. She gagged at the smell of onions and something much worse. Dropping the buckets, she scrabbled at the hand pinning her to her restaurant. Her attacker laughed, a harsh bark of a sound, and suddenly Lailu knew who he was: the Butcher.

"Struggle all you want, little flea. It's not going to save you."

Lailu forced herself to stop, even as everything inside her screamed to keep trying, keep fighting.

"That's better. Now, I have a message from Mr. Boss. He knows about your little dinner party tomorrow night, and when it's over, he wants to hear about it. *All* about it, every last detail: who was there, what they talked about, everything. You hear me?"

Lailu nodded, her head throbbing with her pulse.

"Good. We'll be expecting you at the Crow's Nest tomorrow at midnight, and you'd better give a full report. After all, Mr. Boss doesn't really need two chefs." He tossed her sideways with one hand.

Lailu lurched to her feet, her fingers pulling a knife out of her belt, but the Butcher was already gone.

"Too slow," someone said.

Lailu whirled, but before she could throw her knife, fingers closed around her wrist.

"Relax, it's me," Ryon said quickly.

"R-Ryon?" Lailu gasped.

"None other."

She tucked the knife back into her belt. Ryon helped her stagger back inside, then set about making tea, acting as if it were his kitchen. Lailu sat in the chair and stared off at nothing. She was still trembling and couldn't get that smell out of her nostrils. The stench of *him*.

Lailu had always been able to take care of herself, but the Butcher handled her like she was nothing but a useless child. Even with a knife in her belt, she hadn't been able to do anything to him. As she thought about that knife, a slow, steady anger burned under the surface of her fear. Why hadn't she pulled her knife sooner? She had been at the top of her academy class in hand-to-hand combat, and yet she'd wasted all that time trying to break free while her knife was right there. What had she been thinking?

"Here you go." Ryon held out a steaming mug. As Lailu took

it, she noticed that he'd already brought in the two buckets of water and shut the back door.

Ryon dragged a second chair in from the dining room and slouched into it. "Sorry about that, by the way."

Lailu's eyes narrowed on his guilty expression. "You sent him?"

"Don't be ridiculous," he said irritably. "And drink your tea."

Lailu drank her tea, but not because he told her to. She glared at him as she sipped it, trying to make that clear. "So how did Mr. Boss know about Elister's party?"

Ryon pulled a face. "I told him."

"What?" Lailu realized she was standing, hot tea splashing over her fingers.

"Oh, come on, I had to tell him! What kind of spy am I if I don't sometimes give him useful information?"

"So you admit you're a spy?"

"Obviously." Ryon frowned. "And sit down, would you? You're not tall enough to be intimidating."

"Oh, that's real nice," Lailu huffed, but she sat down. "I thought spies weren't supposed to be obvious about it."

"Anyhow . . . I didn't realize he'd send Havoc out here, or I would have warned you." He ran a hand through his dark hair, leaving it ruffled. He looked cuter that way, Lailu reflected absently, then immediately caught herself. *Cute* was not the word for Ryon. *Tricky, treacherous, sneaky*—these were all proper words.

Ryon straightened. "Well, at least we know one thing: Mr. Boss certainly hasn't given up yet."

"On?" Lailu prompted.

"On trying to be the biggest game in town. He's hoping to find something to use on Elister. If Elister backs him, it would give him a much stronger position to break away from the elves' control. And," he mused, "then they wouldn't be able to continuously search his businesses."

"What are they even searching for?"

"You don't know?"

Lailu shook her head.

Ryon ran a finger along his temple. He looked tired. "They're looking for the other missing elves."

"Missing . . . elves?" She remembered her opening day, how the elves had burst into her restaurant, searching for something. Their own people had gone missing? She shivered. "Why isn't he dead, then? I mean, if they think he's behind the disappearances."

Ryon leaned back in his chair. "It's not that simple."

"They think he has them alive somewhere," she realized. "That's why they're not doing anything to him yet. They want to figure out where he's keeping them. Which means they probably have a sp—"

She stopped abruptly, staring at Ryon with new eyes.

He just watched her.

"Who are you really working for, Ryon?"

He leaned forward, resting his elbows on his knees, and winked. Right in her face. The nerve!

Lailu's hand clenched around her teacup. "You are the sneakiest, snakiest, worst, most obnoxious . . ." She tried to think of other insults.

"Go on. Tell me what you really think," Ryon chuckled.

Lailu took a deep breath. "You're worse than, than a fyrian chicken!"

Ryon snorted. "Worse than a *chicken*? You have got to work on your insults!"

Lailu gulped down the rest of her tea, ignoring him as he laughed and laughed. With any luck he'd choke on his own laughter, and that would be one less problem she'd have to deal with. "Feel better?" she snapped when he was finally quiet again.

"Much," he agreed pleasantly. "I knew there was a reason I liked visiting you."

"Whatever. And just so you know, there's nothing as vile, as treacherous, as *scheming* as a fyrian chicken. They're awful." She could still remember that failed hunting trip, the sound of scratching chicken feet behind her, the heat on her backside . . .

"Well, I'd better go." Ryon stood.

"You've—what? Why? Wait, Ryon!" Lailu spluttered, hurrying after him as he disappeared into the dining room. "You haven't even told me anything! What should I do?"

"You should do what the Butcher told you to do." Ryon paused at her front door. "Go to Mr. Boss at midnight tomorrow and tell him what he wants to hear."

"But, but I don't want—"

"It doesn't matter. Lailu, Mr. Boss is serious. He will kill you and not think twice about it. You need to keep yourself safe and try to stay out of the way." Before Lailu could answer, he leaned forward and ruffled her hair, then left, the door swinging shut behind him.

"I hate it when guys do that." She fixed her pigtails, her face strangely warm.

Lailu was still up cleaning when Master Slipshod came home, slamming the door shut so hard the bell swung wildly. "Seems like we both have flighty friends," he growled.

"What does *that* mean?" Lailu asked.

"It means that once again Brennon decided not to show up. And without him, they wouldn't let me back at the table. Rogues, thieves, and liars, the lot of them!"

"The Butcher came here—" Lailu began, but Slipshod had already stomped past her, and a moment later, she heard him creaking up the stairs. Sighing, she finished cleaning and headed up after him. She'd just have to tell him about it in the morning.

Lailu slept restlessly, dreaming the Butcher had caught Hannah. When she woke the next morning, she had circles from lack of sleep developing under her eyes and her whole body ached, but she could smell the delicious scents of marinating basilisk fish. Finding Slipshod hard at work in the kitchen cheered her up immensely.

Lailu inhaled deeply. The lemon marinade Slipshod was using was a delicious complement to the other herbs and spices, and she knew without even looking at it that it had come out perfectly.

"Morning, Pigtails," Master Slipshod said from his place next to the stove.

"Good morning." She hesitated, not wanting to bring up bad memories when the kitchen was so full of good smells, but Master Slipshod had to know about Mr. Boss's request. "Last night—"

"You know what this means?" he cut her off.

"What *what* means?"

"This catering trip?" Master Slipshod turned and grinned at Lailu. "It means you finally get to use your Cooling and Containment cart."

Lailu's eyes widened, all thoughts of the Butcher vanishing in a rush of excitement. "Mr. Frosty?" she whispered. At Slipshod's nod, she practically danced down to the cellar, then dragged her cart up the stairs and into the kitchen, her chest swelling with pride. Her Cooling and Containment cart had been a gift from Master Sanford, her favorite teacher at the academy. Master Sanford's encouragement and enthusiasm had made Lailu's early days at the academy endurable, even with Greg and the other kids relentlessly teasing her about her secondhand clothing. She was able to lose herself to the pure enjoyment of cooking in Master Sanford's classes and forget that she didn't belong, that she wasn't an elite aristocrat like most of her fellow students.

Lailu would have loved Mr. Frosty even if she hadn't gotten it from Master Sanford; not only was it designed by Starling Volan herself, but it came equipped with a generous spice rack as well as a large compartment underneath capable of keeping food either warm or cold, perfect for the traveling chef. When not in use, it folded down to a compact, heavy rectangle, but as Lailu pulled up on the lid and popped the sides out and into place, it stood just higher than her waist.

After bundling their basilisk fish into the cart, Lailu got back to business as usual, helping Slipshod cook up a delicious carper fish linguini with a side of garlic bread and steamed veggies. After all, they still had their lunch crowd to deal with before they'd close up and head to Elister's. Lunch *crowd*. Just thinking those two words sent another thrill through Lailu, and she couldn't stop a smile from tugging at her lips.

They were just pulling the lasagna trays out of the oven when there was a rap at the door.

Lailu and Master Slipshod looked at each other. "I'll get it," Slipshod said, dropping his tray on the counter and pulling off his oven mitts.

Lailu placed her tray next to Slipshod's, then checked on the steaming veggies.

Suddenly, from the dining room, Master Slipshod yelled, and Lailu heard something clatter to the floor. She peeked around the curtain, then scurried back as her mentor raced past her and straight up the stairs, his face deathly pale.

"Master Slipshod?" Lailu called up after him.

No response.

Biting her lip, Lailu tiptoed out to the dining room and saw a small wooden box lying on the floor, a note nailed to the top. She reached for it, then stopped, taking in the darkened edges. Was that . . . blood? Holding her breath, Lailu carefully pulled the note off, trying not to touch any more of it than necessary as she read the scribbled message:

See what happens to those who disobey Mr. Boss . . .

There was no signature, but Lailu knew the Butcher must have written it. Swallowing hard, she flipped open the lid.

It took a second for Lailu to register what she saw, and when she did, she dropped the box, tripping backward over a chair in her haste to get away.

It was a hand. One long, skinny hand with long, skinny fingers, each one ending in a pointed yellow nail.

WREN

ailu didn't know if Brennon was alive or not, and she didn't want to know. She seated and served customers without really seeing them, every few minutes rubbing her own hands together as if checking that they were still attached. Master Slipshod didn't come down all day, but Lailu left him alone. Brennon had been his friend.

When it was time to close up and head to Elister's, she called up the stairs to him. No response. Taking a deep breath, she walked up, then knocked on Slipshod's closed door. Still no response. Tentatively she turned the handle and slipped inside.

The place was a mess, clothing strewn everywhere, the dresser on its side, books and papers all over the place. Lailu never went in there, so she didn't know if that was normal. "Master Slipshod?" she called, taking one step, then another. Something crunched under her boot. She looked down. Dried noodles? What the spatula did he keep in here?

"Master Slipshod?" she tried again, picking her way toward the bed. Halfway there she knew it was pointless; the blankets were in a giant tangle, but Slipshod wasn't in them. He was gone.

Gone.

Lailu closed her eyes. This wasn't the first time she'd gone looking for someone and found them vanished.

"When is Mama coming home?" she remembered asking all those years ago.

And her father had hesitated, had looked so uncertain, so fragile, so unlike himself. "When she's ready," he had finally said. And then he left, too, disappearing into his work, pretending his wife's absence wasn't like one of his precious carving knives, slicing away at their family.

Swallowing hard, Lailu pushed those thoughts away. People left all the time, didn't they? It wasn't a big deal. It wasn't. Her chest felt like it had been scooped out with a giant serving spoon, but that didn't mean it bothered her. She wouldn't let it bother her.

She retraced her steps, then closed Slipshod's door and leaned her forehead against it. With the sun already setting, she knew there was no help for it; she'd have to go to Elister's alone. She couldn't be late, not for Elister the Bloody. Not when she had to report to Mr. Boss. Not after she'd received a severed hand on her doorstep . . .

An hour later, Lailu found herself standing alone in the shadow of Elister's towering Gilded Island mansion, her carriage ride across town already a blur in her mind. But she knew being scared never got you anywhere. As Master Sanford used to say, fear was the worst seasoning, and best kept on the shelf.

"Here goes." Lailu knocked. The sound seemed to echo on and on. Everything about this place was terrifying, from the austere brick walls to the impossibly arched roof, to the solid iron doors. The front even had a marble statue of a man swinging an ax.

One of Elister's bodyguards opened the door, menacing despite the mustache drooping over his lip. "You the chef?"

Lailu nodded, her throat too tight for words.

He stared at her cooking supplies suspiciously, and Lailu wondered if he was going to demand to search them. "Where's the other one?" he barked.

"T-the other one?"

"I was told there would be two chefs."

Lailu shook her head. "It's just m-me today." Just her. She had never felt so alone, and underneath the disapproving glare of the bodyguard, she had never felt like more of a child. How she wished Master Slipshod were here, too. At least she still had Mr. Frosty. The handle felt warm and solid in her hands, and she squeezed it reassuringly.

Grunting, Mustache stepped to the side and waved her in. "Kitchen's this way." He shut the door firmly, then pushed past her. He was so muscular he had to walk with his arms held out from his sides. It looked uncomfortable, and Lailu tore her eyes away from his broad back to study the hallway.

Torches burned every few feet, illuminating the many tapestries covering the walls. Lailu's boots sank into the thick carpeting with every step, and when she passed one of the torches, she realized it wasn't really a torch at all; no fire ever burned so consistently, without smoke. It looked instead like an ember caught inside glass, like the lights in the Industrial District.

"In here." Mustache pointed to a set of wooden doors.

Swallowing down her rising panic, Lailu walked past him and into the kitchen. And stopped. "Oh my," she whispered. The kitchen was as large as her entire restaurant, and full of, of, well, she wasn't even sure what most of the contraptions were. She recognized a steam-powered oven in the corner. It was similar to her own, definitely a Starling Volan, but this one was a much larger model with more knobs on it. Next to it stood another metal box, slightly smaller, that seemed to serve a similar function. There were also bowls with knobs and buttons on them and pipes against the wall, and the floor and glistening countertops were made of shiny marble.

Lailu drifted toward a basin set into a corner. A series of pipes led out of it and along the walls, two very inviting-looking knobs on top. She turned one, her eyes widening as water came streaming out of the top of the basin in a beautiful fountain. "Amazing," she whispered, turning it off again, then on, then off. She was filled with longing for this kitchen. The things she could do in here . . .

"If you're done playing," Mustache growled, "dinner is to be served in the main dining room at seven bells past."

"What bells?"

"I'll just come get you when it's time," he muttered, stomping away.

Lailu went from one end of the large kitchen to the other, turning random knobs and flicking switches. If it weren't for the fear congealing in the back of her throat, she'd be having a great time. But no matter how much she delayed, she'd still have to serve Elister, and she'd have to spy on him. And she'd have to do it alone. A rush of anger warmed her. How could Master Slipshod have left her alone for this? Maybe . . . maybe Hannah had been right about him all along.

Dong . . . dong . . . dong . . . dong . . . dong!

Lailu clapped her hands over her ears but could still feel the noise grating in her bones until the fifth ring finally died away.

So that's what Mr. Mustache was babbling on about, she thought irritably, wishing he had given her a little more warning of what to expect. Her panic rose as she realized she had no idea when to expect the sixth and seventh bells. She hadn't even begun cooking yet! She still had to lightly sear the fish, mix up the sauce, and make the appetizer and dessert.

A small side door opened, and a skinny girl with curly strawberry-blond hair stepped inside. Her nose was slightly on the wide side, and so was her mouth, but she still managed to look cute and delicate in her rose-colored evening dress and long white gloves. She appeared no more than ten or eleven, but thanks to Lailu's friend Sandy from the Chef Academy, she knew the coppery-headed ones tended to look younger than they actually were.

"Can I help you?" Lailu asked.

"Actually, I was sent here to see if *you* needed help with anything." The girl sounded about as young as she looked. "You know, help with the gadgets in here and stuff." She smiled, showing off her dimples. "I'm Wren."

"Lailu," Lailu said, studying the slight girl. She looked familiar, and sounded even more familiar. "Have we met before?"

Wren shook her head. "I would remember meeting a master chef as young as you."

Lailu couldn't decide whether that was a compliment or an insult.

"So?" Wren shifted. "Do you need help, or no?"

"Um, sure. Which one of these stove thingamajigs would be the best for me to use?"

"It all depends what you are used to." The girl marched farther into the room. "This one here gets warm really quickly; this one here is better for a slow-cook dish; this one here is just terrible—seriously, don't use it; and this one here is most like the older steam modules used by many chefs in their own households." Lailu noticed that they all had an engraved starling in a triangle on them, the signature mark of a Starling Volan stove. "So . . . is it true you don't work for a household?"

"It's true."

"What do you do, then?"

Lailu smiled. "My mentor and I have a restaurant, where we get to cook whatever we want, and people come in just to eat. You should come and try it sometime."

"Sounds really nice, and I would like to, but . . ." Wren stared down at the engraving of a starling on the nearest stove. "It's my mom." She twined her hands behind her back.

"Your mom?"

Wren nodded. "She doesn't like me doing anything she feels is *unnecessary*."

"That's a strange attitude."

"I know, right? I mean, I used to take these acting and dancing classes, back before we moved here, and she'd always make these comments about how I was wasting my life. It got so . . . well . . ." Wren stopped.

"You can tell me," Lailu said, trying to be encouraging. She got the impression Wren didn't get a chance to vent much.

"I shouldn't be complaining."

"There's nothing wrong with a little bit of constructive complaining," Lailu said firmly.

Wren gave her a weak smile. "Well, eventually my mom stopped making those comments to me. She stopped talking to me entirely, actually. So"—Wren traced her finger along the starling—"I stopped studying the arts and started helping her with her work instead."

"Oh." Lailu said uncertainly. "Er, what sort of work do you and your mom do, then?"

Wren jerked her chin at all the equipment. Lailu stared at her, not comprehending, and finally Wren muttered, "The stoves. The ovens. My mom invented almost all of them."

Lailu's jaw dropped. "Really? Your mom is Starling Volan? I mean, *the* Starling Volan?"

Wren sighed. "Yes, yes." She ran a hand back through her brightly colored hair.

"But that's amazing! She completely revolutionized the cooking world with her steam-powered tools." Who *wouldn't* want to be a part of that kind of business? The only thing better than creating all these wonderful stoves, in Lailu's opinion, was cooking on them. "Wow. Just . . . wow."

And then it clicked. She *had* seen Wren before! Or at least she'd heard her. Back in the Industrial District a few nights ago, talking about . . . Lailu hesitated. Talking about a thief. And an experiment. Lailu desperately wanted to ask about it, but she didn't want to admit she'd been eavesdropping. "Er," Lailu tried. "Are you and your mom working on any new experiments now?"

"My mom is *always* working on new experiments," Wren said. "That's what she does."

Lailu brightened. "So is it true, then, that everyone from Beolann is a scientist?"

Wren scowled. "No. We're not *all* scientists." She looked away, toward another contraption in the far corner. "Want to see how this works?"

"Um, yeah. Of course." Even with her limited ability for tact, Lailu understood that Wren didn't want to talk about her mom or her old home anymore. Reluctantly, she let it drop, even though she had so many questions. Not just about the conversation she'd overheard, but about Starling in general. All Lailu knew about the inventor was that she was the first person to ever leave her home country of Beolann, taking her band of scientists with her. But why she left and what she was trying to accomplish here were all mysteries.

Wren turned out to be quite helpful, showing Lailu all the useful gadgets and explaining how the bell system was set to ring at each hour. She even assisted in preparing the fish, and Lailu managed to finish everything in plenty of time.

"Well, Wren, thanks."

"Oh, no problem. I like being helpful." Wren smiled, dimples on full display, and Lailu found herself smiling back.

The main door flew open and Mustache stomped inside.

"Chef." He jerked a fat finger in Lailu's direction. "They're ready for you."

"Good luck," Wren called as Lailu followed the bodyguard out the door.

Lailu carefully wheeled Mr. Frosty, the prepared basilisk fish with its carper fish appetizer laid out elegantly in a platter on top. With Wren's help, she felt she had prepared perhaps her best mystic seafood dish ever. Even her special dragon herb sauce with a dash of pixie paprika turned out better than usual and was dribbled artistically on the silver fish. Slipshod would have been proud.

Mustache finally stopped in front of a pair of mighty oak doors at the end of another long hallway. A steady buzz seeped from the cracks under the door, and Lailu swallowed, her pulse quickening under her high-collared shirt. As the doors swung open, she straightened her chef's hat and stood as tall as her limited height would let her. It was time to face Elister and his Gilded Island friends.

SKULDUGGERY AT
THE DINNER PARTY

All talk ceased as the doors swung shut behind Lailu. She froze, her ears ringing, hands clenched around the handle of her cart. Everyone looked so far away, and it seemed like there were hundreds of them, all sitting there, all staring at her. All those eyes . . .

"Ah, excellent. Dinner." Elister's voice broke through the tableau, and Lailu realized there were only the dozen people she'd been told to prepare food for, not hundreds. She released the breath she didn't know she'd been holding and pushed her cart forward.

Elister looked particularly elegant today in a crimson velvet shirt with a black cravat, and Lailu was forced to admit that, executioner or not, the man had style. Even so, it was the man next to Elister who really captured Lailu's attention.

Dressed in a body-hugging green silk shirt, with his long,

crow-black hair brushed neatly back from his delicate face, he was almost breathtakingly beautiful. His eyes were a light gray-blue that seemed to be silently laughing above his high cheekbones, narrow chin, and long, pointed ears.

An elf? Here? She knew they were technically free to roam anywhere in the city, but they usually stuck to the poorer districts. So what would an elf be doing at Elister's fancy dinner party?

"Where is Master Slipshod?" Elister asked.

Lailu gave herself a little mental shake. "He was . . . unable to make it today."

"That's unfortunate." Elister didn't sound like he cared particularly much. "And what are we having?"

Lailu forced a smile. "Today's s-special," she began, her voice cracking. She cleared her throat. "Today's special . . . is an appetizer of carper ceviche, followed by basilisk fish served over a wild rice bed, with a nice mandrake herb sauce and a side of sautéed vegetables."

"Basilisk fish? Really?" the man across from Elister asked.

"Oh, but the girl is joking, of course!" laughed a skinny brunette farther down the table, her head bowed beneath the weight of a gaudy comb so oversized even Hannah would have found it ridiculous.

"A chef never jokes about food." Lailu wheeled Mr. Frosty closer, carefully serving everyone. When the last platter was down, she stepped back. "Enjoy. And please, let me know if you need anything else."

"I have every faith that the meal will be more than adequate. But . . ." Elister smiled. "I'm sure we could all do with some wine."

Lailu flushed. The wine! How had she forgotten? Slipshod would never have forgotten an important detail like that. "Y-yes, of course." She scurried out of the dining room and down the hall, then slipped inside the darkened kitchen.

"Everything going all right?"

Lailu jumped, nearly toppling over her cart. "Wren!" she yelped. "What are you doing, lurking in here in the dark?"

"Hiding," Wren said calmly.

"Hiding?" Lailu's eyes slowly adjusted to the gloom, until she could just make out Wren sitting on a counter, swinging her feet back and forth. "Hiding from what?"

Wren slipped down off the counter. "I'm supposed to be making myself useful to Lord Elister. You know, showing him how to use all the new inventions my mother installed in here."

"Are you living here, then?" Lailu shivered at the thought of trying to sleep in the same house as Elister the Bloody, but Wren was already shaking her head.

"No, I'm just helping out a little. I am currently a 'disposable resource.'" Wren made a face. "My mom's words."

"I guessed."

"She's making me go to this thing for her tonight, too. Actually, I should probably start heading over."

"But you're hiding instead?"

"Well, I don't want to go. It's in kind of a creepy place."

"Where?" Lailu was instantly curious.

Wren shrugged. "It doesn't really matter. So, did you need anything? Or are you hiding now too?"

"I wish. But no, I just forgot the wine."

"Well, that was awfully silly of you."

"Tell me about it," Lailu muttered.

"Wine is a necessity when having a dinner party, especially with fancy food. To not bring the wine out in the first place will lead to complaints, not to mention—"

"Wren!" Lailu snapped. "I know I shouldn't have forgotten the wine, so you can stop already."

Wren was silent for a second before mumbling, "You told me to tell you about it."

"Well, I didn't mean literally," Lailu said, feeling harassed. She felt a pang of guilt immediately afterward, though. Wren had been a huge help to her today. "Sorry, nerves are making me grouchy. Well, grouchier, I guess."

"That's all right." Wren smiled, showing off her dimples. "I forgive you. You're much more fun than the people I'm normally stuck working with. I'd be willing to help you again, if you wanted."

"Oh, uh, thanks." Lailu finished stocking her cart with the bottles of wine she had set in Elister's icebox to chill. "Good luck at, well, being useful," she called as she headed out the door.

"Thanks," Wren said sadly.

Lailu snuck back inside the dining room, then slipped among the guests, pouring wine and listening hard. She needed something to tell Mr. Boss tonight, after all.

At first she didn't hear anything interesting. But then she made her way over to Elister's side of the table.

"How many?" Elister asked, not looking at the elf.

"Seven. One of them taken just a few days ago, in fact."

A flicker of worry crossed Elister's distinguished face as Lailu filled his wineglass. "Young or old?"

Lailu casually slid the elf's glass in front of him. "Young ones," he admitted, picking it up and staring into it. His eyes were very serious, the rest of his face still as a mask. "All under a hundred. But old enough that no ordinary means would have been able to . . ."

"So you suspect *what*, exactly?" Elister asked.

Lailu stood behind him, holding her breath.

The elf leaned in closer to Elister, his words so soft Lailu had to inch forward to hear them. "There must be a traitor inside our camp. And I believe this traitor is working with your beloved scientists."

Elister tossed his napkin on the table and sighed. "Fahr, I am growing tired of your petty bickering. You know I have recently started backing Starling and her people, and this accusation of yours stinks of jealousy."

"What's there to be jealous of? Their science can never compare to the wonders of elven magic." Fahr's voice dripped contempt. "But where their so-called science is legal, our magic is not. As you well know."

"Yes, well, you're half the reason I helped draft that magic pro-hibition law," Elister said irritably. "You're just lucky you weren't banned from the city permanently. As it is, I still get regular reports of magical interference left over from your turf war, and it's pre-venting my people from repairing the western travel district. And that's not even mentioning the now-deceased goblin population."

"There are still pockets of them elsewhere. . . . Treacherous, lying little creatures—"

"They were useful!" Elister paused, then continued in a much softer voice, "The threat of their alchemy along with your magic was enough to keep the Krigaen Empire away from our borders. Thanks to your little rivalry, we now need to find another source of power to keep them away."

Fahr shrugged. "But your law does leave us at a bit of a disadvantage."

Elister ran one hand across his temple. "I suppose," he conceded. "In any case, my friend, I believe your traitor is someone else. A certain loan shark we both know."

Lailu bit her lip to stop herself from gasping. Mr. Boss? It had to be.

"We haven't found any proof of that yet."

"No? Then I suppose it's time I helped you." Elister turned.

Lailu felt like she'd been plunged in a lake of ice water as his green eyes locked on her. She couldn't move, couldn't breathe, couldn't look away, and she wondered if the word *spy* was written all over her face. His eyes narrowed, and she knew it must be. He knew what she'd been up to. And he would make her pay for it.

18

CAUGHT

Elister stood in one smooth motion, and all talk at the table ceased. "Please, enjoy your meals. I'll just be a moment. I need a private chat with our chef." Slowly the pairs of eyes turned away, and he faced Lailu, his smile vanishing. "Get your cart."

She got her cart, trembling so badly it rattled the whole way out of the dining hall and down to the kitchen. She could feel Elister walking behind her, her shoulder blades prickling as she waited for him to do something. Could she make a run for it? No, he'd catch her before she went two steps. Maybe she could explain herself . . . but no. Elister was not known for his mercy. A man who cold-bloodedly removed all possible rivals to the throne in a single night was not a merciful man. Efficient, yes. Methodical, definitely. But understanding? Lailu doubted it.

Swallowing hard, Lailu pushed the kitchen door open and wheeled the cart in after her.

Elister tapped something on the wall, and the lights in the kitchen sprang to life. Lailu shrank away, still holding on to Mr. Frosty as if it could somehow save her.

"So. Victor sent you to spy on me?"

Lailu hesitated, then nodded, her blood roaring in her ears.

"Normally I dispose of spies immediately."

"I remember," she croaked.

Elister frowned, then his expression cleared. "Ah, yes. That unfortunate incident at the academy last year."

Unfortunate incident? Elister had cut a man to pieces!

Elister must have seen her face. "He was part of the Krigaen Empire, as I'm sure you now know. He deserved his fate." Lailu had heard enough about the cruelty of their country and the ruthless queens who ruled it to believe this, especially with her village so close to the border between the kingdoms. Sometimes the Krigs managed to sneak through the mountain passes and trickle into Clear Lakes and the surrounding villages. They'd steal livestock and anything else that caught their eye, and murder anyone who got in their way before melting back into the shadows and vanishing like the summer snows. The last attack had been before Lailu was born, but her father bore several scars from it, and she'd lost an uncle and two aunts.

And yet, that man had had such a way with spices that it was hard to believe he'd really been a Krig.

Elister tapped his fingers together, studying her. "Still . . . you have nerve, Miss Loganberry."

"W-what are you going to do to me?" Lailu let go of her cart. Even Mr. Frosty couldn't help her now.

"That depends on you, doesn't it?" He paused, letting the weight of his words sink in. He opened his mouth, but before he could add anything, the bells started clanging in loud, vibrating tones.

"I always hated those bells," Elister confided as the last tone faded away.

Lailu's jaw dropped. He almost sounded . . . human.

"Still, they're useful. Keeps the house on track." He sighed. "But as I was going to say, it just so happens I need a spy myself." He gave Lailu a pointed look and she stepped back.

"M-me? I'm not a spy."

"Well, you're certainly not very good at it," he agreed. "A good spy knows when to walk away from a conversation and when to continue pretending to pour wine, for example."

Lailu flushed.

"But you are wonderfully placed within Victor's camp."

"Mr. Boss?"

"Yes. He told me that he owns Sullivan's and your business."

"Master Slipshod . . . We borrowed some money from him in order to open it," she mumbled.

"The usual deal. Clearly he's trying to shake the control the elves have on him. But why? That's the real mystery." He leaned back against the counter. "I am hardly an easier person to deal with. If anything, I'd demand a higher cut of his profits. But . . . my backing would force the elves to leave him alone. Victor is up to something, something he doesn't want them to know about, and my instinct tells me he's in over his head. And my instinct is never wrong."

"No, sir," Lailu agreed.

"So, the real question is, what is our dear old friend up to? If you can help me get that information, I can choose to overlook this little . . . incident."

Lailu kept seeing that severed hand, her mind swirling around images of pale bone and pink, fleshy muscle, but she knew she didn't have a choice. "Um, I'll see what I can do."

"Excellent."

She swallowed. "When . . . when should I report to you?"

"Oh, I'll find you when I'm ready." He straightened, and Lailu tensed at the sudden movement. "I must return to my guests now. One of my boys will deliver the money I owe to your restaurant in the morning."

Lailu's eyes widened. He was still planning on paying her?

Elister chuckled. "Don't look so surprised. I might be black-mailing you into spying for me, but that doesn't mean you won't be compensated for your culinary skills."

"Th-thank you, sir."

"However, if I ever catch you spying on me again, it would take more than a delightfully prepared meal to make me forget." He inclined his head, his eyes so cold Lailu's teeth chattered. And then he left, the kitchen door swinging behind him, but the chill in the air remained.

Lailu pushed Mr. Frosty through the streets of Gilded Island, her whole body throbbing with exhaustion.

She was supposed to be spying on Elister for Mr. Boss, and now on Mr. Boss for Elister, and she didn't know what either of them really wanted. Meanwhile, she was being tossed around, threatened on all sides, her restaurant in danger of closing at the end of the month with the rest of her life signed over to Mr. Boss, and who knew what would happen to her then. It just felt like too much. "I don't know what to do," she admitted quietly to herself, her eyes burning.

Blinking rapidly, she turned the corner, then froze as a shriek split the night. Something huge hurtled toward her, steam billowing behind it, the front lit up with glowing yellow eyes. Only years of honing her hunting instincts saved her, and Lailu managed to leap to the side just in time, dropping the handle of her cart and rolling up to her feet with her knife already in her hand.

"What the hell are you doing, you idiot?" a man screamed.

Lailu's mouth dropped open. It was one of the scientists in his bizarre horseless carriage. He careened around the next corner and out of sight before the normal sounds of the city resumed.

Lailu took deep breaths, her heart beating furiously. Too close, too close. That jerk could have killed her, and he called *her* the idiot? What kind of irresponsible fool would go racing around the city streets at night? She jammed her knife back into its sheath and stomped forward. Catching her foot on something, she landed flat on her face in the street.

"Great, just great." Lailu climbed painfully back to her feet, uselessly attempting to brush herself off. Even in the flickering lamplight she could tell her clothing was done for. Between the roll she'd done earlier and her fall now, her crisp white shirt was a dingy gray, and her pants were torn and bloody at the knee.

Then her eyes fell on the metal object she'd tripped over. A metal object that looked suspiciously like a crushed Cooling and Containment cart. *Her* crushed Cooling and Containment cart.

"No," she whispered, horror-struck. "No, please no." She crouched down next to it. One whole side of the cart was dented horribly, the lid busted beyond recognition.

First her smashed shrine, and now Mr. Frosty. It was too much, it was all too much, and she couldn't stop the tears from flowing hot and fierce as she huddled there in the street.

A few minutes later she was knocking on the door to Greg's restaurant. She wasn't sure why, but it was the first place she'd thought to go.

The door swung open. "Welcome to LaSilv—" Greg stopped, his mouth falling open.

"M-Mr. Frosty," Lailu sobbed, pushing her deformed cart in front of her.

"Oh no." Greg's eyes widened in horror. "What happened?"

As he ushered her inside, all memories of their earlier fight vanished, and Lailu found herself telling him the whole story. "He was a maniac," she finished. "A *maniac*, and he, he destroyed it." She wiped the back of one hand across her swollen eyes.

"And you too, almost." Greg's mouth tightened. "Well, I know someone who's no longer welcome at my establishment."

"Gregorian," a man said softly, hovering nearby. He wore a stiff black suit with tails and a silver vest, his dark, graying hair pulled into a neat ponytail. Lailu recognized him as the famous Dante LaSilvian, owner of half the vineyards in the country.

"Yes, Uncle?" Greg asked.

"Your diners . . ."

Lailu was suddenly very aware of everyone in Greg's restaurant staring at her. She hiccuped, brushing uncomfortably at her torn and dirty clothing.

"Ah," Greg said. "Um . . . I see. Thank you. I'll take my guest in back, then."

Greg's uncle gave him a curt nod, then circled back through the restaurant.

Now that she'd calmed down, Lailu noticed the fine details of the place, like the paintings of wine-themed still lifes on the walls, the cherrywood furniture, and the lovely chandeliers glowing over each table. The whole place smelled of spices and meat cooked to perfection. She took a deep, calming breath, then froze, her nostrils flaring. She recognized that smell. He was still cooking fyrian chicken!

"Lailu, are you coming?" Greg called.

Scowling, Lailu scurried after him, dragging her broken cart. "Fyrian chicken?"

He shrugged uncomfortably. "Most people seem to like it." He pushed open the door to his kitchen. She could hear the muffled voices of people whispering as she followed him in, the sound immediately stopping as the door shut behind them.

Greg even gets a real door to his kitchen, she fumed silently.

"Can you wait here for a moment without doing anything potentially damaging to my kitchen?"

Lailu glared at him. "I would never harm a kitchen."

"Um, yes, of course. I mean, I knew that. I was just, er, checking." Greg backed away, disappearing through another door.

Lailu sagged against a counter, idly studying Greg's kitchen. For someone who had money, he'd obviously decided to stick with the equipment he knew. He had a steam-powered oven much like hers but with a few more burners, and his shelves were stacked full of dishes, with large brass and iron pots hanging from hooks below them. Off to one side of the stovetop, a dirty knife rested on a chopping board, evidence that he'd been in the middle of cooking when she showed up.

The kitchen door flew open and Greg stepped inside, wheeling a slightly smaller version of Mr. Frosty. It was folded down into a rectangle about as long as Lailu's armspan and stood as tall as her knees, the handle curving gently above it for easy maneuverability. "I haven't really been using mine lately," he said, pushing it toward her. "So if you want, you can borrow it for a while until you get a replacement."

Lailu stared at him, then at the cart, then back at him. She burst into tears.

Greg took a hesitant step backward. "Um, you don't *have* to borrow it, if you don't want—"

"No, I want to." Lailu pulled it from him and wrapped her arms around its handle. "Thanks," she sniffled.

Greg smiled, his eyes crinkling. "My pleasure."

Lailu looked away, her cheeks flushing. Why was she blushing? It was ridiculous. She had nothing to be embarrassed about.

"I'm really sorry, by the way. For the things I said before," Greg said. Now his cheeks were flaming and he wasn't looking at her.

Lailu gaped. She had never heard him apologize before. Not once, in all the years and after all the pranks he'd pulled on her. Not a genuine apology. "Um, that's okay," she managed. "We can call it even, since you're letting me borrow this." She hugged the handle of her replacement cart tighter.

Greg relaxed, his familiar smile back in place. "You know, I wasn't sure you'd actually accept it. Seeing as we're, you know, 'rivals and that's it.'"

Lailu frowned down at the cart. She suddenly wanted to fling it away from her.

"Sorry, I shouldn't have brought that up," Greg said hurriedly. "I know you were just angry then. Well, I mean you're always angry. At me, at least. I'm not sure why." He stopped and took a deep breath. "Please, ignore everything I just said. I'm just tired."

"Yeah, you and me both," Lailu muttered. Why *had* she agreed to borrow Greg's cart so readily? That really wasn't like her, relying on someone else. It was a bad habit, a dangerous habit. *She* must be tired, tired and desperate. Sniffing loudly, she rubbed her eyes again. "I'll return it soon." She forced herself to look up at Greg again, not quite meeting his eyes. "I promise."

"I'm not worried. I know you're good for it, and honestly, I have another one."

"Of course you do."

At least he had the grace to look embarrassed. "Speaking of borrowing things," he said, clearly trying to change the subject, "I'm glad you stopped by, because I have something of yours."

Lailu waited.

Greg hesitated, his brown eyes serious. "It's Hannah."

RE-HOMING

H annah lay in bed, facing the wall, her long hair in a dirty tangle down her back. She didn't turn around, but her shoulders stiffened as Lailu stepped inside the room.

"I'll just leave you two alone, then," Greg said awkwardly, stepping back and closing the door behind him. Like Lailu, Greg had living quarters above his restaurant, only his were much larger and better furnished. Hannah was staying in a guest room, dimly lit by a lantern in one corner and a stack of half-melted candles in another. Clothes lay strewn all over the place along with piles of combs and jewelry, like Hannah had really made herself at home here.

"Hannah?" Lailu took another tentative step forward. Why wasn't Hannah at school? Lailu sat down on the edge of the bed.

Hannah turned, peering at Lailu through a tangle of hair.

"What are you doing here? Don't you have a restaurant to run?"

"We need to talk."

Hannah's head flopped back onto the pillows and she closed her eyes.

Lailu waited, but after a few minutes it became obvious Hannah was going back to sleep. "Hey, wake up. I said we need to talk."

"Too . . . tired . . ." Hannah yawned, keeping her eyes shut. "Let's talk later."

Lailu scowled. "Hannah!"

Hannah snored softly.

"Look, either you sit up and listen to me or I'm going to . . . to . . ." Lailu glanced around, noticing again the pile of tangled haircombs spilling out on the nightstand. "I'm going to start breaking combs."

Hannah gasped. "You wouldn't!"

"Oh yes, I would," Lailu said grimly. "I'd break each and every one of them, from that ridiculous pink glittery one to the black one with the feathers. One piece at a time."

Hannah reluctantly sat up. "All right," she whispered sadly. "Say what you have to say."

Lailu rubbed her temple. Her ever-constant headache was getting worse by the moment. "I'm not going to yell at you," she began, "if that's what you're afraid of."

"Are you still mad at me?"

"Not . . . not really."

"So if I needed to crash at your place again, you'd let me?"

Lailu blinked. "Sure."

All at once Hannah's expression brightened. "Oh, thank the gods," she breathed. "I wasn't sure what I'd do otherwise. I mean, Greg took me in, but this is obviously temporary, and he just wants to talk about you all the time anyway, and since I've been mad at you, that hasn't been very good at all," she babbled. "But I didn't really have anywhere else to go, and I've been booted from Twin Rivers's Finest because Gweneth de Vincy has a big fat mouth and told everyone about my . . . well, it doesn't really matter what she told them."

"Wait, slow down. You're still mad at me?" Lailu could barely follow the torrent of words.

"Not anymore. Aren't you listening?"

"I'm trying," Lailu muttered. "Who's Gweneth de Vincy?"

"My old roommate."

Lailu stared at her. "So . . . you got kicked out of school?"

Hannah nodded. "I told you that, didn't I?"

"No, you didn't! You told me you were just having some drama at school."

"Same thing." Hannah waved it off, a trace of the old Hannah in her husky voice.

Lailu frowned, her eyes sliding over to Hannah's comb stash. "You weren't . . . you didn't steal from your roommate, did you?"

Hannah gasped indignantly. "Me?" She put a hand to her chest. "I'm not a thief."

"Sorry, sorry," Lailu began.

"I just wanted to make sure those combs had a proper home, that's all."

Lailu's mumbled apologies stopped abruptly.

"I mean, she had them stuffed in a drawer, can you believe it? She hardly ever wore any of them, except this dreadfully plain comb with fyrian chicken feathers sticking out of it." She shuddered.

Privately, Lailu shuddered, too. Why would anyone want anything that came from one of those horrible beasts? Shoving those thoughts away, she focused on the important matter. "So," she said slowly, trying to keep her voice level, "you've been, uh, re-homing combs?"

Hannah blinked innocently, but gave a small nod.

"How many combs?"

"Just . . . a few."

"A few, huh?" Lailu sighed. "Why do you do this?"

"I just . . . I just wanted to fit in." Hannah's fingers twisted in the blankets. "All those other girls could afford to get as many nice combs as they wanted, but I couldn't. Even with the scholarship, it's cost my parents more than they will say to send me to Twin Rivers's Finest."

Lailu frowned, knowing what Hannah meant. She had always stuck out at the academy as the girl with the secondhand uniforms and cooking equipment. Twin Rivers's new scholarship programs made it so people from small villages, like her and Hannah, could go to school and join the rising middle class, but it certainly wasn't easy fitting in.

"Since all those girls had more combs than hair on their head, I figured most of them wouldn't notice if a couple went missing, so . . . I took some." She smiled ruefully. "Turns out they noticed."

"I'm surprised they didn't make you give them back." Lailu picked up a silver comb in the shape of a starfish.

"Oh, they tried. But since I'd already stashed most of them at your place—"

"You what?" Lailu dropped the comb back on the pile as if it had burned her.

"What? Giving them back wasn't going to get me out of trouble. And besides, I *did* promise them a good home."

Lailu shook her head. "What are you going to tell your parents?"

Hannah smiled brightly. "Oh, that's easy. I figured I just wouldn't tell them anything."

"Hannah!"

"Well, you know how they are." Hannah flapped her hands. "They'd . . . Well. They would not take it well."

That was like saying Lailu kind of liked cooking, or Mr. Boss was somewhat untrustworthy. Lailu could just imagine how Garin Meadows would react if he knew his Hannah, his perfect daughter, had been kicked out of school. He hadn't much liked the idea of her leaving the village in the first place, but to leave and then fail? It would be unacceptable. And Hannah's mother would be even more livid. She viewed Hannah as an extension of herself. Any time Hannah wasn't absolutely perfect, her mother took it as a personal insult. Still, they were her parents, and they had a right to know.

"Hannah," Lailu began.

"Hear me out," Hannah continued quickly. "I'll just come live and work with you. I mean, I'm excellent at waiting on people, and none of your customers have any haircombs worth taking, and then I don't have to go back to our village." She shrugged as if that settled everything.

Lailu gritted her teeth, her headache building to epic proportions. What would she tell Master Slipshod? "Look, you can't just not tell your parents—"

"You're not telling yours anything," Hannah pointed out.

Lailu opened her mouth, then closed it again. It was true. Her last letter to her father had just said business was starting to do well. She hadn't told him anything at all about Mr. Boss, or Elister, or the elves, or really anything. "Fine, fine," she grumbled. It wasn't like they didn't need the help.

Hannah put a sudden arm around Lailu. "Thank you," she whispered. "And . . . I'm sorry. For earlier. For what I said."

Lailu wasn't really much of a hugger, but she put an awkward arm around her friend. "I'm sorry too." They sat like that for a minute, just like old times, just like when they were little and Lailu used to follow Hannah around. Hannah, who was always so confident, so beautiful, so popular. Lailu couldn't understand how it was possible Hannah could feel so insecure and yet seem so . . . perfect.

And then Lailu remembered Mr. Boss. She leaped to her feet. It had to be close to midnight by now. If she was late. . . . She clutched the handle of the chef's knife at her hip. "I've got to run."

"Everything all right?" Hannah asked, eyes wide.

"Er, maybe?" Lailu couldn't lie, not to Hannah. But she didn't want to get into the truth, either. "I'll see you at home. Oh, and can you bring Greg's Cooling and Containment cart with you?"

Out on the stairs she practically knocked Greg down in her haste. "Hey, hey!" He caught her by the waist before she fell. "What's going on?"

"I have to go." It was like the walls were moving in, sucking all the air out as they crept closer, closer. "I really have to go." She pulled away.

"Go? Go where? What about Hannah?"

Lailu stopped. "Greg," she began, swallowing hard. He'd loaned her his Cooling and Containment cart, and he'd taken Hannah in. She remembered the way he cut her free from the net, how he walked all the way to Mystic Cooking to bring her the rest of her batyrdactyls, and as she looked up at her greatest rival, her chest felt strangely tight. "Thank you." And Lailu really meant it. "For . . . for everything."

Greg stepped in close, way too close. "I *want* to help you," he said softly, his brown eyes so intense she couldn't look away. One of his hands hovered by her face, almost but not quite touching her; she could feel the heat from it like it was a brand.

She didn't understand what he was trying to tell her, didn't want to understand, so instead she backed away. "Hannah's going to head back to my place with your cart. I can't wait for her, though, I have to go. I have to go now." And she turned and fled down the stairs and out through the kitchen.

THE CROW'S NEST

*L*ailu had never been there, but she still knew the Crow's Nest when she saw it. A three-story establishment, it towered over the taverns perched sadly on either side, its wooden sign swinging gently in the breeze with what Lailu knew to be a crow painted on the front. In the low light, however, it looked more like a black splotch of ink, the name of the joint scrawled in red above it.

Lailu pulled on the splintery door handle and slipped inside. Sound slapped her in the face and smoke burned her eyes as she wove her way through the thick crowd, focusing on the bar toward the back. She dodged one man's elbow and another's flying mug of beer, then jumped as a rough hand fell on her shoulder.

"Sure took your sweet time," the Butcher said, his gaunt face a mess of shadows and sharp angles in the dim lighting. "And here we were thinking you had decided not to come, even after my gentle . . . *reminder*."

Lailu shrank away, but he just tightened his grip. "Let go of me," she growled, hoping she sounded braver than she felt.

"Or you'll do what? Spit in my food?" His sneer widened, showing off his yellow teeth. "This way, chef. Don't want to keep Mr. Boss waiting any longer, or who knows where someone'll find you." Giving her shoulder one last bone-crunching squeeze, he let her go.

Lailu shuddered, but followed the Butcher through the crowd. Someone bumped into him, and he turned, grabbed the guy, and threw him into the mass of people. There was a loud outburst that was quickly silenced, the Butcher's profile enough to send them all slinking quietly back into the shadows. *Cowards*, Lailu thought bitterly. Then she realized she wasn't any braver. Here she was, like a dog on a leash, and all because she was scared of the Butcher too.

Even the bartender, a beefy man with a missing ear and ferocious eyes, shrank from the Butcher. With a curt nod to the man, Havoc slid behind the bar, Lailu following as far back as she dared. She felt the bartender watching as she climbed the rickety wooden stairs half hidden behind the shelves full of drink.

Mr. Boss's office was on the third floor. Lailu stopped at the top of the stairs as Havoc McHackney knocked three times. He waited a moment, then knocked three times again before pushing the door open and walking in. Lailu wasted a few seconds dreaming of running back down the stairs, through the tavern, and out into the fresh, clean air. But then what? Mr. Boss wouldn't just let her go.

And Master Slipshod . . . Lailu no longer believed he could protect her. She wasn't even sure he'd try.

She took a deep breath. "Into the spider's lair," she whispered. Then she squared her shoulders and walked inside, blinking against the haze that immediately surrounded her, trying not to cough. It was worse than downstairs, as if all the smoke had drifted up here to form one thick cloud.

"And there she is, the woman of the hour." Mr. Boss's oily voice wrapped around her, his small frame practically swallowed by his velvet armchair. Glasses covered the wooden table in front of him, most of them empty. Clearly, he and his cronies had been here for a while.

Ryon slumped in a chair off to the side, next to a dark-skinned man Lailu had never seen before. As the Butcher settled into his seat to the right of Mr. Boss, Ryon gave her a halfhearted wink, his face drawn and tired.

Another man and woman sat beside the Butcher. Lailu had never seen the man before. Chubby and wild-haired, he slowly and deliberately shuffled a stack of cards like they were made of glass. And then Lailu's eyes fell on the woman, and she gasped.

Narrow face, sharp cheekbones, red hair pulled into a severe bun, and large green eyes. Starling Volan. Lailu had gone almost two years without seeing the scientist, and now she seemed to be everywhere.

Starling studied Lailu. She wore another one of her famous tailored suits, her wide mouth quirked slightly to the left. What was *she* doing here with Mr. Boss?

"Introduce yourself, Starling," Mr. Boss said loudly, and Lailu realized she was staring openmouthed at the scientist. "Lailu here would obviously love to make your acquaintance."

A couple of people laughed, but not Starling. She merely inclined her head in Lailu's direction. "I remember you. The chef, yes?" Her face softened into the barest hint of a smile. "You came to see my new stoves. You, with your eyes full of cooking."

Lailu found herself smiling back, a small knot in her chest loosening. Starling Volan, *the* Starling Volan, remembered her. She wasn't sure how Starling was mixed up with Mr. Boss, but it was probably a mistake of some sort. A business deal she had unadvisedly made. Lailu could relate to that.

"No Slipshod?" Mr. Boss straightened, clenching his silver-topped cane. He moved carefully, like his whole body hurt.

Good, Lailu thought vindictively, but she shook her head. "I thought you asked for me."

"True, very true. But I'm surprised Sullivan let you come alone. Not very . . . mentorlike, considering he's the one who roped you into all of this."

Lailu tried not to let those words get to her. "He's a great chef," she said stiffly. And he was. But she was beginning to think that this didn't make him a good mentor.

"So tell me, what did you hear? What was our good pal Elister up to, with his fancy exclusive dinner party?" Mr. Boss's lips gave a small, bitter twitch.

"Uh . . ." Lailu stared down at her feet, terrified at the prospect of reporting on Elister, especially since he already knew she'd been spying on him. Would he find out about this? She remembered the look in his cold eyes and knew if he did, she'd get no more chances from him. Still, she had her restaurant to protect, not to mention herself. She needed to tell Mr. Boss something, so she launched into a description of her food and how well it had been received. "Some of them even asked for seconds—"

"I don't care about the blasted food!" Mr. Boss slammed his cane into the ground with a sharp crack like the world was shattering.

Lailu winced, edging backward.

"All I care about is what that, that . . ." He took a deep breath, and in a more normal tone of voice, he continued, "I just want to know what Elister is up to. Who did he invite?"

Lailu hesitated. The Butcher put his hand on his meat cleaver and narrowed his eyes, and she knew she couldn't avoid the question any longer. Reluctantly, she described the people who had been there. When she got to the elf, Mr. Boss's face darkened.

"He had long black hair and gray-blue eyes?" he snapped.

"Yes."

"It must have been Fahr." Mr. Boss's nostrils flared. "So, did *Fahr* enjoy his dinner with the big man?"

"I don't think he was especially enjoying it." Lailu couldn't look away from Mr. Boss's dead fish eyes. They were red-rimmed, almost like he'd been crying. Or rubbing at them really hard. Maybe he was sick. "I mean, he barely touched the food," she added. "Can you believe it?"

"What did they talk about?" Mr. Boss demanded.

"Not much. The elf mentioned . . . He said he had some sort of problem."

Mr. Boss froze. "What kind of problem?"

"He didn't say, but most people at the table seemed to think it had something to do with . . ." Lailu bit her lip, sneaking a peek at Starling. "With the scientists," she finished nervously.

Mr. Boss glanced sidelong at Starling Volan too. "Was anything else said about the scientists?" he asked.

"Well, a lot of people are very impressed with them," Lailu said carefully "Even Elister. He's backing them now."

Mr. Boss's eyes narrowed. The chubby man with the sideburns stopped shuffling cards, and Lailu swore the whole room was holding its breath. She swallowed, her mouth suddenly very dry. Clearly that was not information she should have shared.

"He's backing them, is he?" Mr. Boss asked quietly. "All of them? Or present company excluded?"

Lailu could feel Starling staring at her. It was somehow worse than facing a basilisk fish, and she wondered if she was slowly turning to stone beneath the weight of that gaze. "Er," she tried. "Well . . ." She thought about the door behind her, and every fiber in her body longed to run to it, to yank it open and slam it shut behind her.

Starling finally spoke up. "Don't be absurd, Victor, you know my people do nothing without my consent. Of course Elister is backing me, and my people *through* me."

"Is he, now?" Mr. Boss ran his thumb up and down the silver top of his cane, the muscles in his jaw twitching. "Since when?"

"It hardly matters. We do *not* have an exclusive arrangement. I go where business calls."

"You . . ." Mr. Boss stopped, took a deep breath, and finally seemed to remember Lailu still standing there. "You, go away," he told her.

Lailu blinked. "W-what?"

"Go. Get out. Leave." He waved his hands at her like she was some sort of pest. "Starling and I have things to discuss. Urgent things."

Starling shifted uncomfortably.

Lailu backed toward the door, hardly daring to believe he was letting her go so easily. She remembered the way he'd tricked her on her opening day, and she didn't breathe until she'd shut the door behind her, blocking them all out.

Lailu sagged with relief. *Well, that went well,* she thought. At least she wasn't dead. Yet.

She started for the stairs, then stopped. She longed to burrow under her blankets, safe inside Mystic Cooking, but there was also Elister. If he did find out she reported on him . . . She shivered. He couldn't know. He could never know. But if he did . . . If she had some information for him in return, maybe he'd let her live.

Lailu took a deep breath and crouched, putting her ear against the door.

"—concoction isn't working." Lailu recognized Mr. Boss's voice, loud and angry. "My time still appears to be running out. I'd hate for your time to run out as well."

"You would be wise, Victor, not to resort to threats." Starling's voice was so cold that Lailu shivered. "I am working hard, as always, but having my supplies disrupted—"

From downstairs came a loud burst of noise as if a door had suddenly opened, and Lailu missed the next few sentences.

"—behind my back," Mr. Boss was saying. Lailu pressed closer to the door, then froze as the floor creaked softly under her.

"Alchemy is expensive. Surely a businessman such as yourself understands this better than anyone." Starling's accent became thicker in irritation. "Elister has money, and he is interested in advancing our sciences. Why should we not work with him as well?"

"Are you giving him the elixir, too, then?"

"No, only you, as agreed. Elister would never approve of our . . . *methods*."

Elixir? With a sick, squirming feeling, Lailu remembered the jar of purple liquid Brennon had given her, and his words. *Mr. Boss is bankrupting himself to buy this junk from the scientists.*

After that whole mess with Hannah she'd forgotten all about it, and now Brennon was dead or worse, and she hadn't even tried to help him. He'd been so desperate, and all she'd done was stuff that jar away in her cabinet. She hadn't even told Master Slipshod about it.

Someone tapped her on the shoulder.

Lailu jumped backward, smacking into the wall behind her. Wren's eyes widened in horror and she put a hand over her mouth as both girls froze and listened.

Footsteps stomped to the door. Wren waved her hand at Lailu, who scrambled back and down the first few stairs like a crab as Wren moved closer to the door and lifted her hand, like she was about to knock. The door flew open in her face and the Butcher shoved his own greasy head out. "What do you want?" he growled.

"I, uh, I was sent to see if, if you n-needed anything e-else," Wren stammered.

The Butcher looked her up and down. "I don't believe you." He grabbed Wren by the front of her dress. Lailu tensed, prepared to leap up the stairs.

"Havoc, leave the girl alone," Mr. Boss snapped. "She's Starling's whelp."

The Butcher reluctantly let Wren go. Lailu sank back down on the stairs, more confused than ever. She looked up in time to see Wren disappear into the room, the door shutting firmly behind her. When several moments crawled by and nothing happened, Lailu picked herself up, then straightened her clothing as she walked slowly down the stairs.

Starling and Wren were clearly up to something. Something big. But what? Wren was just a kid. What could she possibly be involved in? And what was in that elixir?

BLOOD AND LIES

*L*ailu had a long, sleepless night followed by a hectic morning, but as she flipped the sign in the window over to CLOSED, she felt a deep satisfaction. Even without Master Slipshod around, she'd managed to feed her lunch customers and had food prepped for dinner. Hannah had been a huge help, just like she promised, and for the first time Lailu began to think they might just be okay.

As Hannah headed upstairs to nap, Lailu wiped down tables, humming softly under her breath.

Wham!

The front door burst open so fast the bell didn't even have a chance to ring.

"M-Master Slipshod!" Lailu gasped as her mentor staggered in. He looked terrible, his wild hair even wilder, his usually smooth chin covered in the beginnings of a beard that crept down his neck, disappearing into his stained and wrinkled shirt.

Lailu wasn't sure what to feel. Relief that he was finally back? Anger that he'd abandoned her at such a crucial time? "Where have you—"

"Gone, all gone." Master Slipshod stumbled around like he was in a dream. "He's really gone, Pigtails."

"Who is?"

"Brennon. I tried to find him, I tried to look . . . gone! I can't believe it, Victor has gone berserk, totally erratic!" He grabbed Lailu's shoulders. "We can't work for a man like that! Do you have any idea what he'll make us do? What he'll do to *us*?"

Knock-knock-knock.

Master Slipshod's fingers tightened until Lailu's shoulders creaked. She winced, pulling away.

"Don't—" he began, but too late: she was already opening the door.

A boy in a crisp black-and-silver tunic with formfitting black breeches stood on the doorstep, his arms wrapped around a small metal box. He held it out. "Message for you."

Lailu eyed it suspiciously. She remembered the last box they'd received on their doorstep. "From who?"

"From Lord Elister." The boy's tone implied that it was obvious, which it probably was. After all, he wore Elister's house colors. Lailu's sleep-deprived brain just couldn't seem to keep up. "Lord Elister says to expect a visit from him shortly," he added, thrusting the box at her.

"Shortly? How shortly?"

"He didn't specify." Giving a small, formal bow, the boy turned on his heel and marched smartly away.

Lailu shut the door before drifting toward a table, her fingers searching for the clasp on the box. She tried not to think what a visit from Elister could mean. Did he want a report on Mr. Boss already? Or . . . had he heard about her report *to* Mr. Boss?

"What is it?" Master Slipshod asked. He was crouched nearby, out of sight of the door.

"Are you . . . hiding?" This was the man who'd once hunted dragons, who'd served the king, who'd trained the head chef at the academy? Her stomach twisted in disappointment.

"I'm . . . Never mind what I'm doing. What's in the box?"

Lailu sat in a chair and flipped the lid open. Her heart stuttered.

Gold. A small pile of actual living, breathing gold. Well, maybe not breathing, Lailu admitted, but there was something very much alive about the shiny pile of coins, the way the light reflected off all those glossy edges and the crown engraved into each one.

Master Slipshod slammed the lid closed and slid the box away from her. "I'll just put this in the safe with the rest of the money," he gasped, his hands trembling.

"P-probably a good idea." Lailu couldn't wrap her mind around all that money. Apparently there was something to this catering thing, especially when you were catering for part of the royal staff. "Will it be enough?"

Master Slipshod paused in the kitchen entrance. "To cover our loan?" He looked down at the box sadly. "No. Not enough. But it . . . it could be enough for . . . for a backup plan."

"What kind of backup plan?"

He hesitated. But then the bell above the door chimed and he ducked behind the kitchen curtain.

That same blond elf strolled in, the one with the cold blue eyes and hundreds of braids. And right behind him came . . . Ryon?

"All right, little chef, it's been three days," the elf announced. "Where's Hannah?"

Lailu stood slowly. "I d-don't know."

"Really?" He raised an eyebrow. "I think you do know."

Lailu lifted her chin. Could he smell the lies on her? Could he read it in her face? She forced herself not to think of Hannah, asleep and vulnerable, just upstairs . . .

"I told you, Eirad, she hasn't returned here yet," Ryon said. "I've been looking for her."

Eirad smirked. "I'm sure you have." Ryon's eyes narrowed and Eirad's smirk faded immediately. "Fine. Little chef, tell your friend that she needs to bring the item tonight."

Lailu took a deep breath. "What happens if she doesn't have it for you yet?"

"Well, then we start taking other things of value from her." Eirad leaned back against a table. "We'll begin with some fingers, then maybe some toes, and then move on to the ears. That sort of thing."

"She's only fourteen!" Lailu burst out.

The elf shrugged. "Old enough. She knew the penalties when she stole from us."

Hannah, why? Lailu shook her head.

"She'll know where to find us." He gave Ryon a hostile look, then stalked out.

"That went surprisingly well," Ryon said into the silence.

"Thanks for sticking up for me." Lailu collapsed back into her chair.

"For you? No problem." Ryon hesitated, one hand running back through his dark, silky hair. "But he's right. The elves always collect what they're owed, and when they don't . . . well, I've seen their collection of limbs. It isn't pretty."

"I don't think Hannah knows where it is," Lailu admitted miserably.

"Maybe you should go upstairs and ask her."

Lailu's eyebrows shot up. "You knew Hannah was here?"

Ryon shrugged.

"You lied? To an elf?"

"I lie to everyone."

"But can't they always tell?"

"Not when *I* do it."

Lailu frowned, studying Ryon. There was something off about him, something she couldn't quite figure out. "But aren't you working for him?"

"Am I?" Ryon smiled. "Anyway, even if the item is gone, you and your friend can still make it out of this, all limbs intact."

"How?"

"The elves can't resist a good bargain. So offer to cook them something they've never had before. Something . . . extravagant."

"Really? That could work?" Lailu's stomach unknotted as the smallest bit of hope welled up. Still, a bargain with the elves? They were more slippery and dangerous than an enraged kraken.

"It's worth a try. But be careful how you word your bargain. Make sure you're very clear about what you're trading, and what you're getting in return." He stretched. "Anyhow, I'm off to see your boyfriend now. Any messages to pass him?"

"M-my what?"

Ryon's grin widened. "You know, handsome fellow, long blond hair. Knows you as 'Lala.' Or is it 'Lillie'?"

"Vahn?" Lailu's face burned. "He's not my, I mean, he's . . . friend, my brother's . . ."

"Relax, I'm just teasing you. You could do much better."

Lailu highly doubted that. "Why are you meeting him?" She suddenly remembered Vahn's statement: *I never thought I'd be doing a job for* this *particular group.* Maybe the elves hired Vahn to investigate their disappearances? "Are you working together?"

"Not . . . exactly," Ryon hedged. "I've been in the business of trading information for a while now. Vahn is just one of my many customers."

"I thought you were just supposed to be 'spying' for Mr. Boss—"

"That's what I want him to believe."

"—and that instead you were secretly working for the elves," she continued.

"And why would you think that?" He grinned, obviously enjoying this, but Lailu ignored his flippant attitude. She thought again of the jar Brennon had left her to give to Vahn. It had been on her mind since last night. Could she trust Ryon? She didn't know when Vahn would be by again, and Ryon *had* helped her before. Maybe . . .

"I do have something for him. Something strange," she said, making up her mind.

"Oh?"

"Brennon gave it to me."

Ryon froze.

"Wait here." Lailu lugged her pixy paprika canister out of the kitchen and into the dining room, then unscrewed the lid and lifted the jar of purple liquid out.

All the color drained from Ryon's face, leaving him whiter than freshly kneaded dough. "By the gods."

"What is it?" Lailu's heart beat faster. The jar was still warm in her hand, the liquid inside hissing like it hadn't been buried in a dark cabinet for the past few days.

Ryon's eyes found hers. "Elf blood."

22

LAILU HAS A PLAN

*L*ailu dropped the jar.

Ryon lunged forward, catching it a foot off the ground.

"I can't believe it, I just can't believe it," Lailu mumbled. She felt sick, the world swimming around her. She had to sit down.

"It's going to be okay."

"I had no idea," she whispered hoarsely.

Ryon gave a wry chuckle. "I can tell." All laughter faded as he looked at the jar in his hand. "Brennon gave you this?"

She nodded.

"Did he steal it from Mr. Boss?"

"Um . . . I think he said he stole it *for* Mr. Boss," Lailu croaked. "But then he decided not to give it to him."

"Stole it from whom?"

Lailu hesitated. She thought of Starling, and of Wren. *He's bankrupting himself to buy this junk from the scientists.* "I don't know," she lied.

Ryon squinted at her. "Lailu, if you know anything . . ."

"I don't. Not really."

He nodded. "Well, this changes everything." He pulled Lailu to her feet. "Don't tell anyone about this, not even that mentor of yours. If Eirad had searched your place just now, you'd be a smear on your floor. Even I wouldn't have been able to save you." He squeezed her hand, then released her. "I don't know what Brennon was thinking, giving this to you."

"So is he d-dead, then?"

Ryon's eyes were cold. "He'd better be." Pocketing the jar, he turned and left the restaurant, the door chiming cheerfully behind him.

Lailu stood there for a long moment, breathing hard and trying not to think about blood, *elven* blood, sitting in her cabinet for days. Taking one last deep breath, she headed upstairs to find Hannah.

Hannah wasn't in the bedroom. Frowning, Lailu turned to go back downstairs when she heard a scuffling noise, and Slipshod's door opened. Hannah poked her head out, then tiptoed into the hall, shutting the door behind her.

"What are you doing?" Lailu asked.

Hannah jumped, then turned around guiltily. "N-nothing."

"Is Master Slipshod in there?"

"No. I saw him leave out the back."

"And so you snuck into his rooms? Why?" Lailu narrowed her eyes. "Are you trying to steal from him, too?"

"Of course not! Lailu, I swear I left the elves' haircomb on your nightstand. I *know* I did. But I can't find it anywhere. So, I thought . . . I thought . . ."

"You thought my mentor took it?"

Hannah bit her lip, then nodded.

"No way! Why would he . . ." But Lailu remembered how weird Master Slipshod had acted right after Mr. Boss moved up their loan's deadline. And she could have sworn he'd gone into her room that night. Could he have? "No way," she repeated weakly.

"B-but I've l-looked everywhere for it." Tears streamed down Hannah's face. "It's g-gone."

"Are you sure?"

"This was my last hope," Hannah sobbed, indicating Master Slipshod's door. "He must have s-sold it, or gambled it away already."

"If he ever had it in the first place." Lailu shook her head. "Did you really steal it off an elf's head?"

Hannah gave a tremulous smile. "Yes," she sniffled.

"How?" Even if she wholeheartedly disapproved of Hannah's stealing, Lailu was dying to know how she pulled it off.

"We-ell"—Hannah drew out the word—"I was doing the hair of Lady Abigail, and Gweneth, she was my roommate—"

"I've heard."

"Horrible person, by the way. Well, she was asked to do the hair of this elf who was visiting Madame Pompadour. For practice, you know? Our stations were right next to each other, so I just sort of . . . helped her."

"You helped her, huh?"

She shrugged. "It was easy to lean over and—" She mimed the motion of pinching something delicately between two fingers.

"Hannah." Lailu shook her head.

"What? It was a very nice comb," Hannah said defensively. "I couldn't help myself. You should have seen the way the sunlight hit it from the windows. It made the whole world look shiny and green."

"And she didn't notice?"

"Well, obviously she did eventually." Hannah wiped at her face. "But not at first, no." She sniffed again. "I probably shouldn't have worn it afterward. That was a little obvious, now that I think about it."

Lailu wasn't sure if she should strangle her friend or hug her. She exhaled. No sense in delaying anymore; she just had to be blunt. "Hannah, one of the elves was here for you again today. He said if you don't return the comb, he's going to . . . to start taking body parts."

"Oh, dragon dung," Hannah whispered. Then she burst into tears.

"It's going to be all right." Lailu patted Hannah's shoulder awkwardly. "You'll see. It'll all work out." But how? "Dragon . . . dung," she repeated slowly, the beginnings of a plan swirling into place. "Dragon dung . . ."

"Lailu?" Hannah sniffled.

And Lailu smiled. Because she had a plan. A plan not only to free Hannah, but to free herself and Master Slipshod too.

It was time for Master Slipshod to teach her the secrets of dragon cuisine.

Lailu cornered Master Slipshod as he was creeping back inside the restaurant that evening. Before he could even sit down or move or do anything, she had blurted out the whole story, ending with her request.

"Absolutely not." Master Slipshod crossed his arms.

"But it's been in the papers! It's even attacking villagers, and if we don't do something about it, you know they'll send a hero after it."

"I highly doubt that. A hero couldn't handle a mountain dragon." Slipshod's lips curled into a sneer. Lailu knew how he felt about heroes. It was a sentiment most chefs shared. She snatched at it.

"True, a hero might not be able to. But we could. If you'll just teach me—"

"I'm not divulging the ancient secrets of dragon cuisine just so you can help your flighty little friend. Besides, you're not ready."

Lailu clenched her fists, her nails biting into her skin. "She's not flighty!"

Slipshod snorted.

"And I *am too* ready. I haven't done anything reckless lately—"

"You're about to try bargaining with a pack of unscrupulous elves! If that isn't reckless, I don't know what is."

"You could come with me."

"I'm done bargaining, Pigtails. And never with elves. It's a bad idea. I'd stop you if I could."

Lailu narrowed her eyes. "I'm ready," she repeated firmly. "I know I am."

Master Slipshod's eyes were tired and bloodshot, he still had the beginnings of a beard, and he'd run his fingers through his hair so often it stuck up in a wiry mess. But his eyes sharpened as he finally studied Lailu, really studied her. Lailu stood very tall, heart pounding. Eventually Slipshod gave a small nod. "You might be at that."

"R-really?"

He turned away from her, one finger idly tracing the *SV* on the stove. "And you say this . . . this item Hannah misplaced is going to land her in a lot of trouble?"

"Yes."

"And this dragon cuisine. It could balance out that trouble?"

"I . . . I don't know. I hope so," Lailu whispered.

Slipshod didn't turn around, but his shoulders slumped. "Let me think on it some more."

Lailu bit her lip. She wanted to know Master Slipshod would help her before using that as a bargaining chip, but she didn't want to push it, not when he was so close to agreeing. Instead, she gritted her teeth and asked him for another favor.

"You want me to deliver messages now too?" Slipshod's eyebrows drew together in irritation.

"Please. It's important."

He frowned. "Wren, you said? Some scientist's kid?" He shook his head but took the letter Lailu wrote out for him. "Don't really see the benefit to getting mixed up with her, but fine, fine."

She wasn't sure if Wren would even respond, but one way or another she had to know what that girl was up to. With these thoughts weighing her down, Lailu left her mentor behind and headed out for her meeting with the elves, feeling woefully under-prepared but determined all the same.

23

THE TREE FORT

ailu studied the massive wooden doors cut into the side of the redwood tree. An intricate pattern sprawled across the front, swirls tangling together to form a flowing tree across both doors with some sort of writing underneath. Lailu was familiar with wood carving, and she knew instinctively that no tool had been used to make this image. It was as if the tree had grown the picture and words, fashioning the doors from its very essence. Back home she had heard stories about elves with the power to shape nature, to call animals, summon fire, and much more. Staring at this tree, she could believe those stories. This place was not grown so much as *created*.

There were no handles on the door, and she hesitated, about to knock. It felt like the tree was holding its breath, waiting for her.

Lailu looked down at the wooden platform under her feet, her eyes trailing out over the edge to the tiny path carved precariously into the tree itself. It stretched from the ground hundreds of feet below and wound its way up the trunk, each step just a tiny sliver carved into the tree. Had she really climbed that just to be stopped by a pair of intimidating doors?

Taking a deep breath, Lailu raised her fist.

The doors flew open, knocking her back.

"Mind the edge," a woman's cool voice said, and Lailu realized her heels were only inches from the end of the platform. She scooted forward quickly, her heart hammering.

A female elf stood framed in the doorway, her chestnut hair pulled into a bun, emphasizing her prominent cheekbones and large pointed ears. "You must be Lailu, the chef."

"Y-yes."

"We've been expecting you." The elf bared her teeth and stepped back from the doorway. "Welcome to the tree fort."

Had Ryon told them she was coming? Or did they just somehow know? Lailu tentatively stepped inside, the doors swinging shut behind her.

The elf stalked gracefully up a staircase in the back of the small room as Lailu followed nervously behind her.

At the top of the stairs stretched a long hallway smelling vaguely earthy, the polished wooden walls and ceiling adding to Lailu's impression of walking through a forest. Was this all part of the same tree? It hadn't seemed that big from the outside. Lailu shivered, remembering Eirad's words, how he wanted to turn five years of her life into magic. How many years had been stolen to create this place?

Pushing those thoughts away, she glanced into each of the open doors they passed. Sometimes the elves in the rooms would look up, but most of them just ignored her.

When they got to a closed door at the very end of the hallway, Lailu's guide raised a dainty fist and knocked three times.

"Come in."

The elf pushed open the door. Lailu followed her in, her hands like ice.

Reclining in a large chair behind an even larger oak desk sat Fahr, the elf Lailu had seen at Lord Elister's dinner party. His booted feet were propped up on his desk, his long black hair silky and smooth in the flickering firelight. Lailu could feel him watching her with his laughing blue-gray eyes.

"Gwendyl?" Fahr turned to Lailu's guide, a small crease forming between his eyes. "I sent for Livea."

The elf woman slid into an empty chair in the back corner. "She's still out," she said bitterly, "so I guess I'm the note taker today."

"Livea's out?" Fahr's shoulders tensed.

The door opened again and Lailu's heart sank as the familiar blond elf strolled in, his braids tumbling loosely around his shoulders. "I hear you want to negotiate after all." He smiled at her, but it wasn't a nice smile. "You can't imagine how happy that makes me."

"I think I'd prefer not to imagine, thank you." Lailu was proud of how calm her voice sounded.

"Eirad, sit down," Fahr said.

A hint of genuine humor touched Eirad's eyes as he folded his tall frame into a seat. Now Lailu was the only one standing. She clasped her hands behind her back to hide their trembling.

Fahr moved his feet off the desk and straightened in his chair. "Let's get this done then, shall we?" His blue-gray eyes fixed Lailu in place. "We have before us Lailu Loganberry, here to negotiate payment for one Hannah Meadows. Our records show that Hannah owes us an elven heirloom, now lost."

"Lailu, what do you propose in exchange for this *priceless* item?" Eirad asked, taking over.

Lailu tried to ignore the way Eirad emphasized the word *priceless*. If this didn't work, she wasn't sure what would. "I am a master chef," she began.

Gwendyl gave a small snort. "You? You're just a child!"

"Gwendyl," Fahr said warningly, and the elf woman was immediately silent. "Continue."

Lailu's face flushed, but she forced herself to say, "So I propose a negotiation based on . . . food." It sounded silly coming out like that.

"Food?" Eirad arched one thin blond brow, making Lailu feel even sillier.

"Y-yes."

"What kind of food?" Fahr asked.

Lailu hesitated. "Dragon cuisine."

Gwendyl dropped her quill on the floor.

"Are you serious?" Eirad asked eagerly.

"A chef never jokes about food," Lailu said.

"So I've heard." Fahr watched her carefully. "A moment, if you please." The two male elves moved their heads together, speaking rapidly in a liquid, flowing language that Lailu could almost, but not quite, understand. She waited, trying not to fidget.

"Really?" Eirad sat back, the beads woven into his long blond braids clacking against one another. "But that's . . ."

Fahr narrowed his eyes.

Eirad smoothed out his features, his face a blank mask as he turned back to Lailu. "Here is what we propose. We will come to your restaurant in two days' time for a dragon cuisine feast. There will be . . ." Eirad thought for a moment. "Twenty of us."

Lailu's heart stuttered. That would practically fill her small restaurant. And two days to hunt down a dragon and prepare it? Assuming Master Slipshod even agreed to take her. "A week," she said, surprising herself.

Eirad blinked. "Excuse me?"

"I need at least a week to prepare a decent meal. I mean, Master Slipshod and I still have to hunt the thing, not to mention all the other ingredients we'll need to track down."

Eirad shook his head. "These are the terms: two days."

"This is high-quality cuisine we'll be making! We'll need time to prepare it."

"Three days," Fahr interjected, and Eirad's jaw dropped. "It's high-quality cuisine," Fahr said mildly, mimicking Lailu's words. "I think three days is reasonable."

"You really think so?" Eirad asked. "Three days seems like a long time."

"It *is* dragon, Eirad."

Sighing, the blond elf turned back to Lailu. "Three days, and we'll be showing up for dinner on the third day, mind." He narrowed his eyes as if waiting for her to argue, but Lailu knew a lost battle when she saw one.

"Of course." She tried not to think of everything that could go wrong. Like what she'd do if Master Slipshod decided she really wasn't ready, and refused to help her. She remembered that Ryon had said to make sure everything was very definitively stated. Clearing her throat, she added, "Just to clarify, our current deal is that I will cook dragon cuisine for twenty of your people in three days' time, and in return you will consider Hannah's debt paid in full."

"Couldn't have said it better myself." Eirad was smiling again, never a good sign, and Lailu mentally reviewed her statement.

"And since Hannah's debt will be considered paid in full, that means you'll leave her alone. No future threats. No revenge," Lailu added.

Eirad's smile faltered a little. "You are taking all the fun out of this job," he grumbled. He glanced at Fahr, who nodded. "Fine. We accept. Although she did steal from us, and it's a priceless heirloom. And really, I feel we are setting a dangerous precedent by not taking at least one limb as a warning to future thieves—"

"Eirad," Fahr said.

"—but those terms are accepted," Eirad finished reluctantly.

Bracing herself, Lailu went forward with the rest of her plan. "I have another, uh, term."

"Term?" Eirad smirked, and Lailu felt her face go red.

"Yes." Here was the real gamble, the one even Master Slipshod wouldn't take. She was gambling not only on her cooking skills, but also on everything she'd heard about the elves, about how they were incapable of lying, and about the things they were willing to take as payment. "I bet you . . . double or nothing."

"What do you mean by that, child?" Fahr asked.

Lailu took a deep breath. "I won't just cook dragon cuisine for you. I will cook *the best* dragon cuisine any of you have ever tasted. In exchange, you will take care of my debt to Mr. Boss so I am free of him. And of course you'll still consider Hannah's debt paid and seek no further revenge against her." Eirad's eyes narrowed dangerously and Lailu hurried on, "And if I fail, then . . . then . . ." She gulped. "Then I'll forfeit the last ten years of my life to you."

As soon as the words left Lailu's mouth she wanted to swallow them back up again. Ten years. Gone. Vanished before she even had the chance to live them. Still, if this worked, she and Slipshod would be free of Mr. Boss forever. And if it didn't work, then her life would be much shorter anyway. She just hoped it wouldn't hurt, having the elves take her last decade from her.

"No no, little chef," Eirad said. "I gave you a chance to agree to a years trade, and you didn't take it. That is no longer an option for you. Instead, I would prefer to go with our standard deal." He stared unblinkingly at Lailu. "If you fail to cook us the best dragon cuisine we've ever tasted, then we start taking body parts from your friend. And once she's run out of useful limbs to donate, we'll begin taking them from you, until we feel satisfied that we've received payment in full."

Lailu's mouth went dry. Apparently body parts were becoming

the currency of choice in her life these days. It almost made her question her line of work.

Fahr spoke up. "Don't be silly, Eirad. Just think how nice it would be to have our own personal chef cook for us every day." His blue-gray eyes narrowed on Lailu's face, and there was no laughter in them as he said softly, "Because we wouldn't just take your last ten years. No. You said double or nothing. We would take the rest of your life."

"O-of my life?"

"Oh, yes. There is no point in using up the years from a talented chef like yourself. You would be much more useful as our pet." He leaned forward. "Once we own a person, we own them forever. And we elves have ways of ensuring you'll live a long, long time. After all, longevity is in our blood." He smiled at her like they were sharing some sort of joke and not talking about lifelong slavery.

"But that's not giving me nothing . . . that's taking away what little I have," she protested, realizing that bargaining with elves was trickier than even Ryon had warned her about.

"We all have different definitions of nothing."

I think I'd prefer donating body parts, Lailu thought miserably, her pulse beating painfully at the side of her neck. This whole negotiation was running away from her.

Eirad seemed to be enjoying Lailu's misery, his whole face shining. "I take back my earlier complaint, Fahr. I approve of these terms."

"Do *you* accept these terms?" Fahr asked Lailu.

Lailu thought they seemed very unfair. Slavery forever? Still, this whole double or nothing bet had been her idea. And besides, what was slavery to the elves compared to slavery to Mr. Boss? It was all the same, really. "I accept your terms," she whispered, her stomach lurching.

"Then we'll see you in three days, little chef. Now come along and I'll show you out." Eirad stood.

"I can find the door on my own." Lailu didn't want to stay next to Eirad any longer than necessary. She got the impression he did the limb removal.

24

GONE FOR GOOD

Lights shone through the windows of Mystic Cooking. Lailu was surprised, since the sun hadn't even risen. Was Master Slipshod awake already? Excitement fluttered through her. Maybe . . . maybe he was preparing for their dragon hunt.

Her hands shaking, Lailu pushed open the door, then staggered back as Hannah flew at her.

"Thank the gods you're back," Hannah gasped.

"Why? What's wrong?" Lailu gently pried Hannah's arms off her.

Hannah's lips trembled. "I'm so sorry," she whispered. "But . . . your mentor left." She took a deep breath. "He's gone."

"Gone? What do you mean, gone?"

"I mean, he packed up all his stuff, grabbed some metal box from the cellar, and ran. I heard him rummaging in his room.

Woke me up, and when I asked him what he was doing . . ."

"Yes?" Lailu prompted. Her chest felt tight, little spots of light flashing in front of her eyes.

"He said he was running, and that he wasn't coming back." Hannah looked away.

Lailu staggered into a chair and hung her head between her knees. Master Slipshod had told her she might finally be ready for dragons. And to just leave after that? "No, no, he wouldn't."

Hannah crouched in front of her, smoothing a hand down Lailu's tangled pigtails. "He's been abandoning you every time things get tough. It's what he does. He screws up, and then he runs."

"No." Lailu lifted her head. "He's a great chef."

"Yes," Hannah said sadly, "but he's a terrible mentor."

She's so weird, it's no wonder her mother left her. Lailu closed her eyes. It hurt to breathe. It hurt to think. It hurt to *remember*. "Maybe it really is me," she whispered.

"It's not you. Lailu, listen to me." Hannah shook Lailu's shoulders until Lailu opened her eyes. "It's. Not. Your. Fault," Hannah said firmly.

Lailu wasn't sure she believed her, but then she remembered something else Hannah had said. A box. She shot up and raced to the kitchen, throwing open the trapdoor and tearing downstairs to look in their safe.

It was just like she'd feared: The box with Elister's payment was gone, and so was the rest of the money. A wave of nausea washed over Lailu, the room spinning around her like she'd gone up a hill too fast. All that work, and for nothing. He'd taken it all.

Desperately she felt around inside the small iron safe, just in case, but all that remained were a few cobwebs and an old, battered book.

Lailu picked it up. Its brown leather cover was cracked and peeling, but she could still clearly make out the large gold letters emblazoned on the front: *Dragon Cuisine: An Account of the Hunting, Preparing, and Cooking of Dragon (including Mountain, Sea, River, and Desert varieties) by Master Sullivan J. Slipshod. First edition.*

She traced her mentor's name, then carefully flipped the book open. Despite her anger, despite his betrayal, despite everything, she couldn't help the excitement bubbling up in her chest. This was the book. *His* book. The one he wrote, the one everyone referred to for dragon cuisine. She'd seen a copy of it back in the main Chef Academy library, but this one included all of Slipshod's original notes scribbled in the margins next to the official recipes.

Turning the brittle pages gently, she flipped back to the beginning, this time spotting the paper he'd stuck behind the front cover, with a note:

> Pigtails—
>
> I know you're determined to see this through, so I won't insult you by suggesting you run. Just remember to aim for the nape of the dragon's neck. There's a nerve bundle there. And yes, I do believe you're ready.
>
> P.S. I've included a map of the best place to ambush the mountain dragon (see back).
>
> P.P.S. Don't get yourself killed.

Lailu wobbled back into the dining room and sat in a chair, still clutching the book.

"Did he . . ." Hannah hesitated. "Did he take the money?"

Wordlessly, Lailu nodded.

Hannah pursed her lips, and Lailu could tell she was trying desperately not to say "I told you so." Because she had, right from the start. She'd always thought Master Slipshod was bad news. Lailu just hadn't been willing to hear it. To Lailu, Master Slipshod was a legend, a great chef who not only taught her favorite teacher at the academy, but was also willing to take her on as his very own apprentice.

"I'm sorry, Hannah." Lailu sighed. "You're probably right about the haircomb, too."

"I know." Hannah was quiet a moment. "So," she said at last, "we don't have any money at all."

Lailu shook her head miserably.

"What's the plan, then?"

"Same plan as before, I guess." Lailu paused. "In exchange for clearing your debt, I'm going to make the elves dragon cuisine."

"Dragon . . . cuisine?" Hannah went pale. "Really, you have to hunt a dragon? Oh, Lailu, I'm, I'm so, so sorry, I—"

"It's no big deal." Lailu tried to sound casual, but her mouth was dryer than fyrian chicken meat.

"No big deal?" Hannah squeaked. "But it's *dragon*."

"Master Slipshod says I'm ready." A tiny sliver of pride cut through the fear and anger. He left her, but he said she was ready. Maybe she really was. Maybe she didn't even need him. "He left me his book and a map, so I know where to find one, and how to hunt it, and even more important, the best way to prepare it afterward."

"A book?" Hannah looked skeptical. "You're going to do all these things with the help of only a book?"

"I'll probably want some backup, too," Lailu decided.

Hannah nodded. "Backup. Yes. Uh . . . can I . . . can I help?" The whites showed all around her eyes and her lips trembled, but Lailu could see by the tilt of her friend's chin that she meant it. She'd really help her hunt a dragon. Lailu tried not to laugh at the image.

"Thanks for the offer, but I think I need someone with a little more hunting experience."

Hannah took a deep breath. "I may not have any hunting experience, b-but I can still be helpful. I can help you carry supplies, at least."

Lailu started to shake her head.

"Please, Lailu! I got us into this mess. I want to help get us out of it." Her eyes filled with tears. "I can't just sit here, knowing you're out there, knowing it's my fault."

Lailu grimaced, but clearly there was no talking her friend out of this. "All right, fine. But when I tell you to hide—"

"I'll be invisible to the world." Hannah smiled tremulously. "So, now that that's decided, what next?"

Lailu chewed on her lip. She definitely needed more backup. But who? "LaSilvian's," she said finally. Hannah's eyebrows rose, but as much as it pained Lailu to think it, there was no one else she could really trust on a mission like this. She needed Greg's help. Again. "We're going to LaSilvian's."

25

Ambushed!

The sun spilled across the morning air in golden waves, not a cloud in the sky. Lailu munched on spiced coffee beans, uncomfortably aware of Greg walking just a few steps behind her. She wasn't sure if it was the excitement of the hunt or the coffee, but her stomach twisted whenever he looked at her. She'd barely spoken to him since he agreed to come along, so the only sounds were their footsteps and . . .

Wheeze, pant, gasp. "Are we," Hannah huffed, "almost"—huff—"there?"

"Almost, Hannah," Lailu assured her, checking the map Slipshod had drawn for her. It still hurt to think of him, of how he'd left her. But she was too busy right now to waste energy feeling betrayed, even if they were making excellent time. They'd already passed the base of the mountains. "Another hour, maybe two, and we'll be at the spot."

Hannah dropped her bag, staggering to a stop. "Another *hour*?"

"You could stay here and rest, if you'd like," Greg said.

Hannah narrowed her eyes. "No," she said firmly. "I said I'd help, so I'm helping."

"Then at least let me carry your bag." Greg reached for it, but Hannah moved surprisingly fast for someone so red-faced and sweaty, snatching it away and slinging it back over her shoulders. Greg's eyebrows rose. "What are you carrying in there?"

"Stuff," Hannah said, shifting away from him.

"What kind of stuff?" Lailu didn't want to sound suspicious, but with Hannah's reputation for re-homing shiny objects, well . . .

"Just things that might help us." Hannah wasn't looking at either of them now, and Lailu's suspicions rose. "Anyhow, Greg, I can see Lailu was wrong about you," Hannah added hurriedly.

Lailu froze.

"Oh?" Greg asked.

Hannah grinned. "You are actually quite the gentleman."

"Lailu said I wasn't a gentleman?"

"I never said that!" Lailu's face blazed.

"Oh, so you said I *was* a gentleman?" Greg asked, the corners of his eyes crinkling.

Lailu's earlier shyness vanished like cream puffs on a market day. Greg was still just Greg, the same annoying, self-satisfied jerk he'd always been. Lailu took a deep breath. "Let's just keep going."

The landscape dried out as they climbed higher and higher into the mountains, surrounding themselves with scraggly trees looming over loose piles of rock. Occasionally Lailu would consult Slipshod's map, but she could tell they were in the right area. This was exactly the sort of place mountain dragons enjoyed, with plenty of towering boulders and craggy cliff edges, and soon Lailu began seeing long gouges in the hard-packed dirt. Talon marks. The distinct half-moon shape was definitely from a dragon.

It was a good thing she was focusing so hard on their task, since Greg and Hannah seemed determined not to pay any attention at all. Instead, Greg was wasting time telling Hannah stories about their experiences at the Chef Academy. Lailu did not fare well in his versions, but she was doing her best to ignore him. It was getting harder and harder, though, especially now that he'd gotten around to the Incident.

". . . so we walk out, and all around us are these burned patches and charred husks of corn. And get this, even after seeing the size of the chicken hut, Lailu goes, 'This doesn't look so bad,'" Greg said, doing an awful imitation of Lailu's higher voice.

"*What?* No, that's not how it was at all," Lailu said, unable to stop herself.

"No?" Greg asked innocently. "You mean, you knew it would be bad? I thought you said it was just a chicken."

"*You* said it was just a chicken!" Lailu had been terrified, but in the face of Greg's easy confidence she hadn't been able to admit it. Even though the smell of charred feathers had clung to her nose, and there had been all those blackened bones scattered around the creature's hut . . . Lailu shuddered. She didn't like to think about that hunting trip. Why was Greg bringing it up now? This was no time to get distracted.

She sped up, but Greg just quickened his own step, his longer legs keeping pace with her easily, Hannah huffing and puffing next to him. Lailu tried to ignore them both, instead examining the rocks ahead. Searching for . . . There! Blackened rocks, patches of soot-stained trees, and a few places where the dirt itself seemed to be melted and glassy. Clear evidence of a mountain dragon's trail.

"So then what happened?" Hannah asked.

Lailu shot her a dark look.

"What?" Hannah asked. "You've never told me this story."

"There's a reason for that," Lailu grumbled.

Greg's grin flashed wickedly. "So then I told Lailu, 'If this doesn't look so bad, then *you* grab the chicken while *I* collect the eggs.'"

"That's not what you said at all!" He'd actually said if she wasn't chicken, she should face the chicken herself. She'd had no idea he would be using her as a distraction so he could get the eggs. And all the credit from their instructor, too. The only thing Lailu had gotten was a nice, sharp blast of fire to her—

"Maybe you'd like to tell the rest of the story, then, hmm?" Greg was wearing that look again, the one that made her want to punch him.

"No, I wouldn't," Lailu snapped. "Unlike some people, I'm actually trying to work here."

Greg shrugged, her words washing over him like steam from a kettle. "Well, just then the fyrian chicken came out," he resumed, his voice as relentless as the chicken he was describing. "And you have to understand, this was no ordinary chicken. Just looking at its eyes, I could tell . . . it was evil."

Lailu closed her own eyes, momentarily picturing the fyrian chicken in all its ugly chicken glory. Coming up to her hip, it had a large orange beak, and blackened feathers that seemed to be molting, leaving red, irritated bald spots. Its black eyes seemed to focus on her, and her alone . . . but the worst part was the second chicken sneaking up from the side. She hadn't even seen that one coming. Or the third one on the other side. Or the fourth one crouching down behind the others.

She shook her head, trying to clear the image from her mind. And then she realized they were in the perfect place to set up their trap. Thank the gods. "This is the spot." She dropped her bag.

"It kind of cocked its head, gave a large 'buckaw,' and then its friend tiptoed out from the side."

"Its friend?" Hannah asked.

"Oh yes. Apparently fyrian chickens flock together. Lailu and I should have known that, but we were busy, er, discussing our strategy when that little tidbit of information was shared with the class."

"You mean arguing." Hannah grinned.

"This is the spot," Lailu repeated a little louder.

"Arguing. Discussing. With Lailu it's all the same. Anyhow, suddenly there was a flock of chickens, all charging right at us. I dove expertly out of the way, but Lailu . . . Lailu screamed like a six-year-old girl and took off running, arms waving and everything. No matter how fast she ran, the chickens were on her like flies on fruit, their little *bucbucbuc*s echoing around the pen. And if that wasn't funny enough, one of the chickens decided it liked its Lailu well-done. So it opened its—"

"I said, this is the spot!" Lailu glared at both of them.

Greg blinked and looked around. "Are you sure?"

"Of course I'm sure," Lailu said. "*I've* actually been paying attention. Again, unlike certain people who are supposed to be helping me."

Hannah had the grace to look a little embarrassed, but Greg just grinned. "Don't worry, Hannah, I'll tell you the rest later," he stage-whispered.

"I'm counting on it." Hannah dropped her pack on the ground and sat gratefully next to it.

They were in a small dip in the mountains with rock formations rising up on both sides, creating a narrow path. Dragons liked to walk the same trails, and the claw marks Lailu saw earlier proved they were in the right place. Once the dragon came through here attracted by the bait, they'd have it. It wouldn't have enough room to maneuver its way out. Really, Lailu couldn't have picked a better place if she'd designed it herself, and as much as she wanted to hate her former mentor, she had to admire Slipshod's genius in finding it. The fact that he'd scouted out such a perfect spot made her wonder if he'd been planning on eventually taking her hunting here all along, before things got too rough for him.

She pulled out a large hunk of half-frozen orc meat and plopped it on the ground.

Hannah wrinkled her nose and inched away. The meat was a mottled grayish green, and even its long stint in Lailu's freezer hadn't taken away the smell.

"What," Greg said slowly, "is that?"

"It's orc meat."

"Okay. If you say so. But more important, why is it here?"

Lailu scowled. "Bait. Obviously. Mountain dragons eat orcs."

"It looks a little . . . er, unappetizing. Sorry, Lailu!" Hannah added hurriedly. "Please don't make me be the bait instead!"

"Don't worry, Hannah. I'd never make *you* into bait." Lailu eyed Greg.

"Is it just me, or is that orc meat suddenly looking better and better?" Greg prodded it with his boot.

Lailu pulled a long coil of rope out of her bag, then a jar of super-sticky solution made from the honey of the legendary buzzard bees. "Let's just get to work."

Wisely, Greg didn't say anything more. Instead, he took one side of the rope and sat across from her, mirroring her as she tied knots to create a giant net. Hannah watched them, then began tying her own rather more creative knots.

Lailu bit her lip. "Um, Hannah? Maybe you can coat the rope with this instead." She held out the jar of buzzard bee honey. "Greg and I can take care of the knots."

"Oh." Hannah looked crestfallen.

"It's just, it's a really important part of the job, and with your eye for detail, I thought you should do it," Lailu added.

"Oh!" Hannah took the jar, looking much happier.

Greg gave Lailu a small smile. She quickly turned back to the rope, her ears burning.

As they worked, Lailu began to feel better and better about everything. So what if Master Slipshod had stabbed her in the back, taking all their earnings and abandoning her at the worst possible time? She didn't need him. The sun was warm on her back, the smell of sage was all around her, and her plan was going to work, she just knew it.

"Wow, Lailu, you sure are slow. I'm already on the next step here." Greg grinned as he began staking his side of the net into the ground.

Lailu's jaw tightened. "Sorry if I don't believe in rushing and doing a bad job."

"It's a net, not a work of art."

"My nets *are* works of art," Lailu snapped. "But obviously you wouldn't know anything about that."

"You two really are competitive." Hannah looked back and forth between them. "You sound like you must have been so fun at the academy."

"Well, *I* was fun," Greg said. "But Lailu . . . did she ever tell you her nickname?"

Lailu went hot, then cold. "Don't you dare." As if telling Hannah about the Incident wasn't bad enough.

"We used to call her—"

"I said don't, Greg!"

"—Crabby Cakes," he finished triumphantly. "You know, I'd almost forgotten about tha— *Oof*!"

Lailu tackled him, knocking him backward and into the stones piled on the side of the path.

"Lailu!" Hannah gasped.

"He swore he'd never call me that again," Lailu snarled as Greg continued chuckling under her.

"No, Lailu!" Hannah squeaked, so fearfully that Lailu stopped trying to punch Greg in his stupid face and turned.

And found herself face-to-face with a mountain dragon, its yellow eyes narrowed into angry slits in the blue-gray of its rocky face.

THE KILL

ailu stared back at the dragon.

It was huge, much bigger than she'd imagined, its head alone larger than she was, its body covered in dull slate-colored scales, good for blending in with its surroundings. Stony spikes ran down the dragon's back, ending at the tip of its flattened tail, and smoke rose from its nostrils and through the gaps between its pointy teeth.

Lailu was close enough to feel the heat radiating off it. How could she have been so foolish? Here she had a perfect ambush spot, and *she* was the one being ambushed. Trapped in her own trap!

The dragon's snout opened wide, and it roared so loud Lailu's teeth rattled. She couldn't move, couldn't look away as it charged at her and Greg.

Greg's arms wrapped around her as he rolled them both out of the way and onto their feet. "Move it!" he hollered.

Lailu gasped, the world suddenly slamming back into focus, and she dove behind a column of rock. The tail she had been admiring a second before crashed behind her, missing by inches. She turned her dive into a roll, springing back to her feet and sprinting to the next boulder, Greg right on her heels.

Flames filled the air behind them as they tumbled behind the large rock, and Lailu remembered with a pang so sharp she thought her heart would stop completely: "Hannah! Oh, gods, Hannah!" She darted out, but Greg caught her, pulling her back as another blast of fire scorched the air around them.

She struggled to get away from him, but he tightened his hold. "It's all right, Lailu. It's all right," he gasped. "She's hiding. She's okay."

Lailu stopped struggling. "She's okay?"

"I'm okay!" Hannah yelled behind them. Lailu looked around to see Hannah peeking out from behind her own boulder. Set back a little from the main path, it towered over her, reassuringly tall and bulky. Really, it was a great place to hide.

Lailu wilted against the rock. Her hands and knees were scraped and bloody from the sharp stones, but she barely noticed as she forced herself to take deep, calming breaths. Hannah was fine, and they had found their mountain dragon. This was no time for panicking.

"What's the plan here?" Greg asked.

"Er," Lailu said, realizing her original plan was no longer going to work.

"Well, that was informative."

"Hey, my orc meat worked, didn't it?"

"I notice the dragon isn't eating it," Greg said dryly.

The dragon snorted, crunching rocks under its large taloned feet as it stepped deliberately around the discarded hunk of meat and approached them.

"Maybe it's saving it for later?" Lailu suggested.

"Maybe it doesn't like meat that's clearly been stashed in a cellar for weeks?"

"I didn't have time to get a fresh orc, okay?"

The dragon roared, filling the air with the strong rotten-egg odor of the gases in its throat, and Lailu knew it was just a matter of minutes before it could use its fire-breathing capabilities again. She racked her brain. They needed a new plan, one that didn't involve their sadly half-finished net. Or . . . could it still be useful?

"Personally, I think we need to reuse our fyrian chicken plan," Greg said.

Lailu almost fell over. "Why do you keep bringing that up? You are a sick, twisted—"

The rest of Lailu's words were drowned out by the sound of the dragon roaring as it slammed its tail into their rock pile. Lailu and Greg cowered, protecting their heads as stones and dirt showered them.

"Are you two seriously arguing *now*?" Hannah called.

"I just thought we could do the same thing we did with the chickens. Remember? You distract the dragon, and then I'll sneak around and take it out from behind."

Lailu scowled. "Oh yes, I remember. How could I not, when you're so intent on mentioning it. Over and over."

The dragon slammed its tail into their rock pile again. This time the rocks trembled violently before settling.

"Fine, here's the plan," Lailu said. "Greg, you distract the dragon, and *I'll* get it from behind. Got it?"

Greg opened his mouth to object, but Lailu was already moving, diving out from behind the rock and running as fast as she could past the dragon and across the narrow valley. She dove to the side, and was rewarded by the sound of shattering rock as the dragon tried to use its tail to swat her again. Scrambling to her feet, she turned and zigzagged behind rocks and around boulders. Mountain dragons were vicious and deadly, but they weren't particularly agile. Not like the river dragons Slipshod had told her about.

Still, she'd never get behind it at this rate, not unless it was distracted enough to turn. "Come on, Greg," Lailu panted as she rolled behind another pile of rocks. And then she saw him, running silently at the dragon from the other side. Sneaking up on it from behind . . . that jerk! That was supposed to be her!

He was close to it now, close enough to leap, but as he crouched, the dragon seemed to sense him there. Its tail flicked out, the spikes tearing toward his head. Lailu knew he wasn't going to be able to move fast enough, and she was running without even realizing it.

Throwing herself forward, she slammed into Greg and knocked him out of the way as the tail crashed down next to them. Her momentum carried them forward and down a slope in a rolling shower of dirt and rocks until they finally came to a stop against a canyon wall.

Lailu's heart hammered painfully against her rib cage, Greg's body crushing her into the ground. "You idiot," she panted. "You forgot about the tail!"

He gave her a weak smile. "I knew you'd save me."

Lailu growled and pushed at his chest. He rolled off her, pulling her to her feet. As he started back up, she caught his arm. "Look, this is *my* dragon, and I want to be the one to bring it down. Got it?"

"Yeah, I got it. Sorry." He looked down at his feet.

She let him go. "Just as long as that's settled. Now let's get us a dragon." Together she and Greg scrambled back up the slope, each running in a separate direction. Lailu hid behind a rock as Greg pulled a large butcher's knife from the sheath at his waist and sprinted at the dragon.

The dragon's head whipped around on its short, stubby neck as it followed Greg's movements. At the last moment, Greg turned and ran away. It chased after him, its talons flinging up chunks of rock and dirt from the path. Greg lurched to the side, moving straight toward the net, then leaping nimbly over it. The dragon moved too fast to change direction and lumbered right into the ropes staked up on the side. Just as Lailu had hoped, the honey painted on the ropes worked well, oozing in between the dragon's scales and causing the ropes to tangle around its legs.

The dragon roared and crashed onto its knees. It tore frantically at the ropes with its teeth as Lailu inched toward its blind side. *Just a little closer*, she told herself. She just needed to get a little bit closer.

The dragon turned suddenly, its head drawn back to let out another blast of fire. Lailu was too close to it to do anything but stand there, her meat cleaver raised defensively in her hand.

"Lailu!" Hannah shrieked, leaping forward and throwing something into the air.

Bam! Pop! Pop! Pop! Bam!

The clear sky lit up in a multitude of colors and shapes. A loud explosion accompanied each flowering, fiery blossom, and Lailu stared at the display in awe.

She shook herself and saw she wasn't the only one distracted by the colors in the sky; the dragon was staring at them too. Drawing back her cleaver, Lailu ran and leaped high onto the dragon's neck.

It reared, snarling. Lailu slipped down its rough back, desperately searching for purchase. She finally managed to get a good grip on one of its stony spikes, but already the dragon was twisting, trying to get a shot at her, its tail flying dangerously close to her head. Lailu tried to ignore it, tried to ignore the sound of Hannah yelling, of Greg calling out to her, of her heart beating too fast. Instead, she just concentrated on being quiet, still, and centered as she searched for the dragon's single weak spot.

There. Carefully hidden behind one of its bony ridges was the spot, slightly lighter in color than the rest, almost like the scales hadn't grown in right there. Lailu let out her breath, her body empty and light and her mind completely focused. The cleaver left her hand, its aim sure and steady.

As the blade buried itself to the hilt, the dragon gave one last roar, then collapsed.

Lailu tumbled off, rolling across the ground and coming to a stop up against a boulder as Hannah and Greg raced over to her.

"That was amazing!" Hannah crouched down in front of her, grinning, her teeth strangely white against her soot-stained face.

"Amazing is right," Lailu said as Hannah pulled her to her feet. "What in the name of cutlery was that?"

"What?" Hannah asked innocently.

"You know, that bizarre fire all over the sky and everything."

"It was—"

"Nice job, team." Grinning, Greg put one arm around Lailu's shoulders and the other around Hannah's. "Look at you!" he said, staring at Lailu. "You're actually smiling."

"Yeah, well, I'm feeling pretty happy right now. It won't last long, though, I promise."

"Good. I'd hate to think we'd lost our normal grouchy Lailu."

"Who's grouchy?" Lailu demanded, pulling away from him.

"And she's back," Greg said, laughing. "But at least I said 'grouchy,' right? I could have called you—"

"It's called a firework," Hannah said quickly.

"A what, now?" Lailu asked.

Hannah reached into the bag slung across her shoulders and pulled out a long cylinder of some kind of glossy dark material. It had a string coming out of the bottom, and it smelled like . . . like . . . smoke mixed with something sharp and acrid. Lailu couldn't quite identify it, although she thought she'd smelled something like it before. "You light the bottom, here," Hannah said, pointing to the string part, "toss it up, and it'll explode with all those colors."

Lailu took it from her. It was heavier than it looked. "I've never heard of this before."

"It's new. This guy who visited our school, well, he invented it." Hannah took the firework back and slipped it into her bag. "One of the scientists."

"Isn't that kind of a dangerous thing to bring to a fashion school?" Greg asked.

Hannah frowned. "Fashion is danger. And really, he was just there to talk to the head fashionista, looking for financial backing. Lord Golderby has a lot of money. I just happened to be in his office at the time." She looked down at her hands. "You know, being expelled."

"Oh," Lailu and Greg said uncomfortably.

Hannah shrugged. "Anyhow, it might be best if you didn't mention I had them."

Lailu sighed. "Is this another thing you re-homed?"

"Re-homed?" Greg asked.

"It's a nice way of saying 'stolen,'" Lailu explained.

"Hey!" Hannah looked so offended Lailu couldn't help but laugh.

"Still, it definitely saved me this time, so I won't say anything. As long as you promise to stop," Lailu added.

"Oh, I've already stopped. I took these days ago, after all." Hannah grinned, brushing her hair back and leaving a soot stain across her face.

"Well," Greg said as a moment of silence stretched around them, "let's get this started then, eh? We have some dragon to cook."

"Do we ever." Lailu turned and stared at the beast.

"How are we planning to bring it back with us?" Hannah asked.

Lailu and Greg exchanged looks. "Good question," Greg muttered. "Good, good question."

27

OVERHEARD

*L*ailu rummaged frantically in the cabinets, her clothing sticky with sweat. She needed to get the dragon meat prepped right away or risk the poison in the blood leeching through and spoiling the meat. Almost a full day had already passed since they had defeated the dragon, so that didn't give Lailu much time before contamination set in.

The oven and every single broiler and burner were going at full speed. Unfortunately, she was still missing some key ingredients. This wouldn't be nearly so challenging if Slipshod were here.

"Um, can I help you with anything?" Hannah hovered in the doorway of the kitchen, fanning her face with a folded sheet of pink parchment.

Lailu exhaled and closed the cabinet. "No. I can't find my pixie paprika. Or the bay leaf combo. Plus I'm running low on lebinola."

Her shoulders slumped. "I think I need to go to the market."

"Oh, good, that makes this easier." Hannah held the pink parchment out to Lailu. "This message just came for you, but I wasn't sure if I should interrupt you with it."

Lailu took the letter suspiciously. It was very pink. She flipped it open, reading quickly:

Hi, Lailu.

Elixir? I don't know what you're talking about . . . I'll be at the market at noon today.

—Wren

Lailu dropped the letter on the floor. There was no counter space for it.

"What?" Hannah asked. "You're making your serious Lailu face."

"I only have one face," Lailu grumbled. Why would Wren say she didn't know anything, but then tell her where to find her? "I definitely need to go to the market."

"At least you've already gotten a lot done here." Hannah jerked her chin at all the mounds of carefully sliced dragon. After they'd managed to hire a donkey cart to lug the dragon to Mystic Cooking yesterday, Lailu had gotten straight to work, separating the top round roast, bottom round roast, and round steak. She'd been at it all night, eating through her stash of coffee beans to stay awake. Now her whole body felt like it weighed about as much as this dragon. Still, she only had today and part of tomorrow left to finish cooking. She didn't have time to rest.

She flipped open Master Slipshod's book, double-checking the marinade. He suggested a few slivers of mandrake root to counteract the bitterness of the dragon's blood. Lailu thought she'd be better off using the bellarose root instead, since it was just a little sweeter. After a few seconds of deliberation, she went with her choice, stirring it into the bubbling pot.

Hannah perched on the end of the chair, chewing her lip.

"Haven't you heard that a watched pot never boils?" Lailu asked irritably, dumping the chopped meat from her cutting board into her marinade.

"Everything here seems to be boiling nicely."

Lailu sighed. "What is it, Hannah?"

Hannah shrugged, her eyes distant. "Just . . . wondering."

"Wondering?"

"What'll happen if . . ." She chewed her lip harder.

Lailu set down her cutting board. "This is going to work, Hannah. I know it is. We'll both be okay." The youngest in a house full of boys, Lailu could still remember how proud she'd been that someone like Hannah wanted to be friends with *her*. Hannah had fit into her life perfectly, more like a sister than a friend. "We don't need Slipshod or anyone else," she said firmly. "Not when we have each other."

Hannah smiled weakly and dabbed at her eyes with her sleeve. "I still would like to help, though. Want me to go to the market for you? Pick up the spices you need?"

Lailu shook her head. "I need to meet someone there." Besides, she didn't like to trust spice selection to anyone who wasn't a master chef. "But it would be a huge help if you'd get some flyers made."

"Really?"

"Really. After the elves leave, I'll still have plenty of dragon cuisine, and I have a restaurant to run here."

"Wow, you sound so official. But I guess that's true. I mean, with Master Slipshod gone, Mystic Cooking belongs to you."

Mystic Cooking belongs to you. Lailu let those words sink in, but instead of being excited and proud, all she felt was tired and betrayed. She didn't feel ready to run a whole restaurant. She didn't feel ready to be completely on her own. After all, she hadn't actually finished her apprenticeship, so what did that even make her? Not quite a master chef? An "almost" master chef? She wanted her mentor back.

Hannah must have seen the conflict on her face, because she changed the subject quickly. "Want to head to the city together?"

"Sure." Lailu stretched. Fighting that dragon yesterday had really taken it out of her. Everything creaked and popped and hurt. "Let's go."

Hannah's gaze sharpened critically. "You're not going like that, are you?"

"Why? What's wrong with how I look?"

"Lailu, honey, you're going to drive away business. No one will want to eat food prepared by someone who looks like, like, well, like *that*." Hannah jerked her chin at Lailu's stained and disheveled outfit.

Lailu glanced down at herself. Her hair had straggled loose from her standard pigtails and there was blood smeared all across her apron and spattering the edges of her wrinkled shirt. "I don't look *that* bad, do I?"

"Don't make me answer that question. I want us to stay friends."

"Ouch," Lailu said. "Okay, I guess I'll wash up quickly and change."

"Oh, good. I have just the outfit!"

Lailu's stomach sank. "I don't have that much time," she began.

"Then let's be quick, but if you want to keep customers coming, a professional appearance is vital." Hannah beamed and clapped her hands. She looked so happy that Lailu knew, despite her time crunch and her hatred of dresses, she was probably going to end up looking like she'd lost another battle to a garden.

"No high heels," she warned as she followed Hannah up the stairs. "And no pink!"

Lailu and Hannah parted ways in the city, Hannah off to see the scientists while Lailu headed toward the market. She spotted the small booth in the corner, almost hidden behind a vegetable stand advertising GARDEN FRESH VARIETY and a soap shop proclaiming SMELL SCENT-SATIONAL! The man behind the counter smiled at her, displaying a row of extremely crooked teeth in an otherwise pleasant face. "Ah, Lailu, welcome back to the Spice Rack."

"Hello, Bairn," Lailu said resignedly.

"And look at you! My, aren't you just a sight for sore eyes."

Lailu picked irritably at her lavender dress. "Yes, well," she muttered, shrugging off the compliment. She knew she looked ridiculous, what with the puffed sleeves and cutesy flowers sewn along the hems. Hannah had even insisted on thrusting an absurd jeweled comb into her hair, the top also in the shape of a flower, the bottom a long, slim blade like a letter opener meant to stab through a ponytail. Lailu could feel the sharp edges scraping into her skull whenever she moved her head. Hannah claimed this made her look more professional. Lailu had her doubts.

"So, where's ol' Sullivan Slipshod, eh?"

Lailu's heart squeezed, but she forced herself to say casually, "Oh, he's not around. Just me today." And without giving Bairn a chance to ask more questions, she began her negotiations.

Ten minutes later, Lailu was down one full-course dragon feast to be claimed when her restaurant reopened to the public, but she had all the spices she needed without having to pay up front for them. Which was great, seeing as she had no money. In fact, Bairn was so happy with the deal he even offered to have her spices delivered to her door. "Dragon. I'm going to have dragon. That'll be somethin' to tell the ol' grandkids, eh?" he kept saying, rubbing his hands together gleefully.

Lailu shook her head, but she couldn't stop the smile from creeping across her face. The idea that people were so excited about her cooking, *her* cooking, even without Slipshod, filled her with warmth.

As she wove back through the market, she kept an eye out for Wren. The girl hadn't said where in the market she'd be, but it was right around midday now. She had to be here somewhere. But as long moments passed with no Wren, Lailu began feeling more and more anxious. She could practically feel her dragon feast waiting for her.

"Just two more minutes," she told herself, elbowing her way through the crowd of shoppers and stall vendors, trying to get out of their way and still keep a clear view of the market square. Two more minutes and she'd go. She couldn't wait any longer.

Finally, a flash of orange caught her eye. Across the square, a girl with curly red hair was trying to sneak around the booths, and doing a terrible job of it. She darted to the side, ducked behind a stall, then shuffled across the narrow lane, tossing a quick look over her shoulder. In her hands was a large glass jar, wide at the bottom before slanting inward, then rising up in a tall, narrow neck. It was empty now, but Lailu remembered seeing it full of a hissing purple liquid, and as her eyes followed the jar up, she glimpsed Wren's face before the girl darted around another booth and out of sight.

Lailu shot after her, dodging other people and ducking around stalls, the erratic hem of her horrible dress held up in both hands so she could move easier. There! Another flash of orange just up ahead.

"Wren!" she called, dropping her gown with one hand so she could wave. "Wren!" The girl glanced back but seemed to look right through her, turning quickly away and speeding up. She was dressed much better for running than Lailu was, in gray slacks, leather boots, and a loose black vest over a purple shirt.

"Butter knives," Lailu swore, jogging after her. Wren probably didn't recognize her in this dress. Must be the ridiculous flower comb, Lailu decided.

Wren ducked down a small alley into the Industrial District before turning a corner. Lailu hurried after her, glancing around uneasily. She'd never really liked this part of the city, even before she'd had that creepy confrontation with Brennon. It was . . . strange. The buildings here all looked like giant blocks of brick and metal without any windows, holding only large, imposing doors. A few of the buildings had steam coming out of chimneys at the top, and the building closest to her was emitting a strange grinding, whistling noise. She hugged her arms around herself, wishing her knife were easier to reach. Unfortunately, she'd been forced to strap it to her leg; apparently, wearing a knife belt with a dress was a big fashion no-no in Hannah's eyes.

Rounding another corner, Lailu stopped. Wren was leaning against the wall with her arms crossed, the empty vial at her feet. Lailu hesitated. She hadn't really thought this through all the way. What exactly did she want to confront Wren about? The elves? The elixir? Starling's plans with Mr. Boss? Her eyes narrowed on the vial. Everything, she decided. It was time to get straight down to business.

"What are you up to, Wren?"

"No 'Hi, thanks for meeting me, I got your note'?"

"There's no time for that now. I know you and your mom are using elf blood. I'm assuming it's for that elixir Mr. Boss has been taking . . ." Lailu paused, her own words catching up with her. "Wait, he's drinking . . . elf blood? He's actually *drinking* it?"

"What did you think he was doing with it?" Wren asked.

Lailu shuddered. She'd heard of humanoid creatures out in the farthest reaches of the land of Mystalon that drank blood, but this was somehow worse. This was horrifying, monstrous, and downright disgusting. "How could you help him do that?" she whispered.

Wren sniffed, her eyes filling with sudden tears.

"D-don't cry. Please, please don't cry." Lailu shifted uncomfortably. Should she pat Wren on the back? Or give her space? She wasn't sure. She hadn't been expecting tears.

"It's just," Wren sobbed, "I don't want Mama to get in trouble. Mr. Boss is *forcing* us to make this elixir of immortality for him, and he won't ever let us stop. If I show you where the elves are, do you promise not to tell anyone we're involved?"

Lailu hesitated. She still couldn't believe Starling Volan was behind the kidnapping of the elves, but she knew firsthand how Mr. Boss could turn things around on a person. Starling had probably gotten caught up in a bad deal with him too. If she told anyone about Starling's involvement, the elves would kill the scientist for sure, and she doubted they would spare Wren. Not when they were so eager to go chopping off people's body parts over missing hair-combs. "Okay," she said finally.

"You promise?"

"I promise."

"A promise is binding," Wren said solemnly.

"I know."

Wren relaxed, her tears turning off immediately. So immediately it was like they had never been there at all. "Give me a count of five, and then follow, okay? I'll lead you to them, but it can't look like I know you're there. You know, just in case."

Lailu nodded, but Wren was already ducking around the corner and out of sight. Lailu counted hurriedly to five and then followed her.

The alleyway was empty. Completely empty. "What the . . . ,"

Lailu whispered, looking around. She sprinted down it, turning another corner. Up ahead she saw Wren hesitating at the end of the alley. Lailu ran toward her, her eyes so focused on the girl that she didn't notice there was anyone else in the alley with her until she crashed into them.

Strong arms caught her before she fell.

"Careful there," said a familiar voice.

"Vahn?" Lailu's heart skittered.

Vahn let go of her, his eyes widening. "Oh, Lula. I see Hannah's dressed you up again."

Lailu frowned and stepped away from him. This alley intersected another alley, but Wren wasn't anywhere to be seen. Lailu peered left, then right, but saw no sign of her. There was nowhere that Wren could have gone: the street was straight, each side walled off by those strange buildings.

"I'm sorry I scared off your friend."

"What?" Lailu asked.

"She saw me standing here and took off. Strangest thing, a girl seeing *me* and running away." Vahn scratched his head. "Well, Lula, I need to get back to work, so—"

"Which way did she go?"

Vahn shrugged.

Lailu clenched her hands, suddenly frustrated. "Look, Vahn, this is important. I know you're working for the elves." Lailu had thought about it ever since she'd given Ryon the jar of blood: Vahn had to be working for the elves. That was why he was talking to Ryon, and why he suddenly left that day with Eirad, and why

Brennon—Lailu swallowed, trying not to think too hard about him—why he had wanted her to give the jar to Vahn. It was the only explanation that made sense, the pieces coming together like spices in a perfectly blended broth.

Shock wiped away Vahn's smile. "How did you . . . I mean, that's an interesting theory."

"Brennon gave me that jar to give to you," Lailu continued, ignoring him.

"Wait, what? You know about—" He glanced around, then lowered his voice. "About the jar, too?"

"Yes. I know about the jar, and what's inside it. And I can help locate the missing elves, too. But only if I find where that girl went first."

"Well, in that case, let's stop wasting time." Vahn tossed his long golden hair back behind his shoulders and strode forward, turning left at the fork. He hesitated, studying the buildings, his steps slowing. "She was too fast for me this time, but earlier I thought I saw her press . . . aha!" He pushed a small indent in the side of the third building down the row. Now that Lailu knew what to look for, she could see it too, a little circle slightly wider than her thumb that blended with the walls almost perfectly. With a soft *ding!* the wall of the building split in the middle, the sides sliding apart to reveal a small, square room.

"I've seen her here before," Vahn said, stepping inside. "I just never thought she was very important." His lips quirked in the smallest smile Lailu had ever seen on his face. "Seems I have a tendency to underestimate you kids."

"I'm not a—" Lailu began.

"I've got it from here," Vahn said, ignoring her. "Go back to your restaurant and tell Ryon when he shows up where I've gone," he called as the doors slowly slid closed behind him.

Lailu hesitated, staring at the building into which Vahn had completely vanished. She could barely see the slit between the doors anymore. She should go. She still needed to add more spice to the roast, plus rotate all the dragon meat to cook evenly. But she hated the idea of leaving Vahn here, of not seeing this mystery through.

A soft purring sound brought Lailu back to reality as the front of a building down the street slid open, the door rolling right up into the ceiling. She caught a glimpse of Starling marching outside the building with Mr. Boss.

Lailu looked around, but there were no spaces between buildings, nowhere to hide, and they were heading right toward her. She did *not* want to see Mr. Boss. Or Starling Volan, for that matter. Anxiously, she turned and punched the button Vahn had pressed. The doors slid open painstakingly slowly. As soon as the gap was wide enough, she threw herself inside, praying to the God of Cookery that no one had seen her as the doors slid shut and plunged her into an eerie sort of half-light. There was another one of those illumination contraptions on the ceiling, but this one flickered and buzzed more than shone. It made Lailu's head pound and her eyes ache. The only other source of light came from four glowing buttons on the wall in front of her.

"—only when you give me a workable product," Mr. Boss was saying, his voice quite loud.

Lailu held her breath, her heart pounding painfully in her ears as she realized they must be walking right past her hiding place.

"And, as I told you, I have developed a better product, but again, I will be needing the payment first," Starling answered, anger bringing out a hint of her accent.

"Well, now, maybe we can work out a deal."

"No." Starling's voice got louder. "No more deals, Victor! I am *done* with deals until you give me what you owe me. Changing locations will be expensive, and it's thanks to your carelessness that we . . ."

Their voices trailed off until Lailu could no longer distinguish the words being said.

There was another *ding!* and the doors split in front of Lailu. She blinked at the sudden light, then fell back, gasping.

The Butcher stood there, looking grimly satisfied. "Hello, little chef. Hear anything interesting?"

28

PRIORITIES

*L*ailu went for her knife, her hand closing on open air. Too late she remembered she was wearing a horrid dress, her knife strapped to her leg underneath it.

The Butcher slammed into her, knocking her to the ground. Lailu screamed, her head smashing into the floor, spots of color flashing in front of her eyes as Havoc's large, bony hands pinned her wrists down. She could smell the stink of him, all sweat and blood and death. Lailu gagged, struggling, but it was no good.

"Just my luck," Havoc hissed in her ear. "I heard something, thought there might be a rat in our little operation, and here's you, all prettied up. Helpless." He squeezed Lailu's wrists until her bones creaked. A whimper escaped her throat, her heart hammering so hard and fast she couldn't breathe.

She closed her eyes, blocking out the dim light, and forced

herself to remember her training even as Havoc crammed both of her wrists into one large hand. Focus, Lailu, focus, she told herself. She was the youngest chef to come out of the academy in three hundred years. She had earned top marks in hand-to-hand combat, even beating out Greg, and she had just hunted and killed a dragon. What was the Butcher compared to that? Nothing. Just dead meat to be wasted.

Lailu waited for a second, her body limp, and then moved. In one burst of motion she slammed her head into the Butcher's. He howled in rage and pain but she ignored him, ignored the spots dancing in front of her eyes, and got her knee up. Planting her foot, she arched her body up, yanking one of her wrists free as she twisted to the side.

The Butcher made a grab for her free hand, but she was already reaching up under her dress for the hilt of her knife. She pulled it free as she sat up, kicking the Butcher with the side of one leg, but there wasn't much force to it from her awkward seated position. Swatting her leg away, the Butcher slammed an elbow into the side of her face and she went tumbling back down, the knife skittering out of her numb hand and across the floor.

Lailu tasted blood as the world shifted around her. Her head and shoulders were outside the small room now, and dimly she was aware of the doors closing on her. For a second she wondered if she would be cut in half. She wanted to move, *needed* to move, but it was like her bones had been replaced with bread, her blood with stew, everything thick and heavy and slow.

Ding! The doors gently nudged her shoulders and sprang open again. Lailu forced herself to sit up just as the Butcher's heavy body moved, crushing her back down, his hand reaching for her own. She jerked it out of his grasp, her reaching fingers tangling in the cold metal spikes of her haircomb. In one quick motion she had it out, the point pressed firmly into Havoc's throat.

He froze.

"Back up." Lailu pushed the point into the soft part of his neck until his skin dimpled under the pressure. The Butcher slid back just enough so she could get her legs under her to stand. "Now let go of my wrist." He didn't move, so she dug the blade of the comb in until the edge started to slice through his skin as easily as it would have gone through a ripe tomato.

He stiffened, then let go of her wrist.

"That's better." She shook her hand out. The feeling started to come back, chasing pins and needles down her fingers. She gave her hand one more shake, then grabbed the Butcher by his greasy, dirty hair, the comb still pressed firmly into his neck. Now what?

Lailu wasn't really sure what to do. She hunted and killed mystic creatures, true, but the Butcher was a man, even if he was a monster. She couldn't really kill him, could she? But if she let him go, he'd attack her again . . .

"If you're going to kill me," the Butcher growled, "kill me and be done with it."

Lailu hesitated.

"That's what I thought. You don't have the guts. You're just a weak little girl after all." He shoved the blade of the comb away from his throat and lunged at her, his hair coming out in her fingers.

Lailu moved without thinking, kneeing him full in the face, then spinning and kicking him in the temple.

Crash!

The Butcher went down hard and stayed down, his face bleeding all over the floor. Lailu stood over him, panting, the bloody comb still clutched in one hand. She was hot and cold and weak, and she stumbled back, leaning against the wall for support as she tried to catch her breath. It felt like she'd been running, like she was still running, like she'd never breathe normally again. Was he . . . dead? Lailu looked down at him, noticing the slight rise and fall of his back. Not dead. She couldn't tell if she was relieved or disappointed, and that scared her. Was she becoming a monster now too?

"No," she whispered to herself. "No, I'm not." She snatched her knife from the floor and backed away until she could feel the warm afternoon air on her skin.

Ding!

The doors slid closed, trapping the Butcher inside that little room with the four glowing buttons.

Lailu let out a breath, stuffed her knife into her leg sheath, and sagged against the wall, her knees weak and wobbly like cooked pasta.

Her hands shaking, she finally managed to wipe the comb off on her borrowed dress, but then couldn't bring herself to put it back in her hair. Instead, she traced the large fake flower on top, her finger trailing down the length of the blade. She never thought a haircomb would save her life, and she made a quick mental promise to stop making fun of Hannah for her strange obsession.

The image of the Butcher flashed through her mind, his neck bloody, his face filled with rage as he lunged at her, and she shuddered and pushed it away. She couldn't stop to think about what had just happened, so she straightened her dress as best she could and headed back into the center of town, the comb held carefully in one hand. Vahn would be okay without her. She knew he could handle himself.

"Wow, I've never seen you work so fast!" Hannah said.

Lailu kept slicing dragon, cutting the rib eye portion into thick steaks. She could feel the evening trickling away from her. Had this been a normal day, the dinner crowd would already be fading like steam from a frying pan. She was running out of time.

She pulled out one roast from her oven and slipped in the rib eye steaks to cook in its place. They needed to cook overnight to leach out the last of the poison. Off to her right, the sizzling of another batch of meat told her it was about time to switch it out.

"So . . ." Hannah moved farther into the kitchen. "I got you a really nice flyer. It's all over the city by now, or at least it will be in a few days. I mean, I found people to help distribute it, and everyone's all excited. Dragon cuisine! It'll be the talk of the town in no time." Hannah clapped her hands enthusiastically.

Lailu checked on her tri-tip steak. The subtle streaks of green indicating the meat was still poisonous were almost gone.

"I had to promise them all free food, but I know that doesn't bother you," Hannah continued, eyeing Lailu.

Lailu flipped the steaks into a clean pan, then added some phoenix feather meat tenderizer along with her own blend of dry rub before setting the pans back on the stove to cook with the steaks' fatty side up. Turning, she removed a sizzling pan full of chunks of dragon and set it to the side for the soup.

"Ooh, looks delicious." Hannah reached out to take one.

Lailu spun and slapped her hand away. "It's not ready!"

Hannah smiled. "So you *do* see me standing here. I was beginning to wonder."

Lailu exhaled, her shoulders slumping with exhaustion. "Sorry, Hannah. Thanks for getting the flyer made." Then the rest of Hannah's words caught up. "Wait, how much free food?"

Hannah smiled mischievously. Then her smile wilted as she looked Lailu up and down. "What happened to you? Did you bathe?" Her eyes widened. "What happened to my dress?"

Lailu glanced down at her outfit: gray slacks and a black shirt damp from her wet pigtails, half disguised behind a large stained apron. "Honestly, the dress is ruined," she confessed. "I'm sorry, Hannah."

Hannah's eyes narrowed in her lovely heart-shaped face. "What about my comb?"

"Actually, your comb is just fine. I've given it a place of honor." Lailu pointed to a pair of hooks above her stove where she'd laid the comb out in all its ugly glory.

Hannah picked it up, clearly relieved. "Why does it get a place of honor? I thought you hated my combs."

"I used it to stab the Butcher in the throat."

Hannah dropped her comb on the floor. "You what?" Then she realized what she'd just done and crouched down swiftly, scooping the comb back up and clutching it close to her chest.

Lailu put down her cooking utensils and wiped her hands on her apron. "He attacked me," she began, trying to justify her comb abuse. Hannah gasped dramatically, her hands over her mouth as Lailu told her all about her run-in with the Butcher.

"How can you be so calm about it? I mean, Lailu, he *attacked* you. You could be dead! But here you are, cooking away like nothing is out of the ordinary–"

"I *have* to cook. The elves are coming tomorrow evening. It's not that I'm not upset, but if I don't get this done before then, both you and I are toast. We're on our own now, Hannah." Turning back to her now sizzling slices of dragon meat, Lailu carefully flipped them over. She could feel Hannah's eyes on her like a weight at her back. "Let me know if you see Ryon hanging around, would you?"

"Who?"

"That annoying winking guy. The one who was with Vahn that day we went to get my picture taken," Lailu said.

"Oh yeah. Dark hair, kind of skinny? Wears his clothing all rumpled?" Hannah said this last part very disapprovingly.

"That's him. I'm supposed to pass him a message for Vahn when he shows up here again." Lailu yawned. Her whole body felt heavy, so heavy, but she was just about done with the initial prep work. Just a little longer and she could sleep for a few hours.

Hannah played with a lock of her long, dark hair. "What if Ryon doesn't show up?"

Lailu hesitated. "I'm sure he will." She wondered where Vahn had gone. The room had been nothing but a small box when she went in there, but there must have been a door or a hidden passage to someplace else. Vahn would be fine. He'd be *fine*. Wouldn't he? For a second she thought about going back to help him, or searching out Ryon, but then she looked at the beginnings of the full-course feast spread in front of her and knew she couldn't leave now.

She was a chef first and foremost. The problems of the world would have to wait until after she finished cooking.

29

DURING CLOSED HOURS

*L*ailu frantically stirred a large pot, adding vegetables and a few bay leaves. It was the morning of the third and final day. No matter what, her feast had to be complete tonight.

"So I figure I'll head out to the city, see how those flyers are doing," Hannah said. "Unless you need my help here?"

Lailu looked up into Hannah's wide, fearful eyes and realized her friend wanted to be somewhere else when the elves showed up. "No, I think I've got everything under control," she lied. Hannah had already gone with her to face a dragon. She didn't need to face the elves, too.

Hannah sagged with relief. "Oh, good. Not that I wouldn't want to help you, of course, but I'd like to be out of the way when . . . that is, it'll just be better. For both of us."

Lailu nodded, carefully measuring out a pinch of a special

bouquet garni to counteract the acidity inherent in the dragon's flesh. It was well known that when cooking dragon, regular herbs and spices needed a good mix of mystical herbs. Grown in hidden groves and slices of concealed rain forest, mystic herbs were said to help increase a person's imagination, intuition, memory, or even intelligence. Lailu mostly used them as a way to soak up the excess magic of her mystic beasts and dilute it.

"Have fun in town," she called absently as Hannah left.

A few seconds later, the bell above the door chimed again. Puzzled, Lailu poked her head around the corner.

"Did you forget some . . ." Lailu swallowed her words.

Starling Volan stood in the doorway. She cut a striking figure, her auburn hair pulled into a practical bun, a man's vest hugging her lean frame over a white blouse and a long navy skirt. She caught sight of Lailu and her lips twitched into a clever little smile.

"You," Lailu began, when the bell above the door chimed once more and Elister stepped inside, trailed by Mr. Mustache and his freshly shaven twin.

"Ah, Starling, you just beat me," Elister said warmly.

Lailu's stomach cramped in fear. Why was Elister meeting Starling here, of all places? She studied his face, but he looked perfectly composed. If he planned on harming Lailu, she couldn't tell.

"Elister. As always, it is truly a pleasure." Starling cast a sideways glance at Lailu.

Lailu forced her mouth shut and kept her expression neutral, but she couldn't slow her rapidly beating heart. If Starling mentioned that she'd seen her at the Crow's Nest . . . if she told Elister that Lailu had been spying on him for Mr. Boss . . . Lailu's throat went dry.

"And Lailu." Elister turned toward her. She froze, trying to look innocent as all the blood drained out of her face like water through a colander. "Is Mystic Cooking closed today?"

Lailu swallowed. "N-not to you," she managed. What else could she say to him?

A genuine smile split his face. "That's my chef." He clapped her on the shoulder. Lailu staggered slightly. "We have some business to discuss, and I thought your restaurant would be the perfect place." He looked around. "And where is Master Slipshod?"

"N-not here right now," Lailu managed.

"Oh, he's left you alone again? Well, I'm sure he's a busy man." Elister turned back to Starling. "Starling, this is Lailu. Don't let her tender age fool you—she recently served up an excellent dish at a party of mine. Basilisk fish, if you'll believe it. My guests are still clamoring for seconds."

"Really?" Lailu asked, startled out of her fear.

"Oh yes. You'll have to cater for me again." He nodded his head at Starling, adding, "Lailu, this is Starling, a brilliant scientist and a friend of mine."

Starling looked hard at Lailu, then gave her that same sly smile as she put out one dainty hand. "A pleasure to finally meet you. Why, everyone has been positively *crowing* about your work."

Lailu hesitated a second, her blood running cold. Starling's word choice had felt very deliberate, like a subtle warning. Reluctantly, she shook Starling's hand, feeling like she'd just made some kind of pact; if she didn't talk about Starling's dealings at the Crow's Nest, then Starling wouldn't mention hers. They both wanted to keep that secret from Elister.

"Uh, sit wherever you like and I'll, er, get you some appetizers." Lailu ducked into her kitchen, but no sooner had she disappeared behind the cloth then the bell above her door chimed again. What *now*?

She popped back out from behind the curtain to find Greg standing in the doorway, clutching the handle of a large Cooling and Containment cart, his eyes widening dramatically beneath his mop of curly hair. Over in the corner, Elister and Starling stopped talking, and one of the bodyguards stood up, his expression dangerous.

"Greg!" Lailu moved quickly before he could say anything. "Glad to see you. You must be here for your portion of the meat. Finally."

"Uh . . . ," Greg said. She remembered the way she'd felt when Elister the Bloody had first appeared in her restaurant.

"Is everything all right?" Elister asked quietly.

"Everything's fine, just fine." Lailu tugged Greg toward her kitchen. "This is my friend Greg, a fellow chef. We're just, uh, collaborating on a dish."

Lailu could feel all eyes on her as she practically dragged Greg into her kitchen and pulled the curtain back into place.

"What's going on?" he whispered.

"Nothing." She checked on her dragon broth. It was simmering nicely, but could use a little more salt.

"Nothing?" Greg repeated. *"Nothing?"* His voice rose and Lailu shot him a warning look. "That's Elister the Bloody out there in your dining room!"

"*Shh.* I am perfectly aware of who is in my dining room."

"Are you? Because you seem awfully calm about it!"

"I said *shh*, Greg. It's not like it's the first time—"

"Not the first time? Do you regularly entertain him here, then?" Greg's voice sounded strangled. "He's the one practically running the kingdom."

"That's only until the king is a little older," Lailu pointed out. "Besides, the queen is technically the one—"

"You can't really believe that," Greg cut her off. "Lailu, he slaughtered all those people! All those nobles."

"That was to protect the young king," Lailu said defensively.

Greg stared at her. "Really? You really think he did that to protect the king?"

"Why else would he?"

"Um, let's see, so he could be the one running the kingdom?"

"Stop using that voice, Greg. I'm not stupid," Lailu said.

"You sure about that?"

Lailu narrowed her eyes dangerously.

"Sorry, that was . . . that was rude," Greg said. "I didn't mean it. It's just, don't you remember what he's like? How he was at the academy? What he did?"

"Of course I remember. It was right in front of me." Lailu shuddered, trying not to picture the way Elister's victim had looked, and how those crescent-shaped knives had gone through him so easily. "Anyway, it's not like you don't get high officials at your restaurant too."

"That's different."

Lailu narrowed her eyes. "Oh, it's different, is it? Why? Because you and your famous uncle are aristocrats?"

"Why do you keep throwing that in my face? It's not my fault—"

"Oh, I know, and it must be so terrible for you."

Greg sighed and ran a hand through his hair, looking suddenly as tired as she felt. "Look. Aristocratic or not, we've never had anyone sitting in a private conversation in our restaurant during closed hours."

"And why should that matter?"

"He's turned your restaurant into his private meeting area. Into his *territory*. Don't you see?"

"Well, yeah." Lailu shifted uncomfortably. "But it's not any worse than being Mr. Boss's territory, is it?"

Greg frowned. "Why are you doing this to yourself? I mean, why let it be anyone's territory?"

"It's not like I *want* these people here. But Slipshod borrowed money from Mr. Boss, so I'm stuck with him, and Elister seems to really like my cooking, so he keeps coming back. And I have to cook for the elves tonight, so . . ." She shrugged. "What can I do?"

Greg shook his head and muttered something.

"What?" Lailu demanded. "We can't all start out with money, you know."

"You could have come to me. I would have helped you out. I *wanted* to help you."

"I didn't need your help. I can do this on my own," Lailu said stiffly. "And it's none of your business who I choose to let into my restaurant during closed hours. So you can take your portion of dragon from downstairs and go."

Greg stared at her, then past her, his eyes sweeping over all the dragon meat and ingredients in various stages of cooking. She knew the only counter space not taken up by her preparations was where Slipshod's dragon cuisine book was perched. Honestly, the room looked like an explosion had gone off.

"Want a hand with this?" Greg asked suddenly.

Lailu gaped at him.

"I'll be your assistant," he added quickly. "I won't try to take over the cooking, I promise. You just look like you could use a little extra help."

"What about your restaurant?"

"Well, my uncle won't like it, but . . . it can be closed for the day." He had a pained look in his eyes that went against his casual tone.

Lailu's chest filled with something suspiciously like gratitude. She really could use some help, and Greg was an excellent chef. *Almost* as good as she was, honestly. "You'd close your restaurant to help me?"

"Again," he reminded her.

"Again?"

"Well, I already closed it once this week to help you hunt dragon." He winced. "But sure, I mean, since I'm your *friend*."

"I just said that so Elister's bodyguards wouldn't shred you," Lailu said testily. "Don't let it go to your head."

Greg grinned, and Lailu's lips twitched in the barest hint of a smile back. "Fine, fine. You can stay and help. But don't think I don't know your real motive."

"Oh?" He raised one eyebrow and took a step toward her. "And what's that?"

"You just want to learn from the master."

He stopped, surprised, then laughed. "You never change, do you? Cooking really is all you ever think about."

"What else is there?"

Greg opened his mouth like he was thinking of saying something, then just shrugged. "All right, what's first, Master?" he asked instead.

"Master?" Lailu grinned. "I could get used to that." She looked around. "Separate two bowls' worth of broth out of that big pot, and cook it in that smaller one." She indicated a brass pot sitting out on her counter. She'd originally planned on using it to cook up a special sauce, but that could wait.

"You do realize the dragon meat hasn't been boiling long enough to get the real flavoring yet?"

"Of course I realize that. What kind of chef do you take me for?"

Greg shrugged and ladled out the broth. "Just saying," he muttered.

"Now, what I'm planning to do is grab the last of my batyrdactyl bones and throw them in the small pot of soup. The flavoring, as you know, comes out of them a lot faster—"

"—and with a hint of the dragon flavoring spiced with pagora plant, that will be perfect!" Greg finished excitedly.

"Pagora? I was thinking some lebinola spice."

"No way. Lebinola is way too sweet."

"I like sweet. It's like me."

Greg snorted and turned back to his ladling. "Just saying," he grumbled. "But you are the master chef here."

"You seem to be 'just saying' an awful lot for an *assistant*." Lailu narrowed her eyes.

Greg pursed his lips but kept quiet while he ladled the rest of the soup. Lailu could have sworn she heard the words *crabby* and *cakes* muttered under his breath, but in the interest of preserving their partnership, she pretended not to. After all, she really did need the help.

30

Not Leaving

fter agreeing on pagora plant with a hint of lebinola, Lailu and Greg prepared a soup that both of them found suitable as an appetizer. While Greg kept an eye on the lean dragon meat searing in a pan, Lailu headed into the dining room to serve Elister and Starling.

"—highly explosive. Neon has even found a way to make it different colors, like fire flowers in the sky," Starling explained, leaning across the table.

"And how would fire flowers help me with the Krigaen Empire?" Elister asked coolly. "I mean, that's fine for outdoor dinner parties, I suppose, but hardly practical."

Starling smiled, her green eyes glittering. "Do not misunderstand me, Elister. I am not such a frivolous woman. Pretty they may be, but I think you'll be much more interested in their other capabilities."

Mr. Mustache gave a dainty cough that Lailu found completely ridiculous coming from such a large man. Elister and Starling looked up, and he nodded in Lailu's direction.

"Ah, Lailu. What's on the menu for today?" Elister asked. Starling's eyes narrowed suspiciously.

Lailu took a deep, shaky breath. "For today's menu, you get a Lailu . . . and Greg," she added, "one-time special. For your appetizer, we prepared a batyrdactyl soup with a light flavoring of mountain dragon."

Their eyes widened at the mention of the mountain dragon, and Lailu placed bowls of soup in front of each of them before continuing. "For your entrée, you'll be served a top loin cut of mountain dragon, cooked medium rare for the optimal flavoring, with a light drizzle of my very own specialty sauce and a side of steamed carrots, broccoli, and snap-dragon peas."

"Now you see why I chose this restaurant," Elister said. "And here you were suggesting we leave."

Starling glanced sidelong at Lailu. "I merely thought that afterward we should go somewhere a little more private so I can give you a demonstration of my latest invention."

"Did you bring it with you?" Elister leaned forward, clearly forgetting about his soup. Lailu scowled, but forced herself to continue backing out of the dining room.

Greg looked up at her from over a large bubbling pot. "So, what did they think?"

"They didn't taste it yet," Lailu said, trying not to sound bitter. "They're too busy talking."

"What about?"

"I think," she began, frowning as Greg added in some more seasoning, "they were talking about those fireworks that Hannah had . . ." Her frown turned into an outright scowl. "What are you doing?"

Greg jumped, a guilty look on his face. "Sorry." He quickly put down the seasoning bottle. "Just thought it needed a bit more spice."

Lailu stalked over and picked it up. She looked at it a second, then looked at the pot and sighed. "It does need a bit," she admitted reluctantly, handing the bottle back to him.

His lips twitched, but he was smart enough not to smile as he added the seasonings. "So, when is your dinner rush, eh?"

"You mean my date with the entire elf clan to determine Hannah's fate?" Lailu's stomach twisted. "And mine, too."

"Yours?"

"Oh, if I don't make the best dragon cuisine they've ever tasted, I'll be forced to work for them."

"For how long?"

"Well, just, uh, for the rest of my life." Lailu tried to say it off-handedly, but the horrified look on Greg's face made the words stick in her throat.

"You agreed to those terms?" His voice cracked on the last word, and Lailu winced.

"They were the only ones they offered."

"Those are the worst terms I've ever heard! I mean, that basically means you'll be their slave."

"I realize that," Lailu muttered.

"They'll make you work for them until you grow old and your fingers fall off your hands and your eyesight fades from all the fumes of the poisons they'll have you cook up, and—"

"You're really not helping right now."

"It's just, I'd think you of all people would have refused them."

"And what's that supposed to mean?" Lailu put her hands on her hips.

"Just that you're so big on your own independence. I mean, that's kind of what got you into this mess in the first place, isn't it? Otherwise you could have joined a good household, or worked with my uncle and me. Instead, you go and start this venture with Slipshod." Greg's mouth thinned and he shook his head. "Really, what were you thinking?"

Lailu let out a breath. "If they like my cooking, they'll take care of my debt to Mr. Boss. And besides, I couldn't leave Hannah to them, and it was the only way I could think of to help her."

Greg's eyes softened. "You're very loyal, you know that? You're the most loyal person I know."

Lailu's face grew hot and she looked away, fidgeting.

"So." Greg cleared his throat. "When are they coming? I mean, I'm assuming you won't want them to be here at the same time as Elister and Starling, right?"

"No, by all the gods, no. The elves won't be here until this evening. I'm sure Elister and Starling will be long gone by then."

But as the day wore on with Elister and Starling showing no signs of leaving, Lailu's anxiety rose higher than the steam in her kitchen. She alternated between cooking and hovering in the doorway, silently urging Elister to go. At one point he looked up, a bite of dragon steak halfway to his mouth, his eyes meeting hers. "Ah, Lailu."

Lailu jumped, almost tripping over her own feet in her haste to move back into the kitchen.

"No, no, don't hide. Come on out here."

Lailu trudged over to the pair of them. She glanced out the window, her heart sinking as she saw how low the sun was in the sky. It was creeping ever closer to dinnertime. Why were they still here? What could they possibly still have to talk about?

"You have outdone yourself," Elister said warmly, indicating the plates in front of them. "This has to be the finest meal I've had in years. Better even than the basilisk fish you served up before."

"Th-thank you. I'm glad you like it."

"I, too, find this meal to be fantastic." Starling smiled. Her plate was practically empty, Lailu noticed with relief. That must mean they were almost done. "I was just telling Elister here that I'll have to bring my associates to your restaurant. I'm sure they would love it."

"You mean the scientists?" Lailu blurted.

Elister chuckled. "See, Starling? Already famous, even all the way out here."

"Yes, well, that is our goal." Starling tilted her head to the side. "Have you met any of them?"

"I visited Gilded Island earlier, and a scientist took my picture, and I saw a man driving a horseless carriage." A maniac, she amended silently.

"You shall have to meet the others," Starling said. "We'll all come out here for dinner sometime."

Lailu opened her mouth to say she'd like that, but nothing came out. She felt like she already had enough going on, what with Elister, Mr. Boss, and the elves turning her restaurant into their own personal hangout. "Er," she said instead, "have you tried Greg's restaurant? It's right there on Gilded Island and it's . . . well, almost as good as mine."

"I heard that!" Greg yelled from the kitchen.

"LaSilvian's, isn't it?" Elister looked faintly amused. "I remember you don't carry their wine here."

"Yes, well, I prefer *other* brands." Lailu had a sudden idea. "And speaking of wines," she said slowly, "I see that you are just about finished with your meals. How about I bring you one of our dessert wines, on the house? I'm sure you're both busy—"

"Busy?" Elister chuckled. "My dear chef, I have no plans for today. In fact," he continued as Lailu's heart sank to her shoes, "I'm enjoying my meal so much I think I'd like to stay around and wait for dinner. Starling?"

"Dinner sounds fantastic." Starling scraped her fork across her now empty plate. "I'm certainly in no rush, either."

"How about a game of chess, then?" Elister asked. "It's quite popular in our country. You really should learn it."

"A game?" Lailu asked desperately. "Are you sure? I mean, it's pretty loud, what with my cooking . . . difficult to concentrate . . . probably want to leave . . . ," she mumbled. Elister completely ignored her as he explained the rules of the game to Starling. Lailu stood there, watching as the sun dropped lower in the sky, along with her hopes for a successful evening. "I'll get you your dinner, then," she said dejectedly, turning on her heel and walking slowly back to the kitchen.

"Now what?" Greg asked.

Lailu slumped against the wall.

"I mean, I guess you could ask them to leave."

"I can't do that. That's Elister out there!"

"I know, I know." Greg looked far too calm; Lailu had to stifle the urge to shake him. "You could just tell him the elves have rented out this space for the evening."

Lailu shook her head. "I don't think I want him to know about all that. Or, rather, I don't want Starling to know."

"Why not?"

"Because . . ." Lailu hesitated, remembering her promise to Wren. *A promise is binding.* Did it still count if Wren had vanished? "I think the less she knows about the elves' location, the better."

"Well, Elister and Starling are going to know soon enough. I mean, I'm pretty sure they'll notice when the gang of elves shows up for dinner."

Lailu scowled. "Just stir the pot."

Greg opened his mouth to retort when they both heard a soft *knock-knock-knock.* They froze, staring at each other. It was coming from the back door.

31

Making Connections

The sound of Lailu's hammering heart drowned out the knocking outside. Could it be the Butcher? But would he really knock? Master Slipshod? Her heart beat even faster.

"Are you going to open it?" Greg asked at last.

"I'm debating," Lailu said.

Shaking his head, Greg stepped past her and grabbed the door handle.

"Wait—" Lailu began, but it was too late. Greg pulled open the door.

Ryon stood just outside, one hand raised to knock. As soon as Lailu saw him, her fear was flooded in a wave of relief, and she dragged him inside, shutting the door behind him. "It's about time," she huffed.

"About time? For what?"

"I've been waiting for you to show up."

Ryon flashed a slow, cocky smile. "Have you, now?" He winked mischievously. "Missed me, huh?"

"In your dreams," Lailu snapped.

"Um, who is this?" Greg's eyebrows were practically invisible in his thick, curly hair, and his arms and shoulders had gone stiff.

"Ryon, at your service." Ryon held out a hand, and Greg reluctantly took it, wincing as the other boy pumped his arm up and down enthusiastically. "And you must be the infamous Gregorian LaSilvian. I've heard all about you. None of it good." Greg managed to free his hand as Ryon leaned in closer. "Most of it came from Lailu, you see," he stage-whispered.

"Stop fooling around," Lailu said. "Greg, Ryon here is . . . well. Sort of a friend."

"Sort of? I'm hurt."

"You will be," Lailu muttered.

"Easy there, tiger," Ryon said. "I just came to warn you."

"Warn me? Warn me about what?"

Ryon glanced at Greg. "Is it safe to talk freely? I mean, in front of the bystander?"

"I'm *not* a bystander." If anything, Greg's shoulders grew even more tense, and he wore a very Lailu-esque scowl.

Lailu sighed and rubbed her temples. Ryon and Greg were both annoying enough individually. Who'd have known they could be even worse combined? "You can talk freely. Greg is helping me."

"Very generous of him." Somehow the way Ryon said it, it didn't seem like a compliment. Greg's scowl deepened, but before he had a chance to respond, Ryon continued, "Mr. Boss is going to stop by tonight for the money you owe him."

"What?" Lailu's knees gave out, and suddenly she was sitting on the floor. "He can't. I should still have five more days! He has to know there's no way I have his money yet."

"He knows you might have it soon."

"What?"

Ryon pulled a slip of glossy paper from his coat pocket and held it out. Lailu took it, reading the elegant writing stamped across in bold letters:

Coming soon to Mystic Cooking:
Dragon cuisine!
Dine better than royalty, but only for a day.
Exclusive offer open to the first fifty
people to come to the restaurant.
Priced at twenty gold crowns a person.

"Wow, nice advertisements." Greg took the paper from Lailu and studied it. "*Very* nice."

"Hannah had them made."

"Isn't he your competition?" Ryon asked, snatching the paper back from Greg. "Don't go showing all your business secrets or he might copy them again."

"Hey! That's hardly fair—" Greg began.

Ryon crouched in front of Lailu, ignoring Greg. "They're all over the city," he said, tucking her advertisement back inside his coat pocket. Greg fumed silently behind him. "And I must say, they're creating quite the buzz. I have a feeling you're going to have a packed house tomorrow."

"If I live that long." Lailu buried her hands in her hair, her face pressed against her knees. She felt like the world was spinning without her, and the only thing keeping her here was this gnawing feeling of dread filling her stomach. There was no way the elves would clear her debt with Mr. Boss tonight, even if she did win the bet. "Why is Mr. Boss coming this evening, then? Why not wait until after that?"

"Because he doesn't want you to have his money."

Lailu stared up at Ryon. "That hardly makes sense."

"Oh, it makes plenty of sense. He doesn't want you to clear your debts. He never wanted you to."

"Why?"

"Because you're his golden ticket. An academy-trained master chef? If you fail to clear your debts, you'll be in his pocket forever, and he'll be able to use you however he wants. It would destroy you, but it might save him."

"Save him? From what?" Greg asked, trying to nudge himself into the conversation.

"Mostly himself," Ryon said. "He's had a few deals backfire, and a lot of his supporters have left him, including the scientists. I think . . ." He took a deep breath. "I think it's made him a little unhinged. Meanwhile, his health is not good. Honestly, he looks like a corpse. A seriously-in-debt corpse."

"Have you seen Vahn lately?" Lailu asked suddenly, her brain working feverishly. It sounded like Ryon hadn't made the connection yet between the elf blood and Mr. Boss's "health" elixir.

"No, not for a while. Why? Did he find something?"

"Doubtful," Greg muttered under his breath.

Lailu hesitated. If Vahn hadn't found Ryon by now, that meant he was probably still stuck in the Industrial District. It had been an awfully long time. Was he still all right? She tried not to imagine him caught and held prisoner—or worse. No. Vahn could do anything. She knew he would be fine. Spending a whole day and night in some weird Industrial building wouldn't hurt a man who could stop a pack of vibbers without breaking a sweat.

And even though he had told her to send Ryon to him next time he showed up, she decided to wait. It made her feel squirmy on the inside, but if she told Ryon where Vahn was now, then the elves might never know that Mr. Boss was behind their disappearances. She needed them to know.

Squashing down her anxiety, she made her decision. "Ryon, I know where the missing elves are."

"You what?" Ryon straightened. "Where are they? How?"

"I . . . I can't tell you where they are. Not yet."

He frowned. "Lailu—"

"No, listen. You want to find them, but you also want to catch the person responsible too, right?"

Ryon hesitated, then nodded slowly, his eyes never leaving her face.

Lailu let out a breath. "Vahn is with the elves, I think. And I'll tell you where they are, but first I *need* you to get Mr. Boss to come to my restaurant right now." She couldn't work for Mr. Boss, she just couldn't. She needed the elves to catch him. She had to trust that Vahn would be okay on his own a little longer.

Ryon studied her, then nodded. "Okay, I'll trust you. Just don't make me regret it." He gave her his hand and helped her stand up. "Nice hair, by the way."

Lailu's hands flew to the mess she'd made of her pigtails, and she hurriedly straightened them.

"It sounds like the elves are almost here," Ryon said.

"What?" Lailu felt like the floor was tipping beneath her.

"You can hear them?" Greg asked.

"I have very good ears," Ryon said. "I'm going to sneak out the back again, if you don't mind. I'd prefer your other guests not see me here right now." He gave Lailu a hard look. "I'll hurry back with Mr. Boss, but I hope you know what you're doing."

"So do I," Lailu whispered as Ryon vanished outside.

All was silent in her kitchen, aside from the bubbling, steaming, cooking dragon. "Not sure I liked that guy. He seemed . . . shifty," Greg said finally.

Lailu glared at him.

"But of course, what would I know? I'm just your assistant." He picked up a large wooden spoon, then glanced at her over his shoulder. "I may not understand everything that's going on with you at the moment, but I promise it's going to be okay, Lailu. You know that, right?"

Lailu nodded. She didn't know that, but one way or another, at least things would be over with tonight.

She took a deep breath, steeling herself, then went back into the dining room of Mystic Cooking.

A Favor

Elister, Starling, and the bodyguards looked up. "Ah, Lailu," Elister said pleasantly. "Starling and I were wondering how much longer before you would be ready to serve dinner. Chess always works up an appetite."

"I, too, am excited about this dinner." Starling smiled and patted her stomach. "I know we just ate, but one can never have too much dragon."

"D-dinner will be ready soon." Lailu swallowed. "But the group that I closed the restaurant for is going to be here shortly. So it might become a bit crowded in here."

Elister raised a well-groomed eyebrow. "And whose company will we be graced with?"

"The elves," she squeaked, and coughed to clear her throat. "The elves," she repeated.

Elister's other brow rose. "*The* elves? How many?"

"Around twenty."

"Twenty of the elves." Elister gazed across the table at Starling, who kept her face unreadable. "Well, that should be interesting."

Lailu thought *interesting* was hardly the word.

"Do you need us to leave, then?" Elister asked.

Lailu's mouth dropped open in surprise. Would he really make it that easy for her? She started to say yes, but his eyes grew cold again, and she realized there was only one right answer here. "Of course not, sir," she forced herself to say, her lips stretching in what she hoped was a smile. "I have enough room for all of you."

Elister's eyes warmed up. "Very good, very good," he said. "I must admit, I'm looking forward to eating more of your dragon cuisine."

Lailu nodded, trying to hide her pained expression. "Well, sir, I'd better go check on the food." She inched back toward the safety of the kitchen.

"Wait a moment," Elister said.

Lailu froze.

"Before your other guests arrive, tell me, did you learn anything of interest from Mr. Boss? As I recall, we had ourselves a bit of a deal."

Out of the corner of her eye, Lailu could see Starling clutch the edge of her seat. And no wonder, if she was helping Mr. Boss kidnap elves to experiment with their blood. Surely Elister would find *that* information interesting enough.

But then Starling would definitely tell Elister about Lailu's trip to the Crow's Nest. She didn't want to find out how he'd react to that bit of news. And the elves, when they found out, when Elister told them about Starling . . . what would they do to Wren? Lailu had to keep her promise. Besides, Starling wasn't her enemy. Mr. Boss, on the other hand . . .

"Actually, sir, I just discovered something very interesting," Lailu said, making up her mind. If Elister knew about Mr. Boss's involvement, maybe he would support her against the loan shark if things went sour tonight.

"Oh?"

"You've heard about the missing elves?"

"I have."

"Well, Mr. Boss knows where they are."

Starling gasped. Elister didn't take his eyes off Lailu. "Does he, now?"

"Yes. He's been drinking an elixir made from their blood. A life elixir, only I don't think it's working too well."

"No. No, it wouldn't be," Elister mused. Across from him Starling had recovered her composure, her posture very casual. "I do wonder, though, who would be making this elixir for him. It hardly seems like something our dear loan shark would be capable of creating on his own." He glanced at Starling. If anything, her posture became even more casual.

Elister smiled, and turned back to Lailu. "How did you find this out?"

"I have my sources," Lailu supplied bravely.

Elister laughed. "Don't we all. Well, then. Where are they?"

Lailu summoned all her courage. "I was hoping you could ask Mr. Boss that when he shows up tonight."

Elister's laughter faded, and he studied Lailu with an intensity that made her want to squirm right out of her skin. Had she gone too far? But then he nodded. "I see. Clever girl. But I believe *you* should be the one to ask him."

The bell above the door chimed, and the first elf stepped inside, stopping at the sight of Elister, Starling, and the two bodyguards. His pale eyes narrowed. "What's this?"

Lailu took in his height and those long golden braids. "What's what?" Lailu replied obstinately. Of all the elves she'd met, she disliked this one the most.

"Eirad, calm yourself," Fahr said as he entered the room, his long dark hair glossy in the lamplight. "It's just Elister." He strode forward. "Elister, my friend. How good to see you again."

"Fahr." Elister stood to shake the elf's hand. "I'm not sure if you've met the lovely Starling Volan?"

Starling did not stand up, and Fahr's smile faltered. "Not formally, no," Fahr said. "Merely from a distance."

Starling's expression made it clear that this distance hadn't been far enough.

"Oh, good." Elister nodded pleasantly as if the temperature in the room had not just dropped twenty degrees. "We can all sit together, then. I hope you don't mind us crashing your party? Lailu mentioned she was serving you all dragon cuisine, and I must admit, I could hardly leave after hearing that."

"Understandable." Fahr's gray-blue eyes remained fixed on

Starling's stoic face. After a moment he looked away, finding Lailu hiding in the corner near the kitchen. "So, shall we just move some tables together?"

"Oh, of course. I'll take care of that for you." As she started dragging the first table, Greg came out of the kitchen, his brown eyes widening at the sight of the elves still pouring in. Without a word, he picked up the other end of her table.

After the elves were all seated, Lailu and Greg slipped back into the kitchen. "I'll set the tables," Greg whispered. "You finish preparing the food. It's pretty much done, but I thought you might want to check it. I tried keeping everything to your normal tastes, but . . ." He shrugged. Lailu understood; Greg had his own peculiar ideas about seasonings.

"You don't have to stay," Lailu told him, even as her stomach clenched at the idea of facing this crowd alone.

"Are you kidding me? They'd eat you alive out there."

Lailu thrust out her chin. "I'd be fine." Her defiance melted a little. "But if you want to stay," she mumbled, "I wouldn't mind the help."

"What was that?"

"I said you could stay, if you wanted," Lailu repeated, still mumbling and staring at the tops of her shiny black boots.

"I'm sorry, I *thought* I heard a 'Thank you, Greg' somewhere in there."

Lailu scowled, and Greg grinned from ear to ear in response. Taking a deep breath, Lailu forced herself to say it. "Thank you, Greg."

His smile widened even further, showing off his straight white teeth in a way Vahn would be proud of. "You're welcome, Lailu."

She hesitated, then blurted out, "Why are you helping me?"

Greg's smile wilted. "What?"

"I said, *why* are you helping me?"

"You don't know?"

She shook her head. She could hear the elves chattering outside as they waited for the meal that would decide her future.

Greg ran a hand through his curly brown hair. "Lailu, after all this time . . ." He dropped his hand and looked at her. "We're friends."

"No, we're not."

"Yes, we are," he said firmly. "Even if you don't want to admit it, you know I've got your back, and I know, well, that you'd probably like to stab a knife into mine . . ." He paused. "This is not a very even friendship, now that I think about it."

"It's not a friendship at all!" Lailu didn't *want* to be friends with Greg, with his successful, fancy business and successful, fancy family. It was much easier to dislike him. Only lately . . . lately he'd helped her out a lot. Were they becoming friends? Lailu's mind whirled at the idea. Friends with Greg. Friends with the boy who'd tormented her all through school, who had everything so easy.

Greg picked up his chef's hat from the counter. "Fine, then."

Lailu's anger and confusion evaporated, replaced by worry. "You're not . . . I mean, are you leaving?"

Greg paused, then jammed his hat on over his unruly hair. "No, I'll stay," he decided, turning away from her and getting out the place settings from the cupboard in back. "But after this is over . . ."

"Yes?"

"You'll owe me a favor."

Lailu's stomach twisted, but she could hardly deny it. She tried not to picture the kinds of favors Greg might call her in for. At least it was a problem for another day.

33

Dragon Cuisine

Lailu paced back and forth as the empty plates piled up and her front door remained stubbornly closed. What was taking Ryon so long? At least the elves seemed to be enjoying her meal.

Then she spotted Eirad jabbing at his food and muttering, and Lailu felt like the world was slowing down around her. Of course *he'd* be the dissatisfied one. He caught her eye, and in one sharp motion swiped his index finger across his neck, then pointed at her. Lailu gulped.

"Everything okay?" Greg asked. "Your face is whiter than your hat."

"I don't think they all like it."

"Nonsense. They love it." He gave her a reassuring smile, but he couldn't hide the worry in his eyes. "Anything else I can do to help?"

"Can you get the dessert wines out of my cellar?"

"Now?"

"I don't want them to have to wait." She told Greg how to get into her cellar and then watched as he disappeared behind her curtain.

CRASH!

Lailu's front door slammed open so hard it took the bell with it. Silence fell thick and heavy as everyone stopped eating and turned toward the door.

"Chef!" Mr. Boss stomped inside, flanked by the Butcher and Ryon. "I'm here for my money!" He didn't seem to notice the watching elves, only Lailu, his face twisted in a horrifying grimace of rage and pain. He looked awful, with deep, dark hollows under his eyes, dry and cracking lips, and patches of flaking grayish skin. What was left of his hair no longer lay oiled carefully back but instead stuck out around his head, and his expensive clothes hung limply on his frame like they were concealing a skeleton.

"Uh, Victor," the Butcher whispered at Mr. Boss's elbow. "Maybe we should come back later." He wore a bloody bandage wrapped around his head, and the wound on his neck had just started to scab. He glared at Lailu, and she shivered at the promise of revenge written across his face.

"My money, my money." Mr. Boss pulled away from the Butcher, his lips curled back from his crumbling teeth. "You don't have it, do you? You've failed, you've failed, and now you're mine!" He did a little jig, and Lailu found herself taking a step back, terrified by the madness in front of her.

"By the gods, what's wrong with him?" a nearby elf whispered.

Suddenly Mr. Boss seemed to notice they were not alone. As he took in the room full of elves, he froze in place, one foot lifted off the ground, the fingers of his other hand clenched around the handle of his infamous cane.

Ryon slipped past Mr. Boss and knelt next to Fahr. Close together like that, Lailu couldn't help but notice the similarities between the two, especially the eyes. They both had the same laughing eyes—although no one's eyes seemed to be laughing now.

"Victor!" Elister boomed, and everyone turned toward him. He dabbed at his mouth with his napkin, then smiled. "I've just heard an interesting rumor about you."

"A-a rumor?" Mr. Boss slowly put his other foot on the ground.

"Lailu?" Elister gave her a pointed look, and now everyone was staring at her.

Lailu swallowed. "Mr. Boss knows where the missing elves are," she whispered.

Fahr went very still. "Are you sure?"

Mr. Boss shook his head violently. "No, no. You checked, remember? You searched my quarters and there was nothing, I have nothing . . ."

"He's been drinking their blood," Lailu said.

Fahr put a hand to his mouth, his eyes wide with shock.

An elf near Lailu stood abruptly. "Where's Livea?" he demanded.

All around him other furious elven voices chimed in at once, asking about their missing companions.

"I don't have them. I don't know anything about them," Mr. Boss insisted. As Lailu watched him edge back toward the door, her fear dripped away. How had she ever let this man bully her? He was pathetic.

"He's keeping them in the Industrial District. I don't know if they're still alive, but he has them stored away in a strange building near the corner of Steam Avenue and Iron Way. There's a button you have to push. I can show you." Lailu relished the look on Mr. Boss's face as she gave away his secrets, relished the feeling of having beaten him. She'd won, and Mr. Boss knew it.

He went the shade of sour milk and stumbled backward, then raced for the door.

Before he'd gone more than a few steps, a tall, broad-shouldered man appeared, blocking the doorway, his boots clicking against the wooden floor as he stepped inside.

Mr. Boss screeched to a halt.

The man straightened his puffy white chef's hat, adjusted his crisp white apron, and smiled. "Hello, Victor. Going somewhere?"

Lailu's jaw dropped. It was Master Slipshod, but Master Slipshod as she'd never seen him before: clean-shaven, his clothing freshly washed and ironed, his posture upright and confident. This, she knew, was a glimpse of the man he'd been, back when he was cooking dragon cuisine for the king himself.

"S-Sullivan?" Mr. Boss gaped. "I thought you left!"

"Left? How could I leave my apprentice?" Master Slipshod dipped his head in Lailu's direction. "You didn't think I'd left, did you?"

"Um, actually—" Lailu began, a rush of anger filling her chest and blazing across her face.

"No, no, I was investigating," Slipshod spoke over her. "Checking in with my contacts. Learning some very terrible things about you, Victor."

"Things? What things?" Mr. Boss asked.

"Yes, chef. What things?" Fahr demanded, moving in closer, a wall of elves at his back and Eirad and Ryon at his sides. Lailu wanted to shrink away, they looked so terrifying, but Master Slipshod seemed cooler than old Mr. Frosty.

"I found Brennon's family. You remember Brennon, don't you? My old gambling buddy, took one bluff too many." Master Slipshod's smile dropped, his chubby face hardening. "You made a mistake, Victor, when you stopped paying your henchmen to guard them. It was easy to set them free, and they told me what you'd been keeping hidden away." He paused, looking around the room dramatically. "I know where the missing elves are being held."

Fahr sighed. "So do we. Lailu just told us."

Slipshod's triumphant air collapsed like bread left too long in the oven. "Oh, you already know?" Then he recovered. "I mean, I'm not surprised. Best apprentice in the land, she is." He grinned at Lailu. She did not return it.

"I-it wasn't me!" Mr. Boss spluttered as the elves advanced on him. The Butcher just stood there, apparently not sure whether he should try to attack the elves or just stay out of the way. "It was, it was, it was . . ." Mr. Boss looked quite deranged, staring wildly around the room. Then he stopped, his gaze landing on Starling.

"You," he whispered, pointing one shaking finger at the scientist.

Starling looked around as if she couldn't imagine Mr. Boss might be pointing at her. "Me?" She sounded calm—amused, even.

"She's the one! The one who's been trapping those elves," Mr. Boss shrieked. "It's her fault. She made me tell her where they would be, how to find them. She took advantage of me! A poor old man's dreams, turned them to ashes, lied to me, *poisoned* me. It was all a game, an experiment to her, but I have to keep drinking that damn elixir, or I die. I *die*!"

Some of the elves glanced angrily at Starling, but her face was a mask of shocked innocence. Even Lailu, who knew better, was half-convinced the scientist was innocent, but she could tell by some of the elves' faces that not all of them were as convinced.

"Clearly, the man has gone delusional," Elister spoke up, his voice full of scorn. He shifted closer to Starling, a subtle reminder that she was there with him. If she weren't, she might not be leaving Mystic Cooking all in one piece. "Isn't elven blood poisonous to humans?"

"Yes," Fahr said coldly. "When taken in large doses, that is." He turned back to Mr. Boss, his eyes glittering. "It looks like it's far too late for you."

"Lies. *Lies!* I should be younger. Stronger. I'll live forever!" Mr. Boss stood straight up and in one quick, surprising motion, slammed his silver-topped cane into Fahr's temple. The elf made a small sound and crumpled to the floor. Half a second of stunned silence passed, and then the rest of the elves screamed and yelled, scrambling over one another and knocking over chairs in their haste to get to Mr. Boss. He ducked past Master Slipshod, darted through the open door, and fled, a stream of elves on his heels.

Lailu heard dishes shattering and she winced, glancing up in time to see Starling slip out the door, the scientist's hand sliding under her vest and pulling out a compact metal object, pipe-shaped with a handle.

Fahr groaned, and Ryon went to him, his face twisted with concern. "Fahr, are you—"

"I'm fine. Help me up," Fahr said.

Ryon shot a look back at Lailu, then put his hands under Fahr's arms and hauled the elf to his feet. Together they staggered out the door after Starling and the rest of the elves, leaving the restaurant in silence.

Elister picked up his fork and resumed eating, his face impassive like this was a normal day, while Master Slipshod stayed by the door, quietly watching the retreating crowd.

"Little chef," a familiar rough voice snarled, and Lailu's heart sank as she realized the Butcher had also chosen to remain inside. "I owe you."

"You owe me, all right," she said, trying to be brave. After all, she'd already beaten him once, and with only a haircomb at that. Plus, Lord Elister was there. Surely the Butcher wouldn't be foolish enough to try something in front of the king's executioner. "You owe me an apology."

Havoc looked taken aback. "No." He slowly pulled a long serrated blade out of the sheath at his hip. Maybe he was foolish enough after all. Lailu gulped. "I owe you pain." The blade was of decent quality, Lailu could tell at a glance, but the edge wasn't nearly sharp enough for her kind of cooking. Still, it would do the job, if the Butcher got close enough to use it. Lailu had no intention of letting him near her ever again. She reached for the knife at her hip, then froze at the sound of a loud pop coming from outside, much like the sound of the fireworks Hannah had used.

And then she turned back, too late, as the Butcher lunged at her.

Whoosh!

Something sailed past Lailu's head, so close it sliced a few hairs off one of her pigtails, and then a second later the Butcher slammed into the far wall, a meat cleaver pinning the collar of his shirt to the plaster as easily as Lailu had once pinned onions in that very spot.

"You leave my apprentice alone," Master Slipshod growled, a second meat cleaver in his hand.

The Butcher's face was full of surprise. "Slipshod? You wouldn't dare do anything to me, you spineless, worthless, used-up old has-been—"

Another whoosh, and Master Slipshod's second cleaver quivered in the wall a mere hairbreadth from the Butcher's head. "Just watch me." Master Slipshod stalked forward, grabbing both of his meat cleavers and pulling them slowly from the wall. "You have five seconds to leave."

Havoc hesitated, but the look in Slipshod's eyes must have convinced him the chef was deadly serious. With a growl he stalked past him and toward the door. Lailu relaxed like jelly freed from its mold.

"Lailu, I found the—" Greg stopped in the doorway of the kitchen, his eyes widening as he clutched two bottles of wine. "Watch out!"

Lailu turned, but it was like she was swimming through stew as the Butcher lunged at her, serrated knife held high.

"Die!" he snarled.

She fell backward, but too slowly, her death clearly written in Havoc's cold eyes.

34

LAILU'S TURN

A blur passed between them, and then a thick, warm liquid spattered Lailu's face. Havoc's eyes went from vengeful to shocked to completely empty before he fell over, dead. Behind him, Elister calmly wiped down his crescent blades before sheathing them.

He turned to his bodyguards. "Some help you were."

Mr. Mustache and his twin began muttering apologies.

"Save it," Elister said. "Instead, make yourselves useful and dispose of that before it stains the floor." He indicated the Butcher's bleeding body.

"Are you all right?" Greg whispered, crouching down next to Lailu, but she hardly noticed him. Everything seemed so cold and distant. Elister had moved fast, *too* fast. No human should be able to move that quickly. Yet if he had gone any slower, it would have been her body lying there, staining the wood of the dining room floor.

Master Slipshod stepped in front of Lailu, blocking her view of the two musclemen carrying the Butcher's body out of Mystic Cooking. She took his proffered hand and let him pull her to her feet, the world swirling around her.

"Well, that was unfortunate," Elister said. "Technically I'm not supposed to kill anyone if I'm not in my official capacity. It causes all sorts of messy paperwork." He sighed. "But some things can't be helped. And I must say, Sullivan, I was most impressed with your bladework. I'll have to tell the king he was wrong about you. You have not lost your touch from the days when you served his father."

Master Slipshod colored slightly and bowed his head.

"And your apprentice." Elister smiled, his expression almost fatherly as he looked down at Lailu. "My dear young chef, it has been my pleasure. Excellent meal. I shall have to call on you again, and soon. Say, do you have any plans yet for the Week of Masks?"

"Uh . . ." Lailu couldn't wrap her mind around anything other than the day's events, let alone a holiday that was months away.

"I don't need an answer right now, as I'm sure I'll see you again before then," Elister said, not altogether reassuringly. Inclining his head toward her, he put a handful of coins on the table. "For the meals," he explained. Then he turned and walked out the front door.

"By all the spices," Greg breathed. "I can't believe that just happened."

"You almost missed it. What were you doing in the cellar for so long?" Lailu asked.

"I was looking for LaSilvian wine."

"We don't carry that stuff," Master Slipshod said scornfully, and both Lailu and Greg looked at him in surprise. "We prefer other brands."

Lailu felt her anger toward her mentor softening. "That's right."

"What are *you* doing here?" Greg demanded. "You can't honestly think Lailu would still be your apprentice after what you did."

"Of course she's still my apprentice. Best apprentice in the land." Master Slipshod dropped one hand on Lailu's shoulder, then sniffed the air. "Although I daresay the pupil has outdone her master. That is some fine cuisine I'm smelling. Mountain dragon, spiced with . . . is that a hint of lebinola? Genius. That wasn't in my book."

"No, I added that in myself." Lailu couldn't help herself; her chest filled with pride as she grinned up at her mentor, who maybe wasn't so bad after all.

"I did, for the briefest of moments, consider the idea of leaving town," Master Slipshod admitted. "But when I delivered that note to your little redheaded friend, she told me where to find Brennon's family."

"*Wren* told you where they were?"

"She said she had come across their location 'by accident.'"

"Who's Wren?" Greg asked.

"Starling Volan's daughter," Lailu explained, then added, "She helped me prepare a meal once, back when I catered for Lord Elister." Greg's shocked expression almost made that whole experience worth it.

"Anyway," Slipshod said, "you know I would never have truly abandoned you, right, Pigtails?"

"Wait, you just admitted—" Greg began, but Lailu was already nodding.

Greg looked at the two of them and sighed. "Sometimes you can be too forgiving," he told Lailu. "At least toward everyone but me."

"Oh, I've forgiven you many times," Lailu said sweetly.

"You have?"

"Yes, but usually you go and muck it up again right afterward."

"Yeah, that's probably true." Greg grinned. Lailu decided she didn't mind his goofy smile so much anymore, or the way his eyes crinkled at the edges. In fact, if she was perfectly honest, it was kind of a nice smile.

"Well, Pigtails, you ready?" Master Slipshod barked.

Lailu jumped, her face strangely warm, like she'd been caught eating ingredients before they were cooked. "For what?"

"For the real work to begin." He rolled up his sleeves, his expression grim. "We have some serious cleaning to do. I'll start in the kitchen." And he vanished behind the curtain before Lailu could argue.

She looked at the overturned tables and chairs, the broken plates, and the smears of food and blood on the floor.

"I guess we'd better get started." Greg rolled up his own sleeves, looking as tired as Lailu felt.

"We?" she asked.

"What kind of assistant would I be if I didn't stick around to help with the cleanup?"

"A lousy assistant, that's what."

"So does that mean I'm a good assistant?"

Lailu tilted her head to the side, considering. "I suppose you're passable."

"Oh, come on! I'm the best assistant you ever had, and you know it."

"Wren was better," she said, but she couldn't stop a smile from spreading across her face, and with Greg's help, the cleaning didn't take so long after all.

An hour later Greg had gone back to his restaurant, while Lailu and Slipshod were putting the final touches on Mystic Cooking's cleanup.

The door opened silently. With the bell lying in a broken heap on the floor, the only warning they had was the sound of footsteps as Fahr and Eirad marched inside the dining room.

"Is everything all right?" Lailu stood up. "Did you get him?"

"Yes and no." Fahr looked a little dazed, and his face was pale, but otherwise he seemed fine. "We lost him at first—he was darting erratically through side streets and doubling back on his path—and when we finally tracked him down . . ."

"Someone else killed him." Eirad flicked back his blond braids in annoyance.

Lailu gasped. "Mr. Boss is dead?" She exchanged looks with Master Slipshod, who stood frozen near the back of the dining room.

"That upsets you?" Eirad narrowed his eyes.

Lailu shrugged, not really sure how she felt. Mr. Boss was evil, and he'd caused her all sorts of trouble. It had even been her idea to set the elves on him to save herself in the first place. But when she pictured the pathetic creature he had become, all she really felt was pity. "Do you know why?" she asked.

"Why what?" Eirad asked.

"Why he was drinking your blood? I mean, if he knew it would make him like . . . well, like what he became."

"Because the fool man was mortal." Eirad shook his head. "He had no idea how lucky he was. To be able to grow old . . ."

"Eirad, enough," Fahr said sharply.

Eirad pressed his lips together, a small crease forming between his eyes. Lailu had never noticed before how much sadness lay buried beneath his perfect features. He glanced at her, and she looked quickly away.

"How did he die?" Master Slipshod asked, his voice strangled. "Who killed him?"

"We don't know," Fahr said bitterly. "There was this flash of light and then a sound, like a loud pop. The next thing we knew, Victor was falling backward, a hole in his chest."

"A hole?" Lailu asked. "What do you mean?"

"I mean," Fahr said impatiently, "that someone ahead of us managed to use a projectile to put something through Victor's heart."

"Someone ahead of you?" Slipshod asked. "And you don't know who?"

Eirad scowled. "We have our suspicions—"

"We don't know who. Not yet." Fahr gave his companion a sharp look.

"Well, whoever it was knew him well enough to know where he would turn, to know where to wait," Eirad said.

"Right now the more important mystery is, how did Victor trap our people?" Fahr continued darkly. "He would not have been strong enough to do that. Not without significant help."

Lailu bit her lip, thinking of Starling. Would the elves suspect her? There was already no love lost between them and the scientists. What would happen if they learned the truth?

"So now, chef, it's your turn."

Lailu looked at Master Slipshod, then realized Fahr was addressing her. "Me? My turn? For what?"

"To show us where our brethren are being held," Fahr said just as Ryon stepped through the doorway.

Ryon nodded at Lailu, his eyes more serious than she'd ever seen them.

"Ryon will go with you," Fahr said. "Now, show us this building at the corner of Steam Avenue and Iron Way."

Lailu shivered, wishing the sun were still up. The glare of the Industrial District's fake lights set her teeth on edge and made all these buildings look the same. Still, she recognized the split in the center of the door in front of her, and the way the building loomed so tall and skinny, its metal panels distorting her reflection like a cursed mirror.

"This the one?" Ryon glanced around, looking as anxious as she felt, but the street around them was empty. Almost too empty.

"There's the button." Lailu pointed to the small round circle glowing softly against the metallic surface of the building. "Should we wait for the others?" Master Slipshod had stayed behind to prepare Mystic Cooking for the next day's customers, but Fahr was close by with a small army of his elves, waiting for Ryon and Lailu to scout out the place first.

Ryon hesitated, then shook his head. "If it's a trap, better not to drag everyone into it. In fact, why don't you wait here while I go check it out?"

With a pang, Lailu realized Vahn had said something similar, and she hadn't seen him since. "I'm coming with you," she decided, jabbing the button.

Ding!

The door split in the middle, opening to reveal the familiar box of a room. Ryon followed her in, the doors closing behind him.

Lailu silently prayed to the God of Cookery, trying not to dwell on what happened the last time she was in this room. Instead, she studied the four glowing buttons and pressed the one with an arrow pointing up. A soft rumbling began under her feet, and then the room gave a stomach-dropping lurch as it moved upward.

Ding!

The doors slid open, revealing a dimly lit hallway. The air was filled with a soft buzzing sound, and Lailu could smell something sharp, acrid, like nothing she'd ever smelled before.

"You okay?" Ryon whispered.

"Fine," she lied, and moved out of the room.

The hall stretched in both directions. To the right it ended in a small metal door, and to the left it vanished around a corner. Lailu hesitated, but that distinct smell was definitely stronger to the left, so she resolutely turned in that direction. Her feet moved soundlessly on the metallic floor as she fell into her hunting stride, her hand on the hilt of the chef's knife at her hip.

They got to the end of the hall, then paused, listening. Ryon stood silently behind her, his movements even quieter than her own. She couldn't even hear him breathing. All she could hear was the thrumming of her blood in her ears, her own soft, ragged breaths, and . . .

Rumble, rumble, rumble. Drip, drip, drip.

"Round the corner on the count of three?" Ryon asked softly.

Gulping, Lailu nodded and held up three fingers . . . two . . . one. They sprang around the corner.

35

THE AFTERMATH

The long, narrow room in front of them was lit up by more of those glass orbs from outside, their harsh light spilling over everything and turning the shadows to knives. Lailu shielded her eyes against the glare, waiting for an attack that never came.

As her eyes adjusted, the looming shapes against the far wall resolved into a dozen metallic coffins, each set into a raised dais. Wires curled and trailed from the coffins over to a huge circular contraption in the center of the room, steam puffing in steady, pungent bursts from the top of it.

"What is this place?" Ryon asked, but Lailu had no answer for him. Judging by the empty vials lying on a nearby table and the shattered glass on the floor, the people who had the answers had all left in a hurry.

Lailu ran her hands over the top of one of the coffins, then gasped. The metal had changed, becoming transparent like glass. Inside lay a very thin elf, her hair nothing more than wispy white straw, her eyes sunk deep into hollows in her face. Every few seconds a trickle of purple hissed through the wires bulging under the translucent skin of her arms, winding its way to the machine in the middle of the room.

"Ryon, come see— Ack!" Lailu leaped back as the elf's eyes shot open, her chapped lips pulling back from her teeth in a wordless howl of anguish.

"What? Oh . . . my . . . ," Ryon whispered, his own mouth falling open in horror.

A rush of sound behind them heralded the arrival of the rest of the elves, who had clearly not been content to wait for Ryon and Lailu's signal. "They're in the coffins," Ryon told them, turning back to the first one and trying to open it. It didn't budge. Eirad joined him, shoving and pounding at the top, while Lailu ran her hands along the sides. There were no latches, no levers, no buttons of any kind.

"How do we open these?" Eirad demanded, his eyes narrowing on Lailu. "Little chef?"

"I—I don't know—I swear I don't." Lailu took a step back as all around her the elves unsuccessfully tried opening the other coffins. And then she remembered. Vahn! Was he stuck in here too? Was he trapped inside one of these creepy glass coffins? She raced down the row, but saw only pale and drained elven faces.

And then she heard it. A soft knocking noise, but it was

impossible to hear where it was coming from with all the elves pounding at the coffins around her. "Everyone, stop!" she yelled.

Fahr turned to Lailu. "What is it?"

Lailu listened harder.

Tap-tap. Tap!

She spun around, but it sounded like it was coming from . . . the ceiling? Lailu looked up just in time to see Vahn come crashing through it.

He managed to do some kind of fancy roll as he fell, springing to his feet, his hair a wild tangle, his shirt dirty and mussed, but his smile as wide and confident as always. "You made it," he said cheerfully. "And good timing, too."

"V-Vahn?" Lailu almost melted with relief.

"The one and only."

"But . . . the ceiling. You fell out of the ceiling." Lailu couldn't help staring at that jagged hole. It looked like the ceiling was made of multiple flat metal panels and one of them had simply crumbled.

He brushed himself off and bowed to the astonished elves. "Don't worry, I know exactly how to free your people." And he turned and fiddled with something in the side of the large metal contraption in the center of the room. It whined, steam pouring in larger streams from the top, and then it was still.

Around the room the coffins popped open one by one.

"I managed to find a space between the walls right back there with vents so I could see." He pointed behind the coffins, and now Lailu could see how the walls were made of the same metal panels as the ceiling, many of them with small slits carved in to let air escape. "Unfortunately, I wasn't able to get out again to tell you. This place has been under constant supervision since I snuck in here, people coming and going and taking a lot of the equipment with them. I tried finding another exit up through the ceiling panels, and, well, you saw how that worked out."

"And who are these people?" Fahr demanded.

Vahn's smile dimmed around the edge. "Er, well, I never did see who they were. They always wore masks. But I do know they were draining the blood from your people. They were careful, though; they made sure to keep them alive." Vahn lifted his chin, throwing back his hair. "In fact, if you follow my instructions, it is my professional opinion that all your people should be able to make a full recovery."

Several of the elves gave a cheer, and even Eirad looked marginally happy.

"I'm going to take Lailu home," Ryon said, as Vahn instructed the elves on the proper way to remove their kidnapped brethren. "She's done her part."

"Has she?" Eirad asked.

Fahr sighed. "Is this really the time?" he asked his companion. He nodded at Ryon. "Thank you for your help. And yours," he added, looking at Lailu.

Lailu nodded, but she had barely taken two steps when Fahr called out to her.

"Little chef!"

Lailu froze, then reluctantly turned back.

"I thought you would like to know that we decided your meal was excellent—the best dragon cuisine any of us ever tasted," Fahr said.

Eirad coughed.

"Even Eirad agreed." Fahr shot him a look.

Eirad shrugged, but his lips curved up in the hint of a smile as he looked away from them.

"So your friend's debt is cleared."

Lailu sagged with relief. "Thank the gods," she whispered.

"And you are free of Victor Boss and your debt to him," Fahr continued.

"Free." Lailu liked the sound of that word.

"So now you just need to take care of your debt to us." Fahr's smile was cold enough to freeze dragon blood.

Lailu blinked, sure she had heard that incorrectly. "I what?"

Eirad chuckled. It was a horrifying sound. "We were Victor's backers, so when he died, all his businesses reverted to us, and all his loans became our loans. Including yours. So you see, little chef, you are far from free."

"But you were going to take care of my loan to Mr. Boss. That was the deal," Lailu said slowly.

"And strictly speaking, your loan to Mr. Boss *has* been taken care of." Fahr inclined his head, and Lailu could see the inevitability of it all. Her shoulders sagged. He was right; the elves had upheld their end of the bargain. Technically. She just hadn't been specific enough with her request.

"We'll send someone by to go over all the details with you at a later time," Fahr added. "And to draw up a reasonable payment plan for your loan."

Eirad bared his teeth. "Oh, I plan to handle this account personally."

"Even better." Fahr's smile was almost gentle. Still, Lailu thought, it had to be better than the madness that was Mr. Boss and his ever-changing loan due dates. This time, she was going to make sure she got a copy of that contract.

"Come on, Lailu, let's get you home," Ryon said.

She waited until they were past the Industrial District to speak. "Why does Eirad hate me so much?"

Ryon's eyebrows rose in surprise. "On the contrary, I think he's rather fond of you, in his own way."

"Yeah, right," Lailu snorted.

"Seriously. I haven't seen him take a personal interest in a human in . . . oh, it's been a long time."

"I suppose I should be honored, then," Lailu muttered. Just her luck. Elves. She could have gone her whole life without attracting their interest, and here she was, stuck owing them money. "Were you ever working for Mr. Boss, or were you working for the elves this whole time?"

"I told you before, I'm in the business of information. I'm not in the business of freely *giving* information."

"So you're not going to tell me? Even after all this?" Lailu's frustration rose. She hated mysteries.

"We-ell," he said slowly. "I really was working for Mr. Boss. Somewhat. He did hire me a few months back, and I did collect information for him. But he was never my sole client. Never good to put all your eggs in one basket." He grinned. "That cooking reference was for you, by the way."

"Thanks," Lailu said dryly. "But elves . . . why would you work for the elves?"

"Technically, we could make the claim that you are also working for the elves. Everyone has their reasons."

"Yes, but what are yours?"

Ryon glanced sideways at her. "Let's just call them . . . familial obligations."

Lailu thought of the way Ryon and Fahr had looked with their faces so close together. The resemblance. Was Ryon . . . ? But no. Even with all that hair, she'd have noticed a pair of elf ears. She was too tired right now to think properly. Tomorrow, after a good night's sleep, she'd tackle the mystery that was Ryon and his ever-changing loyalties.

"Thanks for helping me out on this whole thing," Ryon added when the silence had grown thick as salamander stew around them.

"Didn't have much choice, did I?" she asked.

Ryon grinned. "No, I suppose you didn't. Still, I enjoyed this, working together."

Lailu waited, but that was it. "No winks?"

Ryon shrugged. "I think I'm all out."

"And here I thought this day couldn't get any better," Lailu laughed.

"Don't start celebrating yet. I'm sure I'll see you again soon, and I'll have a fresh supply."

"You're still planning on coming by?" Lailu felt strangely relieved.

"Of course! We're friends, right?"

She considered. "I guess we are."

Ryon ruffled her hair. "Of course we are. Plus you're the best chef I know. I'll be back."

Lailu smoothed her hair. "Just to eat, though, right?"

No answer.

"Ryon?" Lailu glared up at him. "You don't have any other tasks for me, right? No more ridiculous spying missions?"

Ryon looked her full in the face and winked. "What do you know, I still had one left after all."

"I can't believe I just called you my friend," Lailu grumbled, and she refused to speak to him the rest of the walk back.

The sun had dipped well below the horizon by the time Lailu finished cleaning the restaurant again the next evening, but she still found herself whistling cheerfully. The day had passed in complete chaos, but it was the good kind of chaos. The kind of chaos that involved long lines of people all clamoring for dragon cuisine, and leaving behind large tips.

"Don't you look happy today," Hannah remarked as she helped Lailu finish packing away the leftovers.

"I *feel* happy today," Lailu admitted, grinning. "No more Mr. Boss hanging over our heads, we have enough dragon for at least a week's worth of specials, and Master Slipshod is back."

"Hmm." Hannah pursed her lips.

"I know you don't forgive him, but he's really a great chef. And he promised he'll be a better mentor from here on out. No more gambling."

"Didn't he promise that the last time?" Hannah asked skeptically.

"Yes, but this time he means it. And besides, his gamble worked, didn't it?"

"But he lost all your money!"

"He gave it to Brennon's family."

"Supposedly," Hannah grumbled.

"Plus he replaced your haircomb," Lailu added. *With one that you can wear without having your limbs removed,* she amended silently.

Hannah touched the comb in her hair. "It's not really the same," she began, but Lailu could tell by the way Hannah's fingers lingered that she liked this one, with its opal stones and velvet ribbons. Hannah dropped her hand and folded her arms over her chest. "Besides, it doesn't change the fact that he got us both in a lot of trouble, and he abandoned you."

"He was only on a temporary leave of absence," Lailu argued. "He was helping me grow in character."

"Is that what he told you?"

"Maybe." Lailu shifted uncomfortably under Hannah's angry scrutiny. "Those might have been his exact words, actually."

"What a load of complete—"

Knock-knock!

Both girls looked up as the front door creaked open.

"V-Vahn?" Lailu stammered.

"The one and only." Vahn gave her a small bow, a newspaper held loosely in one hand.

Hannah looked quickly from Vahn to Lailu. "I just remembered something I have to do," she said abruptly, and hurried from the room.

Vahn raised his eyebrows in surprise, then shrugged and turned back to Lailu, who really didn't know what to think. He glanced down at the bell sitting in a dejected heap next to the door. "You might want to fix that."

"Yeah," Lailu said. She felt strange, almost empty. Vahn was as handsome as ever, wearing immaculate clothing, his hair brushed and shining again, but somehow her heart wasn't beating any faster. Looking at him, she wasn't sure how she felt. "Why are you here?"

"Well, I thought I'd thank you for your help, and also collect on that meal you promised me." He flashed his trademark grin.

A few minutes later, Vahn was happily munching down on a well-seasoned dragon skirt steak. In between bites, he filled her in on the outcome of his quest. "Never did figure out who they were, those people behind the masks," he admitted. "The building was rented out under a fictitious name, no connections to anyone. But the elves are okay." He took another bite. "Delicious, Lana, by the way."

"Lailu," Lailu corrected automatically. She stared at him, sitting there in her restaurant enjoying her food, and suddenly she was annoyed. "Why do you always get it wrong?"

Vahn stopped midbite. "Mrmph?"

"My name. It's Lailu. Laaai-luuu. It's not so hard to remember, and I know you know it." She put her hands on her hips.

Vahn swallowed. "Sorry. Didn't realize you were so touchy about it."

Lailu had the strangest urge to slap him. "Touchy? It's my *name*, Vahn."

He inclined his head toward her. "That it is." He grinned, adding, "And a lovely name at that. A lovely name for a lovely girl."

A lovely girl. He had called her lovely. Lailu had waited years for Vahn to say something like that to her, but now she realized they were just words. He didn't mean it. He would never mean it. "Whatever," she said. "Just get it right next time or I won't feed you anymore."

Vahn's eyes widened. "Wow. You've changed, you know that?"

Lailu shrugged. She didn't feel changed. But after all the craziness she'd had to go through, from loan sharks to dragon hunts, she wasn't willing to put up with any unnecessary nonsense. She had enough necessary nonsense to deal with.

"Anyhow," he continued, flashing Lailu a brilliant smile like she hadn't just been yelling at him, "the quest is officially completed, and I have a perfect record."

"That's great." Lailu found herself smiling back. Vahn had a perfect record, thanks to her help. Master Slipshod was back. Business was booming. She felt like she was on top of the world and everything was going her way for once. Until she glanced down, her eyes falling on Vahn's newspaper. On the front page, a headline jumped out at her: *Gregorian LaSilvian Single-Handedly*

Hunts Mountain Dragon, Serves Best Dragon Cuisine Ever!

Lailu scowled and turned on her heel.

"Where are you going?" Vahn called after her.

"To the kitchen," she called back. "I have some serious work to do!" *Best dragon cuisine ever*, she thought to herself irritably. She'd show him!

Acknowledgments

It would be easy to fill another book with all the people we have to thank, so we'll try to keep it brief. But we'd especially like to thank Jennifer Azantian, who has been a tireless champion for our book, and her team, Ben Baxter and Masha Gunic, for being some of Lailu's first fans. Thank you all for pulling Lailu's story out of the slush and fighting to find her the perfect home. We're so happy to be part of Team Azantian.

Another huge thank you to Sarah McCabe and Fiona Simpson, who are two of the best editors a master chef could hope to work with. Our story is a hundred times better thanks to you both.

Also thanks to Angela Li for our amazing cover illustration, and Nina Simoneaux and Karin Paprocki for the cover design. And thank you to everyone else at Aladdin who left their mark on this book: our publisher Mara Anastas and deputy publisher Mary Marotta; Carolyn Swerdloff and Catherine Hayden in marketing; Christina Pecorale and the rest of the Simon & Schuster sales team; our production editor, Katherine Devendorf; and our publicist, Audrey Gibbons. Truly, we are so grateful to all of you.

Lailu and her story had quite a journey before finding a home at Aladdin, and we were privileged to meet many wonderful writers along the way. We would not be where we are now without the help of Stephanie Garber, whose endless enthusiasm and suggestions brought our manuscript to a whole new level; Teresa "word slasher" Yea, who taught us so much about pacing and is the reason this book isn't seven hundred pages long; Sarah Glenn Marsh, whose keen insight helped us shift our story in the right direction and who is always ready to share cute dog pics when needed; and Alan Wehrman, who read our manuscript multiple times over with endless patience and eagle eyes.

Also, so much thanks to the rest of our critique group: Miles Zarathustra, Colleen Smith, Meg Mehagian, and Joan McMillan, who have been with us since the beginning. You guys are the best.

We also want to thank a couple of writers who have been our biggest cheerleaders and supporters as we navigated this road. Thank you so much, Jae Dansie, who we met at our first ever writing conference—someday we'll moderate a panel together! And Brian Taylor, who always knew the best way to cheer us up and keep us going. Justin Stewart, thank you for your enthusiastic support. Also thanks to Liz Briggs—#TeamBriggs forever—and Krista Van Dolzer. Your encouragement has meant more than we can say. And thanks to Ally Carter for being our debut mentor, and the rest of the 2017 debut authors who have been with us, sharing personal experiences and information as we navigate this winding path together.

Also an enormous thank you to all our friends who have cheered us on over the years, including Takeshi Young—we've never forgotten our early days of DMQ; April Stearns, Moana Whipple, and Becky Dickson—it's been a joy and a privilege to share writing time with you ladies; thank you to Conor Driscoll—love the website! And to Nate Boltseridge and Scott Grabowski, for putting us up during our first writing conference. And to everyone who read our early drafts and encouraged us to keep going, including Kim Kauffold, Jennifer Flinn, and Julianne Dunn. Also a huge thank you to Mitch Berman—it was in your classroom that one half of this duo realized she not only wanted to be a writer, but that it was an actual possibility.

And last but not least, we owe so much to our supportive family, but especially thank you to Lyn Lang—glad to be the "wordsmith" in your family; our cousin Christy Buncic, who was willing to slog through our early drafts; Rosi Reed, our very own resident mad scientist and older sister; our dad, Rich Bartkowski, for reading everything we ever write and always, always giving us positive feedback; and our mom, Rose Bartkowski, for being so encouraging every step of the way. And thank you to Nick "Title Master" Chen and Sean Lang, our partners in everything. You are the reason this dream has been possible.

And to everyone else who has offered us support and encouragement on this long, long trek, thank you. This one's for you.